Toklat's Daughter
A novel

Mitch Sebourn

Toklat's Daughter
© 2016 by Mitch Sebourn

Cover design
© 2016 by Mitch Sebourn

Also by Mitch Sebourn

Flying Saucer
Watershed
Sleight of Hand
Hawks & Handsaws
Inner Sequence
Lamentation
The Hawthorn Room

Seven Years Ago

1

WALLACE O'BRIEN HIKED ALONG A sandy riverbed two-hundred miles south of the Arctic Circle. The day was cool and dry. The mountains were shrouded in clouds. He was returning to the Park Road, having followed the braided bed of the Toklat River halfway across the valley before deciding to turn back.

He was in search of an idea. He hadn't published anything significant in two years; he had no teaching job lined up beyond his present position as a visiting scholar in Anchorage, which would expire at the end of the summer. He needed something, a spark, preferably something brilliant, though anything would do for now. That's why he'd driven up to Denali for the weekend. He could only sit in Anchorage and stare at walls for so long. And *this* was Alaska. This was really what he'd come here for.

"Alaska will do you good," his favorite New York bartender, a man named Peevey, had said when he mentioned taking the position at the University of Alaska in Anchorage. "You're stuck, Wallace. It happens. So get out of here and get *un-stuck*."

To an extent, Peevey had been right. Wallace was glad to be out of New York. He felt better. He was (for the present) earning a steady paycheck, a nice one, as he spent the summer months lecturing about the influence of the Romantics on twenty-first century America, and he even (mostly) enjoyed the students. His parents would be proud. Both had been underpaid teachers their entire adult lives, working on the nation's most underfunded, underappreciated front lines in the battle to educate and inspire and send even the poorest kids off to greater things. His father had been a cynical "realist," his mother a constant beacon of light. It had taken both of them to keep each other moving forward.

"I appreciate you wanting to write," his father had said, "but we need *teachers*, son. We need teachers like you."

Except that wasn't true. Wallace had never found the courage to tell his dad that he hadn't a passion, at all, for teaching. He wanted to *get out* of rural America, and he wanted to be great, even if he really wasn't. His mother had always suspected this. She'd always been the one whispering in his ear to go do whatever it was he wanted to do. If teaching was not his calling, for the love of God, *don't do it*, because that's even worse.

So he got out. Good riddance to the Midwest, off to New York it was, so he could grow out his hair and get his PhD and learn his passions and write and act like he was one of the Greats.

He'd left the Midwest thinking Manhattan would place a muse on his shoulder and embrace him and guide him slowly but surely into a promising future. And yes, he appreciated the culture there, the similar personalities and their tireless encouragements, the inspirations, the varieties of workplaces... but New York, he'd long ago decided, was nothing but a foundation.

"Listen Wallace," the city said, "here's a degree and a place to work. Here are a few friendly types to read your drivel and show you how to make it better. When times get tough, here are a few colleges looking for help—don't worry, sir, this ain't Nowhere High School. These kids won't nix your brilliance, okay? Here's Publishers' Row (if you want to take a stroll and make yourself sad), here are the addresses for a few agents, if you want to drive them crazy, and here are some artsy-fartsy magazines when you get bigheaded and ambitious. Maybe you can take the editors for coffee? Have a nice career, kid!"

But he wasn't a kid anymore. He was on the north side of forty, and the clock was ticking, and maybe New York had done what it could for him. It was home base, that was it.

So, like Peevey said, *Get out.* Get *unstuck.*

It was remarkable how wise Peevey's advice appeared to be now that he was very much *outside.*

Up ahead, he noticed a slight shift in the light on the sand and water.

When he looked up, he froze.

He'd heard about these encounters. One must project confidence. You can't quiver. You can't just look at the ground.

The blond grizzly bear, all five hundred or so pounds of her (he would assume it was female) was thankfully further away than he'd originally thought. She was thirty or so yards up the river, swatting with one paw at a rushing tendril of silver glacier melt.

Wallace reminded himself to stand still, shoulders back, no thoughts of running away. What was the saying? *Make yourself big*? Yes, that. And that was very easy for park rangers to say. It was very easy to say, *Yes, of course I'll remember and do that.* Funny how you can prepare and prepare, but you never see the dangerous things coming, and you never feel prepared.

The bear focused on the water for what had to be at least two full minutes. The whole time, Wallace remained still, tall as possible, until the grizzly looked up and spotted him. Her eyes were black glass. She was beautiful and terrifying. The hump behind her shoulders rolled with anticipation.

Wallace didn't think the beast was angry or scared. Just curious. Hopefully not hungry.

Bears don't see us as food, somebody somewhere had told him. Wallace wondered what this somebody would say now.

The bear took a slow, cautious step toward him. And then another.

This is remarkable, Wallace thought.

And this could also eat him alive.

Talk to her.

"You're at home here, aren't you?" He sounded surprisingly calm. "I get that. If you'll just move on, I'll leave. The road's right up there. I can almost see it. I'll just follow the river and catch a bus. If you don't kill me, I'll buy everybody a beer and tell them about you. I'll give you props. Promise."

At some point during his monologue, the bear stopped.

But she was within twenty feet of him.

"Are you a lady? I haven't had a lady's attention in a long time. I'm running out of things to say."

I just want to know, the bear's stare said, *what you are and what you're doing here.*

"I'm a visitor. I'm a writer. Not much of one. But let's not get into that."

She cocked her head slightly, and a low whimper that might've been pitiful if not for the persistence of reality emerged from the back of her throat. *I see too many of you. I really do. Yet I've never seen you this close.*

She stepped closer.

"I write articles. And essays. I…"

For the first time, his voice quivered.

Now she was within easy swatting distance, should she wish to splatter her new writer toy in the river.

"I just need to catch a bus. Let's forget this ever happened."

The last few words barely emerged, *if* he actually spoke them at all. Hard to say, but his brain was about to betray him. He wished to take a step backward, not that it would do any good, but his knees were about to buckle, and then he'd shit his pants, and he could feel her hot breath. He could see his reflection in the drool dangling from her lip.

She was no longer curious.

She was unhappy.

The quake in the back of her throat made it clear she was sick of toying with this pathetic little writer.

And then came something much louder than that low quake, and she raised her right front paw.

2

Supposedly, this was her home state. She'd heard about it for as long as she could remember. She'd seen pictures.

But Emily Rawlins had never seen anything like this.

It wasn't just the mountains and wildflowers and the dayglow nights. It was all of it together, the enormity of even the most modest of hills.

Yesterday, her mother had seen the wonder in her eyes when the clouds over Denali began to break, and she suggested a hike *inside* the park. Go out into the valley. Specifically, she told her about the Toklat and the wildflowers on the mountain slopes.

"You'll wear out your camera," Mary Rawlins had told her daughter, "and you'll fill up your new photo album."

The album, purple and leather bound, had been a gift from her mother as they left New Hampshire. Emily had been interested in nature photography since high school, having filled up two previous albums with the wildlife and flowers of New Hampshire's White Mountains.

Emily had filled almost half her new album *outside* the park; the Nenana River and the slopes of Mount Healy had provided her an abundance of opportunities.

But now, at her mother's strong suggestion, she was embarking for the wilderness.

Emily wished her mother would have joined her, but Mary had been concerned about her health for years, and it was only getting worse. Her mother was in no shape for a hike.

Emily had spent most of the night, and all of the bus ride out to the Toklat River, anticipating this adventure, almost dreading it. She'd reminded herself over and over again that she'd never done anything like this before, and national park or not, she was setting out into the wilderness.

But now, all her reservations were gone.

The sandy riverbed was indeed a natural trail. It lured her easily deeper and deeper into the valley. To her right, the first orange hint of real daylight reflected off the snowy massif of Denali; straight ahead, the jagged fang of Pendleton cut sharply into the sky. She was hiking straight toward the headwall of a glacier that swooped down around its western slope.

"We come from the heart of Alaska," her mother had told her as they were flying out of Boston. "When you finally see it, as an adult, it *will* change you. You'll know you're home."

Emily had waved off this remark as sincere but empty. Mary Rawlins had always been a sucker for the romantic.

But no, she was right. Though Emily had lived in New Hampshire since she was three, she'd already accepted this as home.

She stopped to eat a granola bar and drink some water.

She gazed ahead at Pendleton. It looked so close, but she knew it was still several miles away.

According to her mother, she would arrive at a magical place (she would know it when she got there), where you could look westward, and Denali would be rising out of a foreground of wildflowers.

She put away the water bottle and pressed on. She hiked in silence, she sang rather loudly the lyrics to some of her favorite Snow Patrol and Crowded House songs. But mostly, she observed. The flowers. The water. The distant mountains.

By mid-morning, she could discern details in the glacier's headwall.

At noon, she'd surely reached the vista her mother had spoken of. The glacier was maybe a quarter of a mile away. The riverbed was ascending steeply. The tiny tendrils of water grew denser as they merged together, the water rushing by deeper, faster. Now, yes, Denali was framed perfectly between a blue sky and a slope of grass and wildflowers. She unpacked her Nikon and took pictures, dozens of them. And then she saw the bear.

The grizzly was no more than two hundred yards away, strolling casually amongst the flowers. Emily knelt down, twisted the zoom lens, and watched as the great blond beast lowered its head and sniffed at a patch of flowers. The beast moved slowly, methodically; sometimes, it seemed not to move at all.

Emily waited. Waited.

The bear raised its head and looked at her. Their gazes met, and Emily fired off a series of shots, her breath caught in her throat.

How long did they stare at each other? Emily didn't know. It didn't matter. It only mattered that it *happened*.

She lowered the camera when the bear turned and started away, and in the corner of her vision, she saw a figure on top of the glacier.

It was a *human* figure, she was sure of it, but when she aimed the camera at the headwall and zoomed, it was gone.

Again, she lowered the camera.

A climber, she thought, assuming she'd actually seen anybody at all.

Certainly, there was nobody up there now.

She replaced the camera in her pack, positioning it carefully between a bag of trail mix and her photo album.

She zipped up the backpack and pressed on.

She was so close. And she intended to make it all the way to Pendleton Glacier.

NEW HAMPSHIRE WOMAN MISSING IN DENALI NATIONAL PARK

(Denali National Park) Search parties consisting of park rangers, state troopers, and members of the Alaska Bureau of Investigations are searching portions of Denali National Park for Emily Rawlins, 21, of New Hampshire.

Three search parties were organized late yesterday afternoon after Emily was reported missing Tuesday night by her mother, Mary Rawlins, 40, also of New Hampshire.

According to Mary Rawlins, Emily left the Salmon Catch cabins outside Denali National Park at approximately six 'o clock Tuesday morning. She was going to ride a bus into the park's interior and hike in the Toklat River region, Mary Rawlins said.

Officer Cormac Pearce of the Alaska State Troopers says search parties will "for now" focus on areas around the park entrance, the Toklat River, and the Eielson Visitor Center, the only visitor center in the park's interior…

MOTHER OF MISSING HIKER REPORTED MISSING

(Denali National Park) Ellis Everett, 66, the owner of the Salmon Catch Restaurant and Cabins outside Denali National Park, notified authorities on Monday that Mary Rawlins, 40, was missing from the cabin where she'd been staying.

Mary Rawlins's daughter, Emily, went missing in Denali National Park earlier this month. Mary was staying in one of the Salmon Catch cabins while authorities searched for Emily. Organized searches were called off last week. As of this writing, Emily Rawlins is still missing. Both women are residents of New Hampshire.

Everett said he noticed over the weekend that the Kia SUV Mary Rawlins had rented from Hertz was not parked outside her cabin. When the car was still gone on Monday, he attempted to find her and could not. Everett notified authorities in Healy on Monday afternoon...

I
The Power Play

1

"DID YOU DO IT?" PEEVEY placed a Sam Adams in front of him and tapped an article that thankfully was buried deep in the guts of *The New York Times*.

Wallace O'Brien had read it once. He would not read it again. It concerned a certain writer who'd settled a copyright lawsuit by turning over everything he'd made from a story he'd published in *The New Yorker* almost three years ago. Wallace O'Brien, once one of the most promising young voices in serious fiction. And now what?

No, he would not read it again.

"I did it," Wallace said.

He took a drink.

This was his first appearance in Shavano's since his shame had started leaking to the public. This bar was his second home, and he considered Peevey a close friend.

And when you're ashamed, home isn't necessarily where you want to be. Friends aren't necessarily who you want to face.

The old black bartender chuckled and walked away. He'd be back, and he'd help Wallace sort his thoughts, ask him what the hell he'd been thinking, and what else was he working on?

I'm not working on anything, Wallace would say. *I have nothing. Why do you think I ripped off Leary?*

He'd returned from Alaska in the fall of 2008 with three thousand dollars in his checking account, twelve thousand in savings, and a ten and a five in his wallet. And that was it. The University of Alaska had been a blast. Getting thrown down in the cold water of the Toklat by a beautiful blond had been exhilarating. But the lecturing gig was up, and he was ready for the nights to be dark again. New York was home. Time to write.

No, it was *past* time to write.

He should've been halfway through the first draft of his first novel-length bestseller when his plane touched down in the lower forty-eight.

But, nothing. Nothing, as in, *nothing*. No ideas, no words, just a spiral notebook full of bullshit scribbles and an extremely finite amount of money in the bank.

He wrote an article about Bernie Sanders for a small leftist rag who wanted a writer "of some esteem" to cover a speech the Bern gave at NYU. He self-published a collection of poetry he'd written almost ten years ago, back when he was still under the age of forty and naïve enough to believe he actually *was* a poet. He sold a few hundred copies of the collection, received half a dozen unremarkable reviews, and quit promoting it. Let it die, he thought. It's better that way.

And then, somewhere close to Christmas of 2008, as he was pondering his own no-good attempt at minor league publishing, he remembered something he'd read that summer, while relaxing on the Ship Creek Bridge in Anchorage. A very bad, self-published turd of a novel called *The Power Play*.

That's when the first bad thought had come to his mind.

And you shouldn't have these *bad* thoughts when you're *bad broke*.

Bad things happen.

2

"Now tell me why you did it."

Peevey had just returned. He was hunkered down across from him, elbows on the bar, arms crossed.

Wallace preferred to simply gaze down into his beer. Because he felt like a kid being scolded by his favorite teacher—who happened to be *very disappointed* in him.

"It was a self-published book," Wallace said. "I found it while I was in Anchorage. I looked it up on the internet and didn't even find it on Amazon. It was full of errors. It wasn't very good. You could tell he wrote it and published it almost immediately. What he did was pay for a few hundred copies, learned the hard way it was awful, and never wrote again. It's the kind of book that a struggling *good* writer reads just to make himself feel good and learn what *not* to do. You understand."

Peevey shrugged.

Wallace continued: "It was called *The Power Play*, by a guy named Damon Leary. It's about this low-level factory worker's plan to get revenge on his boss. Ends up killing him. I read it, I set it aside, and I don't think of it again till five or six months later, when I'm dead broke and needing money, and I think, there's a good idea there. There's a *statement* to be made there. I don't know what else to say.

"I ripped it off. I did. I changed the setting and the characters. I made the protagonist black and actually, you know, gave him some character. I changed the title to *The Letter of Conflict*. It was about twenty-five thousand words. I asked *The New Yorker* if they wanted it, and they published it in three installments. It paid well—three times—and won a prize, and it got me a new teaching gig and a few guest lectures. And I know I sound like a *Scooby Doo* villain, but I nearly got away with it. Unfortunately, Leary picked up the wrong—or right—copy of *The New Yorker*."

Peevey walked off, fixed a few drinks, and returned.

"But why did you do it?" he said.

"I don't know."

"You *need* to know."

"I was desperate."

"You're supposed to be above that. I assume you still are, or I'd quit giving a shit about you."

"I bet he would've let me have it if I'd asked."

"And he took every cent they paid you."

"I offered. To be done with it. And do you know what else is just full of disgusting irony?"

Peevey's eyebrows arched.

"He published *The Power Play* on Kindle two weeks ago. It's near the top of three Amazon lists."

Peevey just laughed. "You did it."

3

There was more, the most devastating part: He hadn't written a decent word of *anything* since *The Letter of Conflict*. The writer's block he'd faced before was *nothing* to what he'd faced in the last four years.

"I talked to the department chair at NYU," he said. "We've agreed that I should step away, at least for a while."

"Till you get your dignity back," Peevey said.

"I suppose."

"I know you, Wallace. You need to write. What else are you going to do? Brain surgery? Construction?"

"I don't know."

"So write."

He tried. Truly he did. He spent days writing, then deleting. Nothing worked. And so he turned to research. The best ideas for the most fantastic works, he'd once lectured, were out in the real world, frequently in the news.

He'd acquired an electronic subscription to the Anchorage *Gazette* while he was in Alaska, and he still received it. It was here, as he was digging back through old editions of the Anchorage paper, that he first discovered the story of the missing hiker. It was one of the first issues sent to him, from the summer of 2008. The story was on the third page: NEW HAMPSHIRE WOMAN MISSING IN DENALI NATIONAL PARK.

Her name was Emily Rawlins. Her mother, Mary Rawlins, stated that Emily had gone into the park to hike, and she never returned. They were Alaska natives who'd moved to New Hampshire when Emily was very young.

And that was all.

But it was a *story*, and maybe it was because it dated back to *his* stint in Alaska, but already, it felt like it might be something meant for *him*.

He went deeper.

There was a follow-up blurb a couple of weeks later: still nothing. And two weeks after that, nearly a month to the day after Emily's disappearance, Mary followed: MOTHER OF MISSING HIKER REPORTED MISSING.

Mary had been staying in one of the rustic rental cabins outside Denali, hoping for her daughter to be found. The owner of the cabins, a man named Ellis Everett, said he noticed her rented Kia wasn't parked out front, and Mary was not inside. He didn't think much of it until the next day, when they were both—the woman and the vehicle—still missing. Mary was as gone as her daughter, and nobody anywhere had any ideas.

The *Gazette* hadn't published an update since. Google, likewise, turned up nothing new; a Fairbanks paper had published a story similar to the one in the

Gazette, and a Seattle blogger had mentioned the Rawlins women in a 2010 blog entry.

That was all.

"I have an idea," Wallace told Peevey at the end of this preliminary research. "Alaska again."

II

The Dreaded Fourth

1

SHE WISHED SHE'D TAKEN THE day off. That way, she could've stayed in bed and focused on her misery, or she could've found some way—some *effective* way—to distract herself. But no. The ever-brilliant Morgan McCown had arrived for work on the afternoon of The Dreaded Fourth, and it was every bit as bad as she'd feared it would be. None of them *wanted* to be awful. All of them truly cared, to some extent or another. But they were all awful.

She clocked in at two, and right away, Colleen, the shift manager, asked her when the list would be posted. Four, Morgan said, four on the fourth, and of course Colleen reminded her she would be fine, no worries, and of course, the words only heightened Morgan's anxiety, because Colleen—and Morgan loved her to death, trusted her, considered her a friend—didn't know anything about anything.

Still, Morgan thanked her and went to work. At least the customers who worried only about giving her their drink and food orders didn't know she was internally a wreck who was waiting on the results of the February bar exam.

But there *were* those who were more observant, or knowledgeable.

Two young men in suits entered, sat down, and after she took their drink orders, one of them asked her if something was wrong. Morgan nearly found it in her to smile and blow it off, but in a moment of total foolishness, she told them. They smiled, they sympathized, because they *were* lawyers who'd been through the same thing just a few years ago.

She knew what they wanted to ask her.

What was she doing *here*?

And it's a good thing they didn't actually ask, because she would've answered, and it would have taken a while. She was *here* because she was a fool and she'd said yes, she would come in; she needed to keep her mind occupied, anyway, so she didn't sit around all day and stare at the clock. She was here because she needed work, and work in the legal field had evaded her throughout most of law school, because she didn't really *like it* all that much, and she'd only applied to law school because her lawyer mother over in Bartlett, Tennessee had *strongly urged* her to do so. She'd come *here* because the mom-and-pop law firm she'd been working at was a sorry ass job that made her hate herself, especially after she failed the bar the first time. She was here, yes, at this cozy little pub in downtown Little Rock, and she liked it here; she liked her boss and the tips were good, and it was *temporary*. And no, she didn't know what she would do if she didn't see her name on the pass list *again*—probably something crazy. Or maybe just stay here and wait tables and work the bar and not pay off her student debt and let the feds come get her. Maybe that.

Thank God, neither of the attorneys asked her anything more.

They knew. They understood.

I'm a fool.

I was totally wrong.

Work did *not* keep her occupied and it did *not* make the time go by faster.

It took hours for the two 'o clock hour to give way to three, and the three 'o clock hour mocked her constantly—from her cell phone screen, from the clock behind the bar, even from the shift manager's watch—because she wasn't strong enough to ignore it, but she *did* avoid the urgent need to have a total nervous breakdown.

At four 'o clock, she casually stepped into the ladies' room, locked herself in a stall, and with her cell phone, went to the website where the list of passers was to be posted.

For a second, the list was not there, and she feared the site had crashed.

But then it appeared, and she scrolled down the list to learn that she'd once again failed the Arkansas bar exam.

The empty feeling in her stomach was short lived and was soon replaced with something that honest to God felt like relief.

2

But the bliss of *At least I don't have to worry anymore* was replaced with *I can't believe it* by the time she stepped out of the bathroom. And about the time she went to check her tables, she was angry. Anger became fury, which crashed and became a sick bellyache.

She told the shift manager her situation and left an hour early.

The sky was dark and the air was as heavy as her mood.

There was lightning in the west, and she drove straight toward it, talking to herself.

Until her mother called.

"I know what happened," her mother said. "I saw, or *didn't* see. How, Morgan? What keeps happening?"

"I don't know."

"How in the world are you going to make a career for yourself if you don't pass the bar exam?"

"I don't know."

"I'm sorry, Morgan."

"I know. Thank you."

"But you *must* pass this. I don't know what to tell you."

"I don't either."

She hung up. She didn't want to hear her mother's lecturing, her condescending cruelty.

The rain started as she approached her apartment door. She stood in the threshold for a moment and watched it, and then she shut the door and changed into lounge pants and a baggy John Mayer tee shirt. She hadn't looked at her text messages since early this afternoon. After crashing down on her couch—a hand-me-down sofa from her parents, congratulating her for going to law school and all that—she dared open them up.

And deleted them.

Truly, she wasn't one to think such nasty thoughts, but fuck *all* of them. Did they truly believe she wanted or needed their sympathy? Unfair, but she could be unfair for a moment, because it didn't hurt anything.

At least I haven't cried.

And if she *was* going to cry, she thought it would've happened by now.

I'm settling down.

But she still did not wish to look at her phone or talk to anybody.

Yes, but at least I've settled down.

She looked at her reflection in her powerless television and thought of all the ways this could be a good thing. It proved to be an amusing thought process, very therapeutic, and by the end of it, some of her ideas were actually growing roots.

The rain kept falling. That was fine.

She let it put her to sleep.

3

When she awoke, sunlight was beaming through the window by the door. The dreaded fourth was over, and God, how good that felt.

She took a shower, put on fresh clothes, and dared look at her phone.

Four new messages and somewhere close to nine thousand Facebook and Twitter notifications. She swiped open the phone and braved the effort of sifting through them.

Her mother had called again. She'd return it, eventually. Her uncle had called, too, and she would return that one as well, and she wasn't even *dreading* it. Because her dad's older brother, Rawleigh McCown (*Ray*, actually, but he'd answered to Rawleigh since childhood), was one of her favorite people.

No text messages she cared about, mainly just generic stuff like "you'll be okay" or "the test is totally random" from friends who weren't really friends.

She tucked her phone in her back pocket, retrieved her keys and purse, and set out.

She didn't know where she was going until she stepped into her apartment's main office. It occurred to her what she was about to do... and she was at peace with it.

No. She was *thrilled* about it.

"I'd like to cancel my lease," she heard herself say to the man on the other side of the desk.

"When are you leaving?"

"As soon as I can. Next month at the latest."

"You will be out by the tenth of next month?"

"Absolutely."

He nodded.

As she was stepping back outside, she thought: *That was simple. How long have I wanted to do that?*

Next, she drove to the pub and put in her notice there, too.

This one didn't make her smile as much.

She'd grown attached to her job.

4

"You know we're disappointed," Mother said, "but we of course don't mind if you come back home for a few days. I'd want to get out of Little Rock, too. That city irks me."

"I might do that," she lied.

God no. She would not be making that dreadful drive down I-40 East anytime soon.

She sat in her car in a parking lot less than three blocks from the pub, gazing at the hills west of the city.

"You just have to go at it again, Morgan. You don't have a choice. And you have to make it count this time."

Maybe she meant well, in some weird way. But she had no idea.

"I know."

No she didn't.

You don't have a choice was bullshit. She could do anything she wanted. That's the only reason she'd had the gumption to wake up today and check her phone and make this dreadful phone call.

"Just come home and rest for a few days," Mother said. "We really don't mind."

"I know, Mom. I love you."

And when Mother said she loved her, too, Morgan ended the call.

Next, she would call Uncle Rawleigh.

But first she went down to the River Market for a frozen Coke and found a seat atop a tall rock that overlooked the river.

She was in disbelief at how good she felt.

She was free, in every sense of the word, and it felt incredible.

Maybe one day she would come back here and *think reasonably* (as her parents would say) and shackle herself to the bar exam again. But not right now.

She called Uncle Rawleigh.

He answered on the second ring.

"How are you, Morgan? Darn glad to hear from you."

"I'm okay."

"I figured. I know you pretty well."

Uncle Rawleigh had moved from Nashville to Fairbanks, Alaska almost ten years ago. According to his little brother, Morgan's dad, he'd been miserable, using drugs, maybe going crazy—as suggested by an instance in which he'd nearly killed one his girlfriends—and since he was in desperate need of *something* (only God knew what), Morgan's dad had made some calls and put him in touch with a Fairbanks construction company. Rawleigh had gone and not looked back.

Morgan had barely been school age when he left. But through social media and email, she'd grown close to him and determined that she had *much* more in common with her crazy reclusive uncle than she did either of her parents.

"How is Renee?" she asked, referring to the woman he'd been dating—or sleeping with, or something—for nearly the entirety of his time up there.

"She's all right. She comes and goes. Guess who's coming to Anchorage?"

He was referring, no doubt, to a band; Rawleigh McCown had diverse (and frequently very obscure) tastes in music, and he constantly attempted to spread the good news about the artists who rose into the upper echelon of the playlists on his phone.

Morgan made a few wild wrong guesses.

"*Opeth*," he said. "You hear me, Morgan? Fucking *Opeth*. Before the announcement, I'd have put the odds of them coming to Anchorage in the next ten years at just south of ten million to one."

"Don't they growl?"

"They used to. Not so much nowadays."

"I'll listen." Better to just *listen* and sugarcoat her opinion of them later. Her uncle didn't always appreciate her slightly more… feminine? (no, that wasn't necessarily right)… tastes in music.

"'Course you will. How's Arkansas?"

"Mild." But he didn't really care about Arkansas, and she knew it. "I feel like I can go anywhere. But now I'm lost."

"You'll retake the test?"

"I guess."

"When is it offered again?"

"July." It seemed so far away, but it wasn't. "I don't know if I want to take it then."

Uncle Rawleigh did not immediately respond.

"If you need a break from it, kid," he said, "take one. You're a grown woman. No rush. No need to kill yourself."

"I know."

"I *do* want you to take it again, if you want to. I just read a message board conversation last night about a guy who failed it in Oklahoma twice and was worried he'd just failed it a third time. It happens. You just keep going."

"It's tiring."

"Absolutely. And I know you're sick of it. If you want to take a break, do it. Do what your gut tells you. And listen to the songs I send you. I mean it."

"I will."

She told him she loved him, then ended the call and sat looking at the river, thinking about going somewhere very far away.

5

She did not have to work that night, but she went to the pub anyway when she knew it was time for Colleen to end her shift. Morgan had worked with Colleen for eighteen months; her shift manager had heard more than her fair share of Morgan's ranting and raving about law school and the bar exam and her parents and her anxiety, and... And she'd listened and been honest with her commentary.

Morgan found her clocking out and sitting down at the small table near the back door. Colleen always sat and had a beer to unwind before she walked home.

Tonight, Morgan joined her.

Colleen had her Kindle in front of her, but when Morgan sat down, she closed its case and dropped it in her purse.

"What are you doing here?" Colleen said. She was drinking something—it was probably Guinness—that matched her appearance and personality: bold, no bullshit.

"Wandering around."

"Good place to wander to."

"I thought so. What are you reading?"

"A terrible book I heard about recently. *The Power Play*. Don't bother." She waved over Randy, the waiter on the clock. "Get Morgan a drink. Whatever she wants. And bring us some cheese fries and some ranch dressing."

Morgan told Randy she'd take a vodka tonic with a lime.

After he walked away, Colleen offered her condolences about the test.

"You know it's just random fuckery," she said. "Don't let it get to you."

"I can't get a grip on it."

"Because anyone who does claim to find a grip on random fuckery is nothing but a liar and the beneficiary of a nice dice roll."

The mood lightened once their drinks were down. Colleen sent Randy after another round and said: "Tell me about your plans, Morgan. I know you have them or you wouldn't have put in your notice, and I think they might be exciting."

"I don't know."

Randy returned with their drinks.

"Come on, honey," Colleen said when they were alone again. "I know why you're here. *Really*. Out with it."

Why not? Morgan thought. Colleen was right. This is why she was here, and maybe with it out, she'd see it for what it was and actually make a decision.

"I'm thinking about not taking the July bar."

"I don't blame you."

"I'm thinking about Alaska. Soon, when the weather warms. I have enough in savings, and I could get a job."

Colleen cocked her head a bit. *No, I don't think you're crazy. Just wasn't expecting that.*

"My uncle lives there," Morgan said. "I love him and talk to him all the time. And it's far away. That's the main thing."

"I *know* you don't want to go back home."

"No, I don't."

"So go to Alaska."

"I've thought about it."

Colleen took a large drink of her Guinness and grinned. "It's kind of exciting, isn't it? I can't imagine."

"I can't either," Morgan said.

And that was the point.

III
The Residence

1

I HAVE TO GET OUT.

That was the idea, and it looked like he would. Soon.

It was early May and Manhattan was starting to feel good again. But he could not let the sun and the warmth fool him. He had to get out.

I have a book to write, he thought as he stepped off an elevator. *And this town's not getting it done.*

He knocked on the door of his editor's office and opened it.

Patricia Weaver cleared away the papers in front of her and tucked her pencil into the tightly pulled gray hair just above her left ear. The slightly forced smile on her face suggested she didn't greatly appreciate him being a full ten minutes early, but so be it. She flicked a hand to motion to the chair across from her.

He sat down.

"It's an interesting idea." She dug through some papers at the front of her desk and retrieved a printout of his emailed proposal. "You don't *know* much yet of the disappearances of these women, which is understandable, since you only started pursuing this idea less than two months ago. I like the idea of the nonfiction novel, in the tradition *In Cold Blood* or *The Executioner's Song*, maybe *Into Thin Air*. And the somewhat exotic Alaskan setting will enhance the intrigue."

"I agree."

"It's nothing you can rip off." Patricia had been looking down at the proposal; now she raised her gaze to him. "That's important."

"I agree."

"I understand you're leaving for Alaska soon. But what makes you think you'll acquire enough information to write this? They're both gone. No trace of a family, which is very bizarre. Very little on the internet. What's your plan?"

"I have hours of interviews with two of Emily's childhood friends from New Hampshire, and several of her teachers and college professors. There will be people to speak to in Alaska. And it is a nonfiction *novel*. That entails a certain amount of liberty."

"I suppose it does."

"Are you interested?"

"There is no such thing as bad publicity, remember? Your recent integrity suicide will sell books, as we all look to see if you can reclaim an ounce of it. Of course I'm interested."

"I'd like an advance."

Patricia Weaver's smile didn't waiver. And she didn't even bother speaking, not initially. Just a slight shake of her head.

He wanted to beg. He *needed* to beg. He'd made good money teaching and lecturing, and occasionally a royalty check for one of his two old books would come in, but those never amounted to anything, and that goddamned Leary had annihilated most of his savings, as he'd paid him to go away. And he needed to allow himself at least two months in Alaska. He'd need the rent for his Manhattan apartment, as well as rental vehicles and a place to stay in Alaska. Surely Patricia Weaver knew this.

"I understand your situation, Wallace," she said, "and I knew that's why you were coming here today. *I understand.* I know. I even had a few conversations on your behalf. But it can't be done. Your proposal is less than two pages long. The details are nonexistent. Your trustworthiness, likewise. It can't be done. I'm sorry. I have full faith you'll turn in a brilliant manuscript. I look forward to reading at least three chapters of it and seeing an outline with real details, and maybe then I can get you paid. But right now, no. I'm sorry."

He stood up and wished her a good rest of the day.

He took the elevator down and stepped out onto the sidewalk.

And his phone rang.

2

"Mr. O'Brien, my name's Frank Painter. You emailed me last week about a book you're working on."

Wallace stepped into an alleyway and leaned back against a light pole.

"Yes. Thank you for calling."

"Truly not a problem. I understand you're hoping to write about a past incident here, and you'd like to stay for a while in the park, or as close to it as possible. How long are you hoping to stay?"

"Two months. Give or take."

"We have an artist in residency program, and that allows you to stay in the park under very basic living conditions for two weeks as you create a work of art influenced by the park. I don't think that would work."

"I need more than two weeks."

"I understand. We reviewed your email. We're not sure exactly what you want to say, but we *want* you to say it. Would you be interested in an *expanded* artist in residency with more advanced living conditions?"

Wallace suspected he was, and said so.

"You'd be in the old Toklat River Ranger Station. It hasn't been used since 2007, but we can get you power. You'd have a bathroom and electricity, at least. Two weeks of standard artist in residency—we can add one more. Beyond that, we'd charge you per night the standard rate of camping in Denali at our maintained campsites. Twenty dollars a night—and to be clear, you'd be in the station the whole time, not thrown out in a tent."

Wallace closed his eyes and grinned.

"Pencil me in, Mr. Painter."

3

He stepped out of the alley and walked past a woman who was sitting on a bench reading what looked like a *new* paperback copy of *The Power Play*.

Nothing to see, he thought. No worries. The damage was done. He'd provided Leary some fortune and fame, but it would fade. All he had to do now was get out and focus on his own life. His own *book*.

Late that afternoon, he went to Shavano's and sat down at the bar. He told Peevey he was leaving in a week. Maybe two—but he was leaving, whether he could afford it or not.

"Why wait so long? I assumed you were already gone."

"I'm trying to get paid. I have to write something and get started. Somehow."

Who was he kidding? He wouldn't tell it to Peevey, but be damned if he could string together a sentence. He could try. He could try plenty. Nothing would happen, and he wouldn't get paid. He'd leave here so broke he'd probably come back to… to nothing. He'd come back to nothing.

Fuck you, Leary.

Peevey stood straight across from him, hands clenching the bar's backsplash.

Wallace couldn't place what it was, but something was different about him.

"Beer?" Peevey said.

Somewhat hesitant, Wallace said yes.

Peevey went down to the taps, ran a pint of Boston Lager, brought it down to Wallace, and said: "How much?"

"What?"

"You said you were trying to get paid. How much?"

"What does it matter?" Wallace said—and he immediately regretted it. Peevey didn't mean anything by his prying. Wallace knew he didn't. And here he was acting like a jackass to maybe the only loyal *friend* he had.

Peevey walked away. The bartender filled a tourist's mug and disappeared through the door behind the bar.

Maybe it was none of Peevey's concern how much Wallace needed to get paid, but in a way, it was. You don't spill your guts to a man for years and earn his trust and then act like a prick just because the subject is money.

He has a right to know, Wallace thought. *He's been good to you, and he's accomplished a hell of a lot more in life than you have. This man owns a bar in Manhattan. What do you do?*

The bartender emerged from the back room with a package under his arm. It was a manila envelope, folded over and taped, and when he placed it on the bar next to Wallace's beer, Wallace saw that *O'Brien* was written across the top of the envelope in blue ink.

"Your buddy stepped in," Peevey said. "He said to give this to you."

"Who?"

"You know who."

The obvious hit him. Wallace knew who it was. Leary. But why?

When he started to ask, Peevey raised a hand to cut him off.

"I've noticed him in here a few times," the bartender said. "I had to double check to make sure it was him. He'd just sit at one of the tables, usually reading, occasionally looking up here. I didn't know what he was doing, and I didn't want to ask. Been close to telling you that you might have a stalker, actually. Then he came up to me and handed me this envelope. I haven't opened it." He scanned the room. "And he's not in here now."

Wallace opened the envelope and dumped its contents out on the bar.

It was *The Power Play*, a brand new copy, just like the one he'd seen earlier in the day. Leary had redesigned the cover (kinda better?), *maybe* fixed a few of the errors (Wallace didn't intend to find out), and published it all over again. Demand, probably. God knows the Kindle edition had been selling well.

Wallace said something. He wasn't sure what. He probably called the man an asshole.

"You know," Peevey said, "he seemed like a nice fellow. A little odd, but I wouldn't say he was an asshole, or dangerous."

"Please."

Peevey told him to quit pouting and open the damned book.

"I'm thinking about pouring this beer all over it. It looks like it needs a good drink."

"Just open the book."

"Why?"

"For no other reason than it's a book. Do it."

Wallace opened it.

Why not?

There was a note on the title page:

Do what you want with this. Sell it, or I'm open to criticism. My main purpose is on page 93. You used me, and then I used you. Call it even?

Wallace thought: *What the hell?* And then he turned to page 93 and found a personal check, written for a very recognizable four-figure number: exactly half of what he'd made from *The New Yorker*.

IV
The Wanderer

1

RAWLEIGH MCCOWN SAT ON THE front steps of the Salmon Catch Restaurant and Bar, gazing up at Mount Healy's high and jagged summit ridge. Nearly midnight and the whole scene was still discernible in civil twilight. Rawleigh had been here nearly ten years and he still wasn't quite used to it. He'd never get sick of it, either.

He'd driven down here from his home in Fairbanks about fifteen hours ago.

When he arrived yesterday, old Ellis Everett, the owner of the Salmon Catch and the nine lodging cabins scattered on the hillside behind it, had taken him on a stroll amongst the storm damage.

"The storm rolled right off the top of Healy about two weeks ago," Ellis said. "Started out with all sorts of pretty lights up there over the ridge, like an aurora. Then came the bad weather.

Flooding was a problem. That wash up on the hill turns into a river every time it comes a hard shower. But it was mainly lightning and wind. Lightning struck right over here, right near this one, and these three just burned nearly all the way down. Those two over there need some major work. And look here. Tree collapsed over those two."

It was enough work to keep him busy for at least two months. He'd told Ellis Everett he'd do the work himself, and he wasn't exactly a young fellow anymore, so he'd take his time. They'd agreed on a price, and Rawleigh could stay for no charge in one of the two unharmed cabins, just like the time he'd spent a week here repairing the north wall of the Salmon Catch's bar.

When Morgan told him she wanted to come to Alaska for a few weeks, maybe longer, he'd hesitated. Not because he didn't want to see her, but because he wasn't sure how it would work. He wouldn't be at home, and did she really want to stay here? In a cabin with no electricity and no running water?

Another factor, she wanted to work, and in this area, right outside Denali, job opportunities were sparse.

As it turned out, Ellis told him he could use some help with the bar.

"I could use her any night she wanted to work. It'd get me out of there, and those knuckleheads in there now could quit working ten hour shifts."

Morgan had agreed.

"You'll be living out of a cabin," Rawleigh said. "Has that sunk in yet? As in, a rustic cabin. No power. Community restrooms and showers. Are you up for it?"

"Sounds fun."

"Even if I'll be there?"

"I *am* coming to see you, Uncle Rawleigh."

And God knows, Rawleigh now thought, he *was* looking forward to seeing her. He loved this place. He loved Renee. But there'd been times, many of them, when he wished he'd made some different choices, perhaps not abandoned his family.

When Morgan got here, he'd give her a big hug, buy her a drink or a meal, and they'd catch up. If she wanted to talk about the test, he'd listen to her. He hated what she was going through.

The pressure's from her mother.

He believed this. If not for that bitch his brother had married, Morgan probably wouldn't be going through this.

Maybe it's a good thing he was here. Maybe she needed to come visit him. Maybe…

He looked down at his hands.

Tomorrow morning, he'd start hauling off the scraps of the ruined cabins. Maybe he'd get it all done. Maybe not.

Tomorrow night, he'd drive down to Anchorage and meet his niece at the airport.

2

He'd come down to the Salmon Catch for an evening cup of decaf and conversation with Ellis Everett. They'd downed a full pot of coffee and continued talking long after the tourists and other locals went their own ways. Ellis spoke of his son—he was a troublesome boy who'd once attacked his own mother, and after the kid had a close encounter with a violent crime down in Anchorage, Ellis convinced him to come on up here and get out of the "big city." Ellis shook his head and chuckled, said he worried about him all the time.

"Will you introduce your niece to your lady friend?" Ellis asked, after he was sick of bitching about his boy, and Rawleigh lied and said he probably would. Truth was, about a week ago, right before Morgan had called and said she was going to come visit, and she was sure about it, Renee had wandered off.

She'd done this before. She'd disappear for days at a time, not answer her phone, not send emails or letters, nothing. And then she'd be back. In the empty house across the street from his. In his bedroom. In a grocery store in Fairbanks. Anywhere, anytime, anything was a possibility.

This was part of her.

Renee was simply a mysterious woman.

3

That night, his first night staying in his cabin, he dreamed something that may not have been a dream. With her, it wasn't always easy to tell.

He followed the gravel driveway around the corner of the Salmon Catch and up the hill to the start of the cabins, then set off on a footpath, through the ruined buildings and past the community showers and toilets, until he was unlocking his cabin door.

Inside, he shut and locked the door, took off his clothes, pulled the comforter back, and climbed into bed wearing only his underwear.

Almost immediately, he *thought* he was drifting off to sleep.

But then the door opened—the *locked* door—and Renee entered the room. She sat down at the foot of the bed.

She was, he thought, somewhere around fifty. She was also very attractive, and she'd been there for him. At times, he wasn't sure which of those factors meant the most to him.

"I understand you enjoy your work," she said, "but I can't imagine why you'd want to stay in one of these things and spend your time rebuilding and repairing all this. Seems like hard work and a lot of hassle for minimal reward. Among other things."

He sat up against the wall behind the bed. "When did you get here?"

"A minute ago. But I didn't come to talk you out of your work. Keep a close eye on your niece, if she's going to stay here. I worry about her. And I worry about you."

"Don't worry about me."

"I don't like that storm that came off Mount Healy. Watch her. Watch yourself."

She leaned up the bed and kissed him, squeezed his side, made sure he felt how warm she was—but of course she wasn't going to treat him to anything. She was generous, but she also loved to leave him wanting.

"Be good, Rawleigh."

She kissed him again and walked out the door.

And immediately, it's like she was never there.

He was asleep again… Or maybe he wasn't.

But he thought he was.

4

Around four 'o clock in the morning, his eyes opened again, and he spent a minute or two staring up at the ceiling, trying to determine what it was that woke him: his bladder or the soft sound of footsteps from outside his door. Not that it mattered. He *had* to piss, and doing so required going outside and facing the footsteps' source.

But when he opened the door, nothing.

All the way to the bathroom, nothing.

It was only upon his return trip that he saw the human-like figure walking amongst the ruined cabins.

He almost called out to it, if for no other reason than to determine whether or not it was really there. In the poor lighting, it was truly hard to discern reality from the flaws of his tired eyes.

The figure stopped, turned, and yes—it was definitely there, standing amongst a pile of toppled boards that had once been a cabin.

Renee?

She was a woman who loved her mystery. But this figure did not look like Renee.

Now he *did* call out to it.

"Need something?" he said. "Are you okay?"

He expected a response. He truly did. Because *somebody* was standing there. But whoever it was did not respond. Just stood… perfectly still.

Rawleigh remained still as well, hoping to wait it out. And at some point, it did continue on its way, moving away from him, up the slope, toward the forest.

Who was it? A lost hiker? A sleepwalker from the Mountaintop Lodge down the road? Somebody in need of help?

A ghost?

He decided to leave it be.

But when he returned to bed, he could not sleep.

He got out of bed, dressed again in the sweatpants and flannel shirt he'd used for his bathroom trek, and used the poor lighting of 4:30 in the morning to follow the path up the slope to the ruined cabins. He was alone, and he knew it, but as he walked amongst the storm damage, he spoke—in a perfectly normal, level tone—to whoever it was who *might* (he now thought) have been here before.

Of course nobody answered.

But a scent brushed his nose. Faint, but noticeable. Smoke. Not quite like the building or the woods were on fire. And certainly not cigarette smoke. But smoke. A blown out match?

He used the light on his cell phone to study the area.

Still nothing.

The smoky smell quickly faded.

I need to go to bed. I have to work tomorrow. I have to drive to Anchorage tomorrow. Get out of here and go to bed.

But a gentle breeze coiled out of the trees and brought with it the unmistakably clear sound of somebody breathing.

He froze and told himself that was absolutely false. He should not act like a fool in a fucking movie. The night was still, there was a breeze, and he'd heard the *breeze*—that was it.

But the figure had returned. He knew it before he saw it.

And when he turned to it, this close up view—the thing was less than ten feet away—revealed that it was not at all human, though it was trying to be.

Amidst its dark and smoky form, there were black filaments, coiling, curling, wavering, rising from blood that was bubbling out of the ground.

V
A Face in the Midnight Sun

1

OVER THE YEARS, MORGAN HAD downloaded several albums her uncle had recommended to her. Most of it was progressive rock that on first listen almost always sounded disjointed and bizarre. But out of respect, she occasionally put on her headphones and dipped back in, and sure enough, it grew on her. *Like all the finer things,* he'd say, *it takes time.*

She'd lost herself in some of this music since flying out of Little Rock. Opeth she wasn't yet sure about. Opeth wished to, at once, lure you into a dream and take your face off. She wasn't into the face-removal stuff, but she nevertheless enjoyed many of his recommendations, and she read about forty percent of Stieg Larson's *The Girl with the Dragon Tattoo* on her Kindle.

She switched planes in San Francisco and returned to her music and Larson book. She let herself doze off for an undeterminable period—returned in dream and memory to the intense departing battle with her mother—but when she felt the plane beginning to descend for the second and final time, she sat up in her seat and raised the window shade.

How otherworldly (to this southern girl, anyway) that it was nearly eleven 'o clock p.m. local time, and there was still such substantial daylight peering over the edge of the sea. She'd not yet totally processed this thought when, below them, the clouds broke and snowy mountaintops materialized.

The plane dropped again and turned sharply toward the west.

Shortly after, it hit the runway.

She had only her pack and carry-on bag, and so once she was off the plane, she was quickly out in the lot, cell phone pressed to her ear, cursing her uncle for not answering. After several tries, she sat down on the curb, rubbed her temples, and considered going back inside and renting a car.

Yes, Uncle Rawleigh had said repeatedly that he had an extra vehicle she could drive, an '04 Frontier he'd paid three-thousand for shortly after his move to Fairbanks (he'd since bought himself a Silverado). But if he wasn't going to answer his phone, what was she supposed to do? Spend the night at the airport? Get a taxi and check into a hotel for the night?

She told herself she was jumping to conclusions. He wasn't around his phone right now. That didn't mean she had to—.

Her phone rang. Uncle Rawleigh's number was on the screen.

Thank God.

But the person on the other end of the line was not her uncle. He was a nurse at Anchorage Regional Hospital; Uncle Raweligh had entered the emergency room about two hours ago.

"Just go through the front doors, honey," the nice man said. "They'll tell you where to go."

2

She couldn't bear to think about it, about how unfortunate it would be if she'd come up here just to watch her Uncle Rawleigh die. What did he do? Lord—was it something *she'd* somehow done? This was an absurd thought, but it was *there,* because she was the type who'd somehow find a way to blame herself, and when it was all over, she'd become a loathsome creature of self-pity, asking repeatedly *why* things had to be this way. What had she ever done?

But her uncle wasn't dead. Nor was he dying.

He was sitting up in bed reading a local magazine called *The Unexplored.* He looked her over when she entered the room and grinned, and the grin was wide and sincere. She couldn't believe she was looking at him. And she *certainly* couldn't believe, after everything, that she was *finally* seeing him and he was in a hospital bed. But here he was, and at least he was alive and smiling.

"Sorry about your calls." He set the magazine on the stand by the bed. "The nurse had it on silent and sitting over there in the window."

Morgan pulled a chair up next to his bed and told him not to worry about it; she was glad he was okay.

"Now tell me what happened," she said.

His smile remained, but a subtle change came over his face as he explained that he'd thought, just earlier tonight, that he was having a heart attack.

"I was already on my way down here to meet you. And I was just getting into Anchorage when my heart just, I don't know, *lurched* a couple of times, and I panicked. You do that when your heart does something like that and you're my age. And then it's beating like mad, just *thump thump thump* about ninety miles an hour. I'm sweating, I know something's wrong. And do you know what? I panic, and it starts to hurt. Heart attack, I know it. I just know you're gonna get off the plane and find me dead."

After a minute or so of awkward silence, Morgan said: "So what's wrong?"

"Hypertension that I don't control very well. And a panic attack." His smile returned. "Swear to God."

"I gave you a panic attack, Uncle Rawleigh?"

"I guess you did." He was beaming, but there was still something subtly restless about his expression. "No, of course you didn't. I had a bad night's sleep last night. I don't know if I slept at all. And I had the worst dream. I actually think I went sleepwalking. It was lack of sleep, I think. I asked the doctor about that. She said it could be. But I think she was telling me what I wanted to hear."

"What did you dream?"

"I don't remember all of it. I don't remember *much* of it. I just know, or I think, I saw something—it wasn't a person—looking at me. I *clearly* remember thinking: *This isn't a person, so what is it?* And that's all I remember."

"Like a ghost."

"Like a ghost, yes." The grin again. "Welcome to Alaska, Morgan."

VI
Healy Overlook

1

WALLACE FOLLOWED TOMMY PAINTER, THE man he'd spoken to on the phone, across the back of the Denali Visitor Center's parking lot toward the Park Road. It was a short walk to his temporary living quarters, Painter assured him.

"I followed an eight-hour flight with a three-hour drive," Wallace said. "I'm not worried about walking."

"So you just got here," Painter said.

"I made it last night. I'm running on what fuel you get from five hours of non-sleep in an airport Comfort Inn."

Painter laughed too dramatically.

They were following the Park Road through a sunlit canyon of evergreens; the ascent was gradual but unrelenting. Wallace regretted neglecting his physical health for the better part of the last three years.

"We're excited to have a prize-winning author here, working on a novel no less," Painter said.

Wallace didn't correct him.

Finally, they crested the slope. Up ahead on the left, a narrow gravel drive led out into the trees. Painter made the turn. This skinny little man was resisting with all his might the urge to take off and jog, while Wallace trudged after him one regrettable step at a time.

Exercise, Wallace thought. *I drink too much and worry too much and I have to.*

"I hope the people will enjoy the book, and I hope it will raise awareness about our park." The ranger's voice echoed through the silence and the trees. "I understand the nature of it isn't exactly a celebration of nature, but I hope it casts our park in a positive light and makes people curious."

Wallace wheezed that he hoped so, too, and probably, he actually meant it.

Now they were coming up on a two story brown building that was hidden from the Park Road by a gentle swell in the landscape.

Painter led him up a set of wooden exterior steps to a door on the building's second level.

"We're still trying to make the Toklat Station habitable," he said. "So for now, we're going to put you here with the live-in employees. This room unfortunately won't have the romantic appeal of staying out in the middle of the park, but it's here, and it's quiet."

He unlocked the door and handed Wallace the key.

The two men stepped inside.

It looked just like a hotel room, Wallace thought. Maybe a step or two in the rugged direction.

Painter said: "It's yours till we get your cabin ready, which should be a week. Or two."

This will be fine, Wallace thought. *This will work.*

He looked at Painter and nodded.

"Good," the ranger said. "There is a laundry room downstairs and a cafeteria and workout room further up the path. If you pine for escape or a drink, the Salmon Catch is about your only choice. But it's good and it's right outside the park. Make a left on the highway. You won't miss it."

"Thank you," Wallace said.

"We're glad to have you. Write a good book. And welcome to Denali."

2

The view through the window was not one of sweeping mountain ranges and gray glacial rivers. Just trees. But that was preferable, actually. In time, he'd be out in the mountains, settled in the remains of what had once been a ranger station, and the only reminders he'd have that there were indeed human beings still on this planet would be whatever scattered evidence the Park Road periodically sent his way on its shuttle buses.

For now, this, and this was fine. This was not New York. He could write here.

He opened the bathroom door.

Not pretty. But so what?

He pocketed the key and went outside and down the steps, then trekked back up to the Park Road, where he made a right and returned to the visitor center. Before going inside, he stopped to inspect a sign at the back of the parking lot. It was posted next to the start of a wide dirt path that led north into the forest... toward a rugged mountainside.

HEALY OVERLOOK TRAIL, the sign read.

He looked up at the mountainside and decided *that* would certainly go a long way toward getting him in shape.

3

The view again, the trees, just the trees, and the hour was getting late, but it wasn't yet time to go get drunk and waste himself away; he was writing—attempting to piece together a rough narrative based on his notes and interviews and what he knew and thought he knew—and he was far away from everything that pissed him off. He was writing *something*. And that's what mattered.

Maybe it wasn't yet Great and Important. But it *would* be. It was based on fact. It would be *filled* with facts. It would be filled with this *place*.

I'm not writing.

No, he was staring out at the trees.

I don't know anything.

Not true. He had enough of the women's backgrounds to begin the narrative, or at least begin to structure a very thick outline.

Mary was a native of Alaska, but nobody knew her. *Nobody.* None of the kind folks he'd spoken to knew much at all about her, aside from what they'd learned in casual conversation. Yes, they'd known Emily very well, particularly the teachers and professors he'd spoken to: she was—*had been*—a good kid, a fine student. Responsible, intelligent, well-liked by everybody who knew her.

According to a young lady who'd claimed to be her best friend while they were in junior high, Emily had been born in Fairbanks (supposedly on a quilt in Mary's living room floor). Mary had moved them to New Hampshire after Emily's dad died. Mary had never married the man, according to Emily's friend. Mary had disclosed to this friend, after she'd indulged in a bit too much wine, (and while Emily was using the restroom) that she'd *never* had any intention of marrying Joseph Paul Hillward. She'd only wanted a relationship and a kid.

She got both, and after Joseph Paul Hillward's extension ladder slipped out from under him while he was painting a garage gable and "what brains he had" were revealed to the open air by the very rock that was supposed to hold his ladder in place, Mary threw a dart at a map—New Hampshire—and they got out. Why not?

"I didn't know how it was going to go," she'd said to the friend during her wine-fueled monologue, "but I thought I'd see. I thought my daughter could have something closer to a normal life in the lower forty-eight. I didn't really care where."

Wallace had asked the friend why Mary had been so convinced that Emily wouldn't have normalcy in Alaska. The friend had shrugged and said it was probably something to do with the dad (or the cold, or the dark winters, or the constant daylight in the summer months, or all of it).

Wallace's final piece of research before flying to Alaska had been to dig into the existence of Joseph Paul Hillward.

It was very boring.

The man had been a preacher and a builder. He'd married twice. Both ended in divorce. According to his only sibling, an older sister, he'd cheated on his second wife with Mary, but it was what it was, and she thought he truly loved Mary. He and Mary never did move in together; nor did they ever consider getting married. But they stayed together for a long time, having fun and never getting serious. Mary wanted a kid but thought she'd never get pregnant, and Joseph Paul Hillward disclosed to his sister more than once that he never even bothered "using anything." And then Emily was born. Shortly after, Joseph Paul Hillward's brief and fairly vanilla existence came to an end.

There would not be much of this man in the book, Wallace thought.

If there was a book.

He wrote for another hour. He did not let himself look up. Just wrote. It was a good start, important stuff, and it was only when several of his fingers began to ache and twitch that he set the pencil down and let himself indulge the idea of a few drinks at the Salmon Catch.

It was nine p.m. when he stepped out of his room.

He looked up at the gray, early stages of what passed for twilight here this time of year and thought: *I feel good. I accomplished a lot more than I thought I would. And it's not even late.*

He climbed in the Escape he'd signed a long-term rental deal on and followed the Park Road out to the highway.

He turned left and immediately began to look for the bar.

4

"Food or just the beer?"

Wallace told the young bartender he was just drinking tonight.

The Salmon Catch was built into a hillside, and the barroom was at the top of a short flight of steps, which separated it from the more family-oriented remainder of the restaurant. The bar ran the length of the room's back wall. Behind it were the typical mirrors and whiskey bottles and beer taps. Throughout the rest of the room were tables and booths. A flat screen television hung on the furthest wall. It was tuned to ESPN, and most of tonight's patrons were gathered in its vicinity watching an early season baseball game.

Of the half dozen patrons who weren't honed in on the Mariners, five of them were in a booth sharing a massive bowl of nachos, and one had just sat down on the stool right next to him.

He'd moved over from the end of the bar, a skinny kid with an intense, chiseled face who was almost certainly a local. He was working on (Wallace figured) his third or fourth tall one.

"What are you drinking?" the kid said.

"Alaskan Amber."

"I go cheap. Name's Cochran. They call me Cork, so that's it."

Cork extended a hand. Wallace shook it and told him his name.

Thankfully, Cork didn't recognize him and ask why he'd plagiarized a book and then fled up to the frozen wilderness.

"Where are you from, Wallace O'Brien? Don't mind me saying so, you sure as hell ain't local, so don't say you are. Maybe it's the uncombed long-ish hair and the way you look around the room. You know."

Wallace couldn't help but grin. He said he was a writer from New York, and Cork nodded along as if he were truly surprised (yet not surprised) to hear this.

And then Cork launched into his story, how he'd worked in the logging industry since he was sixteen years old. Had spent a long time down in Anchorage, till his dad convinced him to move up here where it was more peaceful. Wallace studied him the whole time he talked. He'd originally thought of the kid's face as *intense*, and while that was accurate, that wasn't all of it. His mouth twisted around every word he spoke, and his left eye was about half an inch lower than his right one. *Intense,* yes. Strange? Indeed. And more.

"I've been coming to this bar since I moved up here," Cork said. "It's all we got, so it's a good thing it's a good one, right?" He nodded at the bartender who'd served Wallace his beer. "Most everybody in here is from out of town, even the workers. That dude's been here forever, like ten years. He remembers when the crazy guy crashed through the north wall."

Cork's volume rose with the last sentence, and the "dude" turned to him and grinned.

Cork continued: "So one day, this dumbass brings his truck right through that wall, right below where the TV is. If it happened tonight it'd wipe out all those people, you know? Right there. Happened early enough in the day that there weren't many people up here. Nobody got killed."

Cork drained the last of his beer and brought the glass down with a solid *thump*.

Dude took it and ran another round of Budweiser into it.

Cork drank up and kept on: "I know him, yeah, he's worked here forever. And there's a few of 'em down in the restaurant I know, but I don't eat down there much. Lots of times someone new shows up, like..." He scanned the length of the bar. "Like her, way down there, the girl opening the Heineken. I don't know her. She must be new."

The kid should have seemed entirely harmless, Wallace thought—except for the perpetual *intense* strain on his face.

"She's probably cool," Cork said. "Oh yeah, that Alaskan beer is good, by the way. I go the cheap route. So what are you writing about?"

The question, Wallace thought. He knew it was coming.

Wallace said: "I'm writing about a disappearance."

"Like of a person?"

"Of two people."

Cork leaned close. "The Rawlins, eh? Want to hear something else? About that wall? Something I forgot?" He didn't give Wallace a chance to respond. "They always talk like it was the weather that sent crazy truck guy through that wall. But that's not the whole story. Some say there was a woman. A *ghost*."

Wallace hadn't expected to give a damn.

But he kind of did.

"Somebody was in the road," Cork said, "if you believe the driver. But they, you know, never found anybody. Spooky to me. I believed him."

Wallace might *give a damn* about the story; indeed, it *could* be extremely relevant, but that didn't mean he believed it. Local folklore might be significant, but after thinking about it for approximately five seconds, he decided it was a tired old tale.

"Look it up." Cork had his eyes on the new female bartender. "Want another beer?"

5

When he left the Salmon Catch just shy of midnight, he was not thinking about ghosts in the highway. He had his own story to tell, one that was much more serious. In time, he'd talk with the owner of the Salmon Catch, the same owner who'd rented a cabin to Mary and Emily Rawlins... But he'd seen no sign of the owner, and Cork had distracted him. And he'd drank too much.

Drunk for sure, but not so far gone he couldn't walk. Probably he could drive back to the visitor center. It was only two miles, right? Or less? Probably. But probably he should not. So walk. He was sober enough to do a straight line, one foot in front of the other, all the way to where he started. Go. That's all it was, and he grinned at the idea that *he* was the ghost in the road now.

He walked along the highway. He'd do a good job of staying on the shoulder, but then he'd veer and return... again and again.

He'd gone he didn't know how far, a quarter of a mile, or half a mile, when he looked back. He wasn't far from either location, but he felt so incredibly isolated, and the night, while still much brighter than he considered the norm for such an hour, was nevertheless dark enough to stir uneasiness.

Your head is clearing, he thought. *The Escape is back there. Your bed is up ahead. You drank too much, and you've realized your situation.*

His head *was* clearer, yes.

And this wasn't the first time such a thing had happened to him.

He'd go for a walk tomorrow, go back and get the Escape. For now, he... He what? Needed to go to bed? No, he didn't need his bed. He felt pretty good, actually. He'd indulged a few too many. But he felt okay. He wasn't stumbling anymore (was he?) and he walked on and thought about his conversation with Cork and the words he'd written earlier, his first words in Alaska. He thought about how this place was exactly the same as he remembered, but it didn't remember *him,* did it?

His heart thudded rapidly.

The beer's lingering effects, the gradual ascent of the highway... it felt good.

Funny, the land's effect on his mind.

It'll be the best thing I've written, he thought.

But was it even his?

It was their story. He was just the messenger.

Nevertheless, the book would hit with a bang and pull him out of the ever-shifting storm that was his current financial situation. He'd inevitably be nominated for a few awards, and he'd surely win at least one of them.

It was all in front of him, his story or not, if he could just finish (start?) the damned thing.

Don't squander this opportunity.

Don't you feel your heart racing, Wallace? Don't waste it.

The turnoff for the Park Road emerged from the dim midnight glow.

He turned and walked toward the hulking shadow of the visitor center.

But before he ever reached the building, he reached the start of the HEALY OVERLOOK TRAIL. He stood and pondered it, knowing that taking off down the trail was a dangerous, foolish, absurd thing to do at such an hour—but he hadn't come here because he was a practical sort of man. Correct?

He did not need sleep, so he started up the trail.

6

He did not think much.

The mere act of following the trail in such poor lighting (and in such a poor mental state) occupied the remainder of his mental capacity.

He told himself that was the point of it.

Through the trees, the trail wound up and up the Healy massif's forested southern slope. For long stretches the trees hovered closely over both sides of the trail, and there was no light at all; he could just as easily have been in a cave.

The trail went on and on. His legs tired. Finally, he let himself collapse.

What in the *fuck* had he been thinking? But he wasn't thinking (*and you still aren't, you damned fool*), and yes, he was too tired to start now.

Close your eyes.

But he was in the middle of a trail, and…

And he did it. It was simple.

And they stayed shut.

7

He awoke and winced at the pain in the side of his head, from the rock he'd used as a pillow.

He sat up.

The sky was still dark, but he removed his phone from his pocket and saw that it was five a.m.

He remembered nothing—until he remembered it all. He grinned at how stupid he was. He wondered how drunk he'd been, and then he remembered pondering that very issue just a few hours ago. So he couldn't have been *that* drunk, could he?

At least he could see the path now.

He did not debate his options for long. He stood and continued forward.

Less than a hundred yards from where he'd slept, the trail broke above the trees, and a sharp wind hit him immediately.

Now he was awake and sober, and more driven than he'd felt in a long time.

He hiked up and up through the rocks until he was just twenty or thirty feet below what had to be the overlook, where the trail ended, but the ridge swept off to the north toward the distant cone-shaped summit of Healy itself.

A corner of the sky was partially aglow in various shades of pink and orange, and the landscape before him was alien. The rocks were bare, the ridge jagged and dramatic, a knife edge broken by rolling summits and rising towers of bare rock.

He took a step toward the overlook—and stopped.

Someone was on the ridge above him.

This figure had not been there a few seconds ago. Or maybe Wallace had confused him or her for a rock.

The figure wavered in the wind like cloth, barely visible. Maybe moving towards the summit? Maybe not.

Wallace almost called out, but what would he say?

He had no time to decide.

The figure was gone.

He finished the trek to the overlook.

Trees, mountains, ridges. Far below him, the Nenana River, the gray roof of the Salmon Catch, the Mountaintop Lodge perched upon a hillside. Behind him, he thought the other hiker might've come back into view.

But when he looked, it was just the ridge, and the distant, dawn-painted summit.

I'm not alone, he thought, as if he knew whether or not that was a good thing.

VII
Ghost Story

1

WHEN SHE SOMETIMES WONDERED WHY she was here (something she'd pondered repeatedly since arriving), Morgan reminded herself how little she'd thought of the bar exam or of her mother and that gosh-awful fight they'd had shortly before Morgan left. Since she'd left Little Rock, none of her former life seemed to matter. She thought of Uncle Rawleigh and how happy he'd been to see her. And even considering all that, her being here didn't make any practical sense, which meant she'd made the right decision.

At six a.m., she drove out to the Denali Visitor Center and set off for a jog up the Park Road. She'd barely been gone for half an hour when, on a whim, she flagged down one of the shuttle busses and caught a ride deeper into the park. Now, she was making her way along the gravel bar of the Toklat River, dodging its various woven tendrils of gray water, constantly looking up and around, as if some part of this vast, mountainous landscape might evade her.

It was always the same, yet there was always something new.

"Be careful out there," Uncle Rawleigh had said. "I'd go with you, but I'm already behind."

Indeed, she'd stepped out of her cabin this morning at 5:30 to make a trip down to the restrooms, and he'd been throwing cabin scraps in the back of his truck. She'd offered to help but he told her she better not. "It's going to be a beautiful day," he said. "Go see the park. You'll know why you're here."

The air was crisp and cool, and though she hadn't (and wouldn't) wander far from the road, she seemed to be the only person in the world, a tiny lone speck in the middle of the wilderness.

She reached a wide, dry place in the riverbed and sat down against a rock. This location offered a compelling view of the mountains' lower slopes; the upper reaches were obscured by clouds.

No matter. She hadn't come out here for any specific purpose. She just wanted to sit and think and thank God for the present. Better to serve drinks in paradise than law it all up in Hell, and all that.

She slid her butt forward in the gravel, tucked her windbreaker behind her head, laced her hands together just below her breasts, and closed her eyes. In her mind's eye, she still saw the mountains. She let herself drift away, until a slight rustle in the silence jarred her.

When she opened her eyes, she saw, on the other side of the gravel bar, a blond-colored bear. So close! The great beast moved slowly along the edge of the river, seemingly oblivious to her.

Morgan eased up on her elbows.

She was somehow not frightened.

The sight of the bear fascinated her, and she knew that if she just sat here and let her be (she already thought of the beast as a girl), enjoyed her company, she would be fine. Correct?

The bulge in the bear's back rolled, and for a moment their gazes met.

The bear looked at her until something in the water caught her attention. She dipped a paw in the glacier melt and swatted. Eventually, she moved on down the river.

2

Upon returning, Morgan went down to the bathrooms for a shower, then went to her cabin and passed out on the bed for over an hour.

She awoke to the faint smell of smoke, but by the time she got out of bed and dressed, the smell was gone, and she almost convinced herself it hadn't been there at all.

No. It was there.

Not cigarette smoke, either.

Her legs did not feel sore or numb from her brief foray, so she took a lengthy stroll around the area. Her uncle was not around; she assumed he was hauling off a load of cabin scraps.

At six 'o clock, she went down to the Salmon Catch, put a speed opener in her back pocket, and dove into duty. And *dove* was an apt term; the Salmon Catch bar was awash with the strongest evening crowd she'd seen in her brief time as one of its employees.

Eventually, too, *he* came in.

All she knew about him was that he was a local who frequently drank himself into a stupor. And one of his eyes was too low, he looked like a creep, and he was called *Cork*.

He sat down on an open stool at his usual end of the bar. And since her help had supposedly developed a bladder infection half an hour after she arrived, Cork was her responsibly.

"Budweiser," he said when she placed a napkin in front of him. "We'll go from there."

She ran his beer, cut off some foam, ran some more, set it on the napkin, and went on down the bar before he could speak again. He really wasn't all that bad, but he made her uneasy, and yes, she was getting tired. Tonight was busy—whiskey and water, please, Sam Adams, in a bottle is fine, just a Pepsi right now, Coors, can I get a water with a lemon?—she had no help, and maybe she was feeling the effects of her hike.

She looked out at the room, at this different world.

And then her uncle came through the door. He spotted her, waved, and sat down at Cork's end of the bar. He told her it had been a hell of a day, but unlike the last two, it had been a *productive* day. And so a drink, please, whatever, he'd just have one, maybe two.

She went off to pour his drink. When she returned, he was conversing intently with two tourists from Oregon who were treating him, a real-life local, like he was a member of an endangered species.

Cork called to her.

He raised his empty glass with one hand and gestured for her to come over with the other.

He did not lecture her about the consequences of letting glasses sit empty, not this time—he asked her if she'd met the writer yet, O'Brien was his name.

She stepped away and filled his glass.

"I guess I haven't." She handed him his beer.

"Strange guy. I talked to him a long time. He sat right here next to me." Cork animatedly looked around the room. "He might be in here tonight. Or maybe I scared him off."

Morgan smiled. "No, not you."

He returned her smile; it was uneven, a folded up and awkward thing. "I told him the story about the ghost lady in the road that caused a guy to drive through that wall. So maybe?"

"I don't know. I've never heard it."

"Well then. There's something I need to fix."

3

"They like you." The owner of the Salmon Catch locked the door behind them.

It was one in the morning. Morgan had spent most of the night thinking she'd be locking up on her own, but sometime around ten 'o clock, Mr. Everett had noticed she was running the bar by herself.

"I enjoy working here," she said.

He sat down on the front steps and patted the space next to him.

She sat down.

"Thing is," he said, "this place has pretty much been the entirety of my life since 1990 or 91. You'd think I could remember, but I can't. It's a successful place, and I've had a lot of good help. But not much in the last few years, I'll be honest. I understand if you want to work this job for a couple of weeks or a month, stick around while your uncle's down here, and then leave. That's what I expected when Rawleigh told me about you. You aren't from here and may not want to *ever* say you're from here. I get that. But..." A few bobbles of the head, indicating cautious thought. "But a lot of people come up here with similar intentions and end up staying. I've seen it more than a few times; they fall in love with the mountains or the solitude and stick around. I've watched you these last few days. You're intelligent and educated. You work well with people, even the worst ones. And most importantly, you work your ass off. If you want to stick around a while, I'll help you any way I can."

She blushed and thanked him.

"You're a good kid, Morgan."

4

She slid a note under her uncle's door that read *Good night & I love you* and went to bed.

The next morning, she awoke at seven, showered, dressed in tights and shorts and a Nike sweatshirt, and rode a bus back into Denali. This time she went deeper into the park, all the way to Eielson. She jogged west into the wide open land. Most of the mountains, including Denali, were hidden by clouds.

She made it back to the park entrance by early afternoon, and by then, the whole sky was completely clouded over.

She stepped off the bus and circled around to the front of the visitor center. And he was there, at her uncle's Frontier. Cork had lowered the tailgate and was sitting on it, feet dangling, hands folded in his lap. From here, she could see the slightly unnatural glimmer in his eyes, particularly the right one, the one that sagged halfway down his cheek.

She looked around.

Less than ten spaces down, a family was piling into a Dodge Caravan. Several tourists were gathered around the building's front doors; a few kids were emerging from the Healy Trail at the back of the lot.

He's not going to do anything. You're just paranoid.

But she *wasn't* one to be paranoid. She'd always been bold, self-reliant, and trusting in the sense that she figured most people might not be *decent*, but most at least had some semblance of self-control.

And here she was, making sure she wasn't alone in the middle of the day on a parking lot in a national park.

Because of Cork. No, because of Cork's *appearance*. If he looked like a television hero or a football star, she wouldn't be having these thoughts, would she? Christ, how shallow she was!

She approached the truck like he wasn't there and tossed her pack in the passenger seat.

"What are you doing here?" she said.

"I came to tell you a ghost story."

She did not sit down next to him. She did not walk away. Nor did she lecture him about touching other people's stuff. She simply leaned against the side of the truck and asked him why he wasn't at work.

"Took the day off."

"How did you know I was here?"

He did not answer. Simply grinned.

"Do you want to hear the ghost story here?" he said. "Or would you like to go get some coffee at the gas station? They have good coffee."

She only thought for a moment.

She did not want to go get coffee with this guy. But sitting in the station across the highway from the Salmon Catch sounded better than being *here*. This was awkward. And in the deepest parts of her imagination, she could imagine him coming up with some not-quite unreasonable story to lure her into the woods. And then?

It's just the grin.

And the eye.

And the fact that he's here.

"Let's go get coffee," she said.

5

They sat at one of the picnic tables at the end of the building. The highway ran on one side of them, the Nenana River on the other, at the bottom of its shallow gorge.

It didn't take long for Cork to leap into his ghost story.

He started with the man driving his truck through the Salmon Catch Bar's north wall and went backwards. No, the man hadn't been drunk or stoned. No, at first the man wasn't sure what happened. And then he recalled the lady in the road—no, the *shape* of a lady in the road.

Definitely a woman, yet *not* a woman.

The grin was back. She wished he would stop.

"You don't hear much about her," Cork said, "but I've seen her. Sometimes she looks human. Sometimes she doesn't. Some people think it's the Rawlins mother. I'll be glad to tell you all about *that,* too."

He went silent and raised his coffee cup as if to salute her.

The Nenana roared at the bottom of the gorge.

VIII
Progress & Therapy

1

WALLACE O'BRIEN WORKED. SOMETIMES ALL night and into the dark hours of the morning. He typically slept through breakfast and slouched into the cafeteria for an early lunch after waking and drinking coffee during the course of a short walk. And after lunch, he went back to work, writing, outlining, scratching his head, cursing, writing some more. Most nights, he took a break in the evening for dinner (and drinks) at the Salmon Catch.

One night, a little over a week into his stay, Tommy Painter stopped by his room to see how he was doing.

Ordinarily, Wallace would have been annoyed by the interruption, but he'd just returned from dinner and a walk, hadn't yet returned to work, and truth be told, he didn't know if he could. There was a necessary angle he did not have. He'd procrastinated about talking to Ellis Everett, and only God knew why.

And, to hell with it. Painter was a good excuse to not work, especially since the good man had brought along a six pack.

They took seats by the window, and Painter immediately asked about the book. Wallace told him the truth: it had been going fine, but he'd reached a point where decisions must be made, and he wasn't yet equipped to make them.

"The old Toklat station is coming along," Painter said. "Cleaned up pretty well, just waiting on electricity. We'd like you to be able to make a pot of coffee and charge your phone or computer. 'Course, it looks like you do most of your writing the old fashioned way."

Wallace's current Moleskin and mechanical pencil were on the table between them.

"First drafts, yes." Wallace thumbed the notebook's pages. "That's how I think."

"Is it true about the bear?"

"On the Toklat River," Wallace said. "Years ago."

"That's amazing. Ed Merkin out at Eielson—he's worked here since the end of the Cretaceous Period—he told me you were the one who'd been slapped down by the bear. 'Long haired artsy guy? Writer, right? I remember him.' He said you came into the Eielson Center delirious, couldn't even talk about it till you had a drink."

Wallace grinned. "That man has a hell of a memory."

"We've been seeing bears frequently out in this area. Be careful."

"I'll do that. Thank you."

2

He'd scribbled notes on the back of an envelope. The top half of the envelope was a list of names labeled ACTORS. The two at the top, Emily Rawlins and Mary Rawlins, were separated from the rest with a thick black line. These two were gone, likely dead. He wouldn't be talking to them. Below them, he'd listed and checked off the *actors* he'd contacted in New Hampshire. They'd provided him nearly a full legal pad of notes. Below the New Hamsphirites were the Alaskans, and the first name without a checkmark was Ellis Everett. Next, someone Painter had just mentioned: Ed Merkin. Merkin had been mentioned in the news articles. After Merkin, a State Trooper named Cormac Pearce. And just now, he scribbled the name *Cork*.

From Ellis Everett down, no checkmarks. He needed checkmarks.

Painter's last two beers were on the windowsill, as if they contained some decorative value. He stared at them for several minutes, and then his gaze went beyond them to the dim nighttime and the black shapes of leaves and limbs.

He needed conversations. He needed more. He needed checkmarks.

He went to the bathroom, took a long and extravagant piss, stripped, and collapsed onto the bed.

Sleep came instantly.

He awoke only once, at 7:15, when he heard the first bus of the day rumble by, not too far in the distance.

At ten 'o clock, he got out of bed, put on jeans and a long sleeve shirt, and went down to the cafeteria for the scraps they left from breakfast.

He did not immediately return to his room.

He needed to wander and think.

So he started up the slope toward the Park Road, just in time to hear the soft, regular patter of shoes on pavement. And then, to his left, an approaching glimmer of pink between the trees.

He stepped up to the road in time to see a young female jogger dressed in athletic shorts over tights and a bright pink nylon pullover approaching from the park's interior. She waved and smiled pleasantly when she spotted him watching her.

Wallace watched her disappear toward the visitor center.

She looked familiar, and that night, he knew why.

She was behind the bar at the Salmon Catch.

"So you're the jogger," he said after he picked his poison. "You're not named Peevey are you?"

She gave him a funny look as she ran his beer from the tap. "Morgan."

"Sad. I'd hoped you were qualified to discuss my problems."

"Peevey is your therapist?"

"The best bartender in New York."

"I'm sorry," the pretty jogger said. "I doubt I'm the best bartender *here*."

She smiled pleasantly as she set off for the end of the bar.

Wallace drank his beer.

When she returned, he asked her if the owner—Ellis Everett—was around somewhere.

"Sometimes he's here this late. But not tonight. He'll be back tomorrow."

Wallace thanked her.

He'd come back tomorrow then, for lunch, and get his checkmark.

IX
The Cabin Next Door

1

RAWLEIGH WAS EXHAUSTED.

The tearing down and initial cleanup was a much larger task than he'd envisioned. Yes, he was taking his time. He awoke these days with sore knees and a stiff back. He usually quit by midafternoon so he'd have the willpower to drag his ass out of bed the next morning. Lord knows, this was never going to get done with record brevity.

But he was exhausted. And it was taking forever.

Two full days just to haul away the ruined remains of the cabins that were totally gone. And he'd spent all of today doing exactly what he'd been doing yesterday: taking a sledge hammer and pry bar to the cabins that had been severely damaged by the fallen tree. Pounding, prying, loading in the truck bed, hauling off. Rinse, repeat, and damnation, he was sixty-two years old and half broken down. He'd prefer to spend his days with a joint and a playlist of Blue Oyster Cult and Led Zeppelin, maybe some wild and crazy modern shit like Opeth or Riverside thrown in the mix to spice it up, take him away pretty far. Yes, that's what he should be doing.

But no, he was a sucker for punishment, and punishment it was.

It was after ten. He'd tried to listen to music and doze off, but he was too tired (and sore) to doze off.

And when he closed his eyes, the thoughts came.

It was easy to convince himself they were crazy—*Do the dead speak? Do the dead harm us?*—but were they?

He knew better.

He listened to the night.

Maybe he should return to his music.

But he imagined Renee coming in from the outside, and she'd stand near the door for a moment, then sit down on the side of the bed, and she'd make fun of him, ask him why he wanted to be so foolish and crazy. All day long, he was fine, and then the night comes, and... And what?

He saw something? He didn't?

Of *course* he did.

Right out there.

And what was it?

I'm tired and sore. Take an Advil. Go to sleep.

He stared up at the ceiling... and thought, and thought. He heard a rattling noise. A door? Not *his* door, the noise was too muffled... He would know it if it were *his* door. The wind?

He held his breath and listened.

There was a breeze.

Morgan?

Maybe Morgan was going to the bathroom. Maybe she'd left her door open and it was blowing in the wind.

Maybe.

It was a sane thought, wasn't it? Though he wasn't sure that was it. Was there a breeze? Could the breeze produce such a noise?

For the sake of going to sleep, he preferred to think so.

2

Morgan, he knew, had taken to starting each day by jogging several miles up and down the Park Road in Denali.

But she delayed her jog that morning.

She found him at a quarter past six as he was pushing a wheelbarrow of scraps toward his truck.

He could see that something wasn't quite right.

"Are you okay?" he said.

"Can we talk?"

He nodded, said yes, sure they could, and he released the wheelbarrow and took off his gloves.

Ten minutes later, they were drinking coffee on the steps of the Salmon Catch.

"Something happened," she said.

A sour ball of acid rose into Rawleigh's throat. He choked it back.

Morgan said: "When I got off work last night, I smelled smoke. I've smelled it before and not thought much about it. I went to sleep. I heard my door rattling. Someone was trying to get in. I thought I was dreaming. I sat up in bed and tried to wake up, but I was already awake, so I waited for it to stop. It did. But someone was trying to get in."

"Did you go to the door?"

"No. I was scared." She sipped her coffee. "I still am. But I'm better."

"It was windy last night."

This silenced their conversation. At least for a few minutes.

"Cork told me about the 'ghost lady' in the road."

"Ah," Rawleigh said, "the wisdom of your boss's living disappointment."

It didn't take her long to realize what he'd said.

"Cork is—?"

"Ellis's son, yes."

"Neither of them has ever mentioned that."

"Why would they? Cork isn't a reliable source about anything, and Ellis has every reason to be embarrassed of him. Cork is supposedly a smart guy. But he's not worth shit."

Rawleigh regretted his words as soon as they were out. Morgan had never heard him speak like this.

Again, their conversation stalled.

And again, Morgan was the one who salvaged it: "Have you heard the story?"

"About the ghost? That all started after a bad driver put a hole in one of the Salmon Catch's walls. It's not a story so much as an excuse. I heard it then, but I haven't thought much about it since."

"Cork said it's probably the missing Rawlins woman, the mother. I read about them. There's not much, but I got the gist. Do you think she'd be rattling doors at night?"

He was silent for a minute. "I doubt it."

"But maybe?"

He shrugged. "It's a thought."

3

Morgan went off to Denali and Rawleigh returned to work.

He loaded the contents of the wheelbarrow into his truck bed and set off to gather another load.

I heard it, Morgan. I doubt it was the wind.

The driver who'd taken out the north wall of the Salmon Catch bar had been a tourist from California. He'd been driving a rented 4x4 Tacoma, and had spent that day exploring the back country along the Nenana. The man had not been drinking, and he hadn't *appeared* to be lying. He'd told the cops repeatedly he knew how to drive, he'd been paying attention. And for a few minutes, he'd avoided bringing it up, but they wanted a reason. If he wasn't drunk, if he was paying attention, what had steered him into the building? Why would he do that?

Rawleigh hadn't *been there*, but he'd talked to Ellis about it the next day, when he met with the owner to discuss repairs.

"Said somebody or something was out in the road. A lady. He didn't say this to the authorities, but he said it to me: said she looked like death, and she grinned at him. He said he looked at her for about two seconds too long, then cut to the left... And that's how we're here."

Rawleigh, of course, had told Ellis he didn't believe it. The man hadn't been paying attention, missed a curve in the road, and had offered up a Stephen King story to cover his ass, though why he'd gone with something so unbelievable was admittedly bizarre.

But regardless.

Truthfully, Rawleigh *did* perhaps believe it, at least a little bit.

But he couldn't say such a thing to just anybody.

The storm stirred something up.

Oh, for the love of—.

A familiar red Tundra came up the drive.

Ellis Everett pulled in behind Rawleigh's truck and rolled down his window.

"Cleaner back here." The old man was smoking one of his foul menthol cigarettes. He'd claimed for years he was trying to quit; it never happened.

Rawleigh approached and said there'd eventually be some construction going on.

"Take your time, you geezer," Ellis said. "I wrote the whole summer off, anyway."

4

Later, he sat down on his tailgate and opened a bottle of Gatorade, but he didn't sit for long.

He walked over to Morgan's cabin and inspected the door.

Pulled it.

The door rattled, of course.

Pulled it again, held it, tried to determine if a strong breeze could somehow rattle it.

He decided it was possible. But not likely.

5

The lunch crowd on the Salmon Catch's lower level was going strong, but Rawleigh found something closer to peace and quiet in the bar.

He also found Ellis Everett sitting with a long-haired stranger in a booth by the window.

Ellis caught Rawleigh looking and waved him over.

Rawleigh wasn't sure what he was in for, but what the hell? He stepped over to them and slid in beside the Salmon Catch owner.

"We've got a celebrity here," Ellis Everett said. "This is Wallace O'Brien, published writer. He's staying in the park and writing a novel about the Rawlins women. You remember that, I'm sure. They disappeared right before you came down here to fix our wall."

Raweligh nodded and extended a hand to the writer.

Wallace shook it.

"They were staying in one of the cabins that got destroyed a few weeks ago," Ellis said. "Rawleigh's helping me repair them. Anyway, no, I didn't talk to either of them very much. Not at all. I know they were from New Hampshire, and Mary told me they *were* returning to Alaska full time. But Mary wanted her daughter to experience Denali, and they rented one of my cabins for... I'd have to look. A month? After the daughter disappeared, Mary hung around here for a long time. I *do* remember something memorable: she showed me a trick one night, was sitting over there at the bar. What she did was, she vanished a coin, picked a quarter up off the bar, squeezed a fist around it, opened it, and it wasn't there anymore. She looked up at me and flashed me the weakest, saddest smile you've ever seen. All because of a missing quarter? No, of course not. I'll always remember that. She hung around here, hoping they'd find Emily. She wanted to be here if they did."

The writer retrieved his phone from his pocket and set it to record.

"I want to talk about your business," Wallace said, "and then we'll get back to Mary and Emily..."

Rawleigh got up and said he was going to the bar for some food and water. Leave them be, he thought. He'd had enough of such talk.

And he was hungry.

X
A Lurking Presence

1

MORGAN WANTED TO SLEEP AFTER her two-mile jog along Denali's Park Road. But after she returned to her cabin, stripped down to her panties and tee shirt, and collapsed on the bed, she thought of home—specifically, she thought of her mother, shaking her head as she stared into her eyes, disappointment and disbelief, so much in those eyes, and then her mother faded away, and sleep evaded her still.

This was not simply a case of her eyes refusing to stay shut because of a busy mind or a caffeine overload; this was an unrestful slumber in which her head went numb and her eyelids grew heavy, yet she could *not* sleep, not a chance. And she couldn't get up, either.

I'm too tired.

And uncomfortable. This, perhaps, most of all, because—.

The smoke.

Surely not, but yes, a wisp of that not unpleasant odor passed briefly beneath her nose, gone as soon as it was there.

Get up.

She did so. She sat up and looked around the room.

Dim, just the daylight around the door and around the closed window above the bed. Nothing unusual. Not even smoke. So why was her heart beating so rapidly? Why was she so unnerved?

Because I'm bleeding.

It was a silly little realization that occurred to her only when she felt something *off* and looked down. The sight effectively brought her back to reality, this little spot that wasn't altogether alarming (but wasn't normal, either). She'd just dealt with this *little reality* less than two weeks ago. But it wasn't much, and she didn't even have to go to the bathroom to deal with it. She took a pad out of her toiletries bag, put it in place, and crawled back beneath the covers. Soon, she'd all but forgotten about it.

I need to sleep.

Yes. I do.

I came up here to visit my uncle and jog and look at mountains and flowers. Not listen to creepy cockeyed guys tell ghost stories. Give me a break.

She closed her eyes.

Sleep was close.

At last, it came.

She wasn't sure how long it lasted, and when she opened her eyes, she knew immediately that she was being watched, and the voyeur was most likely above her.

It could have been a trick of the light or her imagination (or pure insanity?)—or maybe something was actually there—but yes, she was being watched from behind the bed.

There is a wall *behind the bed, dear. Just a wall.*

No, there was a window, too. It opened like a hatch and could be hooked into a loop on the ceiling. But it was closed now. Nobody watching her through this window.

Ghosts?

"Stop it," she said.

I need to rest.

This was a nice thought.

But for now, she simply was not going to rest.

2

So she put on some sweatpants and her Nikes and went around to the back of the cabin.

She was no detective or crime scene investigator, but she was confident that there were no signs of a sneak.

She turned and gazed up into the forest.

There.

She scowled at her paranoia, but what the hell? She wasn't going to sleep anyway.

She started up the slope into the trees.

What was she looking for? Perverts? Ghosts?

She found neither.

But thirty or forty yards up, she came upon markings in the dirt.

She thought of them simply as faint footprints. They began near a large rock and went less than ten feet before fading entirely. There were no patterns in the footprints, no swirls or other indications that the person had been wearing shoes... Nor were any part of the prints deeper than the rest. It was as if whoever had been here had been barely touching the ground, and had only been here for a short while.

Like a ghost.

Again, she scowled.

I came here to relax and I'm acting like a fool.

No, no she wasn't.

She stood silently for a moment or two, as if waiting for the trees to tell her something.

But they had nothing to say.

So she went back down.

3

Once she was out of the woods, it was easy to tell herself that the markings were nothing more (or less) than what they appeared to be, thus signaling absolutely nothing. She put them in the back of her mind and returned to her cabin to read, call her parents, and prepare for work.

Her mother was every bit as gloomy as she'd been in Morgan's imagination over an hour ago.

Yes, she was glad to hear from her, and yes, she was still in disbelief that her daughter was in *Alaska* of all places... and with Rawleigh McCown at that. The latter seemed to be, to use the cliché, salt in the wound.

"When your break is done," Mother said, "you have to return to reality. You know that."

"I know."

As if the ground beneath her feet was not real. But she didn't go there. What would the point be?

Mother put Daddy on, and Daddy was marginally more supportive. After encouraging her about the bar exam, telling her it's okay, it happens to the best, he told her to enjoy herself, and tell Rawleigh hi.

This put her in a slightly better mood.

She actually cracked a smile as she hung up the phone.

She went down to the Salmon Catch and ate a light supper of chips and Pepsi. As she did so, she took out her phone and reread an old article about Mary and Emily Rawlins. There was a grainy (*ghostly?*) black and white photo of Mary at the end of it. She didn't look at it for long before she cleared off the table and reported for duty.

"How are you, Morgan?"

Ellis Everett patted her on the back as he walked by.

She told him she was doing well, and she almost asked him why he hadn't told her that Cork was his son.

But Cork was a bizarre little drunken man and she knew very well why he hadn't told her that. So no.

Mr. Everett had been good to her, after all. No need to upset him.

She did *not* mind upsetting Cork, though, and when he walked in a couple of hours into her shift, she set his usual in front of him and stood over him long enough that he began to grow uncomfortable.

He cocked his head and squinted his upper eye. "What is it?"

"What's your last name?"

"Name's Cork, I told you."

She grinned. "But your *last* name?"

He dramatically sloshed some beer around in his mouth. The muscle movements did bizarre things with his lower eye.

"Everett," he said. "My dad doesn't like it, but there you go. Only kid he's got."

She went down the bar, served a few drinks, and when she returned to him, he asked her how she knew.

"I heard."

"He didn't tell you, did he? He never tells anybody."

"No."

After that, she didn't talk to him much that night. He did not seem to mind. He was content to drink quietly and give her occasionally bizarre glances as he sloshed beer around his mouth.

He left earlier than he usually did.

4

It was a slow night, and she closed the bar early.

She was back at her cabin by midnight, and the smell of smoke hit her immediately when she opened the door.

Nothing, of course, was actually burning.

5

The numbness returned.

The feeling that she could not sleep and could not get out of bed.

She bled slightly.

When she finally fell asleep, she had a nightmare she could not remember, and she awoke in the floor at the foot of the bed.

6

"There might be something going around," her uncle said a few days later, as they sat on the shore of the Toklat. "I haven't felt great myself." He thought for a moment. "I feel better now."

It was a dreary day. But dreary or not, she felt better, being away from the cabins, away from the woods, out in the park.

She'd told him she hadn't slept much the last couple of nights. She had *not* told him about her (occasional) preoccupation with ghosts, or all the times she'd smelled smoke, and she certainly hadn't told him about the other issue.

"If you want to get out of that cabin, we can go up to Fairbanks for the weekend," Uncle Rawleigh said. "Might do you some good to get away from there."

She told him that was an excellent idea.

XI
Table Mountain Folk Songs

1

THE TOKLAT RIVER RANGER STATION was luxuriously not luxurious. It sat approximately a hundred feet off the Park Road, just west of the river, a one-level, three-room building covered in brown siding.

Inside, the furnishings were either bare or nonexistent. There was a bed, a bench, and a table and chair in one room. A small refrigerator and a coffee maker in another. And the third room was a bathroom, stocked with a pedestal sink, toilet, and a stand-up shower.

Wallace set his notebooks on the table and tossed his backpack and suitcase in a corner.

It was Monday morning.

He supposed he was officially an artist in residence at Denali now, one with preferential treatment, who would thus be around longer than the rest. He was writing a book, after all.

No longer was he within easy distance of civilization. From now on, he'd have to catch a bus out of the park should he need supplies or a decent meal.

Any and all distractions were, theoretically, over an hour away.

Which was the point.

2

He tried to come up with a general plan for his days.

First quarter of the day, get up and make coffee, eat a lousy breakfast, probably a granola bar or a Pop Tart. Hike, maybe. Or, if need be, go up to the park's only interior visitor center at Eielson. Second quarter, write. Third quarter, wander. Fourth quarter, write until it was time to have a makeshift supper, or perhaps catch a bus out to civilization.

He went up to Eielson that first day and introduced himself to the rangers there. Ed Merkin, the oldest ranger in the park, who had an office at the Eieleson Center, was out at that time. Wallace told them he might be getting in touch with Merkin in the near future.

And then he rode back down to Toklat and started writing.

The skeleton of his book was now complete, and many scenes were growing and developing. Emily Rawlins's childhood in New Hampshire was the most complete section of the story. It occupied almost fifty single-spaced Moleskine pages. He'd approached the narrative in the third person omniscient, perhaps to a fault; he worried he was becoming a bit *too* influenced by Mailer's deadpan, uninterested voice in *The Executioner's Song*. This could and would be remedied, eventually. There were gaps in his narrative, of course. Once he left the relative comfort of New Hampshire and reentered the mysterious Alaskan terrain, the narrative faded to a dense outline, which eventually became a brief list of vague bullet points… but he was thus far satisfied, and besides, any small and inconsequential gaps could be stuffed with the near-reality of nonfiction fiction.

Certainly, he had enough fuel in the tank to carry him into the heart of the story. His lunch date with Ellis Everett had been exceptionally lucrative; Everett, after a bit of prodding, had told him of several conversations he'd had with Mary and Emily Rawlins, and he'd provided mounds of material about the history of the Salmon Catch and the surrounding community, which had largely developed *because* of the Salmon Catch and its cabins.

Yes, he had material.

But God! He did not have near everything. There were more people to talk to, and these conversations would hopefully yield *more* conversations…

He stopped writing when his hand began to cramp, and he noticed something he'd written and circled on the envelope containing his notes: END?

He had no recollection of doing this, neither the writing nor the circling, which wasn't surprising.

He'd written some of his finest material amidst total mental blackouts.

END?

"I don't know how it ends," he said.

Hence, this innocent little note? *End?*

As great as the narrative was coming, it would all be in vain if he did not decide how to handle the possibility that he might never find the answer to a certain key question. He'd come up here to tell a true story, to compose the Greatest Nonfiction Novel since the genre's finest hours in the heydays of Capote and Mailer. This was not pulp material. This could not end in a "cliffhanger." He must either *answer* the question entirely or embed the mystery deep in the book's foundation and make it an essence of its construction. No matter what, this oh-so-significant gap could *not* be filled by his imagination.

End? Yes, *End?*

That was a fine question, wasn't it?

3

There was a knock on his door that evening.

He was leaned back on the bed, reading a novel, not expecting such an interruption.

He jumped.

The knock came again, and he went to the door.

A tiny, almost frail-looking woman with mocha skin stood before him. Her long dark hair was pulled into a ponytail. She was dressed in tight jeans and a plaid shirt. An acoustic guitar was strapped to her back, its strap cutting between her small breasts. Wallace put her at thirty. Maybe forty. The lighting was poor.

She smiled an insecure smile.

"Hi." She extended a hand, which Wallace shook. "My name's Dolores Gunn. I assume you're the writer."

"Wallace O'Brien."

"I'm a musician. I'm here for the next few weeks to write an album. Or, that's the idea."

He stepped out of the way and asked her if she wanted to come in.

She did so.

She unslung her guitar and the pack on her side and sat down on the bench across from his bed.

"Roomy," she said, "and you have a refrigerator. I'm jealous."

"I have water, beer, and coffee," he said.

Ultimately, he got them both water and pulled the chair at the table over near her.

"I won't bother you long, or often." She reached into her pack and retrieved an iPad. "I've been out hiking and recording, just strumming different things, brainstorming. I use the Garage Band app to take down ideas. If you don't mind to listen to something..." She tapped the screen a few times, and soft acoustic strumming began to play from the device's tiny speaker.

Decent, and calming, Wallace thought. *But why am I listening to this?*

In the midst of her third time through the chord progression, he got his answer.

A tiny, muffled voice came through the speaker, from somewhere beyond Gunn's guitar. Barely there, then a bit louder, mostly indiscernible.

"That's not me," Gunn said. "I was not speaking or singing. Surely you can hear that."

Wallace nodded.

Gunn paused the music.

"I was alone." She backed the music up about twenty seconds and played it again.

Wallace leaned toward the speaker.

The voice was *definitely* not Gunn's, though it *was* a female's, seemingly one somewhere off in the distance. Carried by the wind? And what was it saying? Most of it was unclear, but he did catch a few words: "…shouldn't. Thank you." And a few seconds later: "…climb?"

Gunn paused the track again. She agreed when he told her what he thought he'd heard.

"It could have been somebody in the distance," Wallace said. "That's what I'd bet on."

"I thought of that. I'm not saying you're wrong, but I know I was alone. I was up near Table Mountain, and there was nobody around. And the iPad microphone isn't *that* good. It's not good at all. It sounds to me like she's talking to somebody. Do you agree?"

He did.

They both thought about it, but not for long.

"I need to go so I don't miss the last bus back to my cabin," she said. "If you have any ideas, will you let me know?"

He told her it was nice to meet her, and yes, he would.

4

The next morning, he went out to Table Mountain.

He could see the plateau from his cabin, seemingly just a short stroll away, but distance out here was deceiving, and it took him almost three hours to reach the mountain's western slopes.

He had no idea where, exactly, Dolores Gunn had been when she captured the voice. It probably didn't matter. There wouldn't be anything to find, would there?

Still, he'd come here, and he wasn't tired, so he might as well look around.

He cut south and followed the base of the mountain for about a quarter of a mile, to the crest of a steep slope. At the crest, he was gifted a remarkable view of the snow and glaciers of the Alaska Range, the Toklat River and surrounding valley, and beyond it all, the considerable wall of clouds that hid the Great One.

He searched the area, both sides of the crest and up the mountain slope, looking for anything, any indication of who might have been captured by Gunn's iPad.

But he was out in the wilderness, and there was nothing here *but* wilderness.

All around him, silence. No voices. No music. Just the wild, the way it was meant to be.

He sat down on the slope and gazed out across the valley.

He was definitely going to the bar tonight.

XII
Lightning

1

THEY SPENT THE WEEKEND AT Uncle Rawleigh's house in Fairbanks. They watched movies, tossed a softball in the lawn, went shopping, and did not discuss anything relevant to anything. It was a good weekend. Morgan slept well. She felt well. It was rejuvenating.

They got up just before five on Monday morning and made it back to the Salmon Catch by seven.

Uncle Rawleigh set to work on his destructive construction project, and Morgan went into her cabin to reacquaint herself with its walls and bed and whatever else it might contain.

She was not stressed.

Even if the smell of smoke returned, even if she started thinking about ghosts again, all was well, because she was *here*, and far away from *there*.

But she hadn't talked to her mother in over two days.

I'm not stressed. I will not stress.

She'd talk to her parents again. Eventually. But not today.

She dropped her bag in the floor and went back outside and helped her uncle for most of the morning. She stopped when it was time to eat lunch and rest up for her night at the bar.

As usual, she climbed into bed and closed her eyes, and after an indiscernible amount of time, it all came back to her. Perhaps it was worse this time.

A wisp of smoke beneath her nose. Dread. The feeling that she could not get out of bed even if she wanted to. A foul feeling in her stomach. Burning in her throat. She felt hot, and then cold, and maybe it was all in her head, or maybe—.

A dark, skeletal figure nearly human in shape was in the corner, just to the left of the door. It stood near the table, perhaps stood *in* the table; the black filaments that formed what little body it had wavered in a nonexistent breeze, and its odors of smoke and cancerous rot passed briefly beneath her nose.

Neither the image nor her thoughts made sense, and for a few panicked seconds she could not breathe; she thought she might pass out, or at the very least be sick, but it was gone... if it had ever been there at all.

She sat up and spent a few quiet minutes taking inventory of her condition.

Her stomach hurt, but that seemed to be the extent of it.

The rest was gone, like none of it had happened.

She told herself she was okay. Somehow, she believed it.

2

Her uncle was gone when she stepped back outside, and that was good, because she needed to talk to somebody. But this time, it couldn't be her uncle. On a whim, she walked down toward the highway where the phone signal was the strongest… And she called her shift manager from her former job.

Colleen answered on the third ring. After she confirmed that it was Morgan—truly Morgan—calling her, she laughed and said she didn't think she'd ever hear from her again.

"You're not already back, are you?" she said.

"I'm still up here."

"How's it going up there, honey? You sound stressed. You're not supposed to be *stressed*!"

Morgan told her she was indeed enjoying herself. A lot. But…

Gravely, Colleen said: "But…?"

This is the part I hate, Morgan thought.

She'd called Colleen because, aside from her Uncle Rawleigh, Colleen was the kindest, most open-minded person she knew—and Colleen was a fellow *woman.* Who else had a better brain to pick about certain things?

Still, it was hard to begin.

"Come on now, Morgan," Colleen said. "I know you want to talk about something, so be out with it. You know you can talk to me about anything. Surely you've gathered that by now."

Yes, she thought. *Hence, this call.*

She paced along the side of the road, opened her mouth, and began talking: "I just want to know I'm okay and not going crazy. Before I got here, my uncle saw something. He joked and said it was a ghost. I don't know if it's a joke. I'm staying in the cabin I told you about. I've smelled smoke that's not there. I feel panicked for no reason. I've *seen it too*. I know I have, and it does things to me. It's not just a matter of seeing something. My head hurts. I don't get a lot of sleep at night..." She paused. "I've been bleeding, and we've talked about this, Colleen. I'm a clock. It's never like that. We got out of this place over the weekend, and it all went away. I don't want to feel *crazy*."

When Colleen did not immediately answer, Morgan dove back into it—why not? She talked about the Salmon Catch, her job at the bar, her uncle working on the cabins... and finally, she stopped long enough for Colleen to respond:

"You sound like you're having a blast, girl. I'll tell you a few things. Okay? I believe in ghosts. I've seen one before. My grandmother's friend, at the junk shop where she used to work—where she died. I saw her, I know it. So you might have seen a ghost. So what? It doesn't make you crazy. I've read ghosts can make you cold. You see something, smell something you think shouldn't be there, your heart rate goes up. You get a headache. Your nerves are frazzled and your stomach messes up. You don't sleep a lot because your mind won't shut off. One thing leads to another. And

Morgan, let me tell you, don't sweat the period thing. It happens."

Morgan smiled. She already felt better.

Colleen said: "It *does* happen. You think you're like a clock, but that's cause you get frazzled and you start revising history. I remember one time I just *knew* this mole on my neck was different. I thought I was dying. I toughed up and showed it to my mom, and she nearly slapped me. 'That's always been like that. Quit panicking yourself.' You get scared or nervous or stressed, stuff happens. If you've seen a ghost, that's cool. And that sounds like a kickass bar you're running, girl. Enjoy it."

"I will."

"You didn't want to discuss all this with your uncle? He's not *that* cool?"

"He's cool."

"I get you. I might've, just to see his face, but I get you."

"Thank you, Colleen."

After a few more minutes of pleasant conversation that did not involve ghosts or body functions, they said goodbye.

And Morgan set off to prepare for work.

3

Usually, Ellis Everett arrived sometime in the middle of the morning. His office was on the first level of the Salmon Catch, but he seldom spent time there; typically, he gathered whatever it was he was working on and took it up to the bar, where he'd work for an hour or two and then leave, usually to return again late in the afternoon or in the early evening.

Today seemed like a usual day. At ten after ten, he pulled into his normal parking spot.

Morgan was sitting on the front steps waiting for him.

He smiled warmly and asked how her morning was going.

She told him it was going well and asked if him if he had a minute to talk.

"Of course I do," he said. "I've been meaning to show you something, anyway. Come on inside."

After they were seated in a booth upstairs, Morgan asked her boss if he had any idea who the mythical "lady in the road" was.

"If I answer that, is it a given that I believe that story?"

She told him no.

"Okay then. Assuming there is a 'lady in the road'—and I don't think there is—I've always assumed, like everybody else, it's that poor mother who disappeared. The timing is right. The story is classic, just clichéd. There is a writer around here working on a book about her." He studied her face. "I'm guessing you've got some reason for asking me about her. You've seen something?"

She didn't want to go into it. She had her answer—Ellis Everett was a perfectly sane old guy who'd apparently never seen a spook; or if he had, he'd blocked it from his memory and did not intend to talk about it.

"Curious," she said.

Cork told me about it, she almost said. But she didn't want to go there, either.

"You know what I think stirred up all this talk—and maybe a ghost or two?" He grinned. "That storm. And I was going to show you this, show you what burned down my cabins and put your uncle to work."

He pulled his phone out of his shirt pocket, flipped through a few screens with his index finger, and handed it to her.

On the screen was a dramatic picture of a lightning strike over Mount Healy; the bolt split in dozens of directions from a swollen thunderhead that seemed to be painted with wisps of an evaporating aurora.

"I confess," Ellis said, "I didn't take that picture. I don't think this old phone could *ever* take a picture like that. A tourist took it and sent it to me. But I sat here on my front steps most of that evening and watched the storm build. Not unusual to have storms fire up and roll over the valley. The mountains make their own weather. But you could see that one was going to be a doozy. And it was. The hardest part lasted about two minutes. It did its damage."

She handed the phone back to him.

Ellis said: "Your uncle's a good man. I've known him a long time. He'll take a little longer than some, but I know he'll do good work."

XIII
Dragon Canyon Road

1

DRAGON CANYON ROAD, DESPITE ITS name, is not a road. It is a dirt trail for its first four miles, a rugged path only fit for the most capable of four wheel drives for a mile or so beyond that, and finally, as it rises into its namesake canyon, it fades into a boulder field.

Nowadays, the road is almost entirely forgotten, and its beginning, on the west side of the Denali Highway approximately twelve miles south of the park entrance, is faded to the point of being unnoticeable.

Rawleigh knew of a low, rocky spot on Dragon Canyon Road that was perfect for dumping and burning scraps. He was out here this morning, dumping what he hoped was one of the last loads of cabin wreckage. He was sick of this process, but if he wasn't such a lazy old fool with a self-diagnosed case of attention deficit disorder, he'd have finished it a long time ago. He'd averaged less than a load a day, and the bed of his double cab Silverado wasn't all that big. There were days when he hadn't wanted to haul scraps, and so he'd mess around with a hammer or a pry bar, acting like he was working, accomplishing a lot of nothing.

So be it. Everett was a friend. He wasn't going to get mad. And yes, lots of folks would've worked faster, but none of them would have done any better. And they certainly wouldn't have done it cheaper. *Saint Rawleigh is at your service, and he will take his time.*

He climbed up on his lowered tailgate and flung more scraps out into the pile.

He'd learned of this road from Everett's creepy kid, and Cork, he assumed, had learned of it from his job with the timber company. Before he began this project for Ellis Everett, he'd last been here when he fixed the Salmon Catch's wall. And before that? Well, that had been a long time ago, hadn't it? He'd been in a jacked up Wrangler with, yes, cockeyed Cork… and a fellow closer to his own age, a quiet blob of a man named Devin who was no longer among the world of the living.

It was Devin's Jeep. And Devin was driving. At first it wasn't so bad, and the joyride was actually kind of boring, as the road's first few miles were no challenge at all for the '91 Wrangler that sat damned near two feet off the ground. But then the grade grew steeper, and the terrain roughened considerably as they neared the boulder field that led up into the canyon.

"You better hold on," Devin said, leaning into the wheel with one hand on the gearshift, his man boobs bobbing up and down like all those goofy bracelets on his wrists as they approached what looked like a vertical wall of boulders, some nearly as large as automobiles, none smaller than a basketball. "We're going as far as we can go." Yes, but how far was that? And where were they going, and why?

Treasure hunting, Devin had said.

Treasure hunting. Because Devin had been one lazy motherfucker. Why work for a living when you could find treasure? Cork had encouraged it. He'd probably told Devin about Dragon Canyon at a bar… Because Cork was a lazy (drunken, creepy) motherfucker too. He could use some treasure of his own.

The Jeep hadn't made it up the boulder field. Not the whole way. They'd trekked a few miles on foot… and they hadn't found any treasure that day.

But that was all irrelevant.

2

"You're very fascinated with the idea," he said, after she brought up the *ghost lady*. "Are you still feeling okay?"

He'd been back for about twenty minutes, and they were sitting on his tailgate drinking water and Gatorade.

Yes, she said, she was feeling fine.

He could see that she wasn't being totally honest, but he didn't press the issue.

"Do you have any theories?" Morgan said.

"About the 'ghost'?"

"Not just that. About the Rawlins. What happened to them? Why did they never find them?"

"It was a total disappearance," he said. "First the daughter. Then the mother and her car. That's a key point."

"What do you think it means?"

"I have no idea. Maybe they were killed and the car disposed of somehow? Maybe the mother split town? But the car was never found, and I would think it would've been by now if she'd just driven off."

"It makes sense that the 'ghost' is the mother."

"If you believe in that sort of thing, yes. I agree."

"But you don't? You saw something."

"I did see something, yes. And there's always the chance I was asleep."

And he looked directly at her to emphasize this could *very well* be true for her, too.

She smiled and shook her head. She wasn't having it. She seemed enthralled with the ideas of ghosts and playing Nancy Drew.

He said: "I just want you to enjoy yourself and be okay. If you're *not* okay, please tell me."

"I am."

"I believe you. But if that's ever not true, will you tell me? We'll rethink this, I promise."

"I'll tell you. You know I will."

"I believe you," he said.

3

She insisted on helping him load and burn the scraps and walked up to the restaurant to tell Ellis that she might be late for work. With two of them, it didn't take very long to fill the back of the truck, and soon they were on their way to Dragon Canyon Road. Rawleigh told her he encouraged her to hike and explore all she wanted, but he spoke from experience in saying that Dragon Canyon Road was—*pardon my French, honey*—"a fucking nightmare."

"But don't worry," he said. "Today, we're just gonna go a little ways and set some stuff on fire."

And that's what they did.

They threw the last round of cabin scraps onto the pile, doused the mess in lighter fluid, and threw a match on it. Much of the heap had already been charred, but there was enough raw wood and other materials in its gut for the blaze to catch.

For the better part of an hour, they sat on the tailgate and talked—not about ghosts, not about smoke or headaches or missing strangers, but about everything else.

"This is a good time, Uncle Rawleigh," Morgan said.

Rawleigh put an arm around her and squeezed.

She hugged him back.

XIV
Table Mountain Cover Songs

1

DOLORES GUNN RETURNED THREE DAYS after her initial appearance. She had her iPad with her. It was early morning, and Wallace was less than halfway through his first pot of coffee.

Gunn accepted a cup, sat down on the bench, and began her story: "Without going into too many boring details, I've been working on lyrics, and I've been stuck. I don't even know what to say. And when I get stuck, I wander. Sometimes I play other people's songs.

"I went back out to Table Mountain yesterday, and I started strumming somebody else's song. I had one of those moments in which I wondered how I sounded, so I hit record. Do you know the Crowded House song 'Don't Dream It's Over'?"

"Who doesn't?"

"Fair enough. I have one of Neil Finn's guitar picks." She produced a bright green Dunlop pick from the pocket of her jeans as if he might not believe her, then swiped open the iPad and tapped the Garage Band icon. "Anyway, listen…"

Wallace thought he knew what he was about to hear, and he was absolutely correct: Gunn's strumming was very familiar, an excellent acoustic rendition of Neil Finn's intro. And then she started into the first verse, and for a few lines, it was just her, her voice and hers alone, a slightly dry but not unpleasant baritone, but by the time she reached the chorus, the voice that had emerged sneakily from the background was nearly as loud as Gunn's. This new female singer knew the lyrics well and for two or three lines in the chorus, she was singing the song loudly, clearly, beautifully.

She faded away midway through the second verse.

"Again," Gunn said, "I was totally alone."

Wallace asked to hear it again. Gunn replayed it.

"What do you think?" Gunn asked when the track ended.

"I wish I knew what to think."

"Aren't writers supposed to be good detectives?"

"I doubt it," he said.

2

He truly was curious. He had to be.

He was not here to play the role of the Romantic, the writer who indulges himself in Nature to reap the

Rewards of Her Wisdom; he was here to research a story and write it.

And here was a ghostly voice on an iPad. A ghostly *female* voice, no doubt, and...

And what?

It was maddening. It was distracting. *Who* was it? *What* was it? Did he honestly believe it was her? Dead, alive, didn't matter. Did he actually believe it?

He thought he might, though there were two other possibilities that were just as likely—no, that were *much more* likely. One, it was somebody else. Two, that it was all a trick by Gunn. Yes, she seemed like a nice and intelligent woman who was much too grounded in her art to be playing such petty tricks on others. But he didn't know her.

He paced the floor, trying to decide if he truly believed there was a *chance* that the voice on Gunn's iPad was that of Emily Rawlins.

It's not likely, he thought. *It is* much more *likely Gunn's messing with you.*

To what end? To distract him? Why would she care to do that? Did she simply want attention? That didn't seem to be the case.

Maybe it *could* be her. She'd vanished somewhere close to the Toklat; Table Mountain overlooked the river. Maybe her voice had carried...? Maybe? Could it be her? This was certainly an intriguing thought.

Because, if she *were* here, could he find the end of his story?

3

He went up to the Park Road and caught a bus to Eielson.

Painter was there. They stood at the back window and looked out at the clouds and mountains and talked, until Wallace told him he'd come to talk to Merkin.

Painter then led him through the exhibits in the main room, past the restrooms and soda machines, and through an open door to a room containing several desks—all of which were empty except for one.

The man behind the desk was old, but he looked to be in good shape. His gray hair was long and swept back. His eyes were stern and unblinking and glaring through his glasses at a page in a paperback book.

When Ed Merkin looked up, Painter said: "This is Wallace O'Brien, a writer. He wants to talk to you, if you don't mind."

"Not at all." Merkin nodded at a plastic chair in the corner as Painter left the room.

Wallace dragged the chair over to Merkin's desk and sat down.

Merkin leaned back in his chair and scratched at the stubble on his chin.

"What's on your mind, Mr. O'Brien?" he said.

Wallace dove straight into the proverbial deep end: "I'm writing a book about Mary and Emily Rawlins. What few articles I found, you were mentioned in them. The girl apparently disappeared in this park. I'd like to know everything you know."

Merkin shifted in his seat. "If you've read the articles, you pretty much know everything I know. Have you talked to the police? To Mr. Everett at the Salmon Catch? Family?"

Wallace didn't care to have Merkin's approval regarding his research.

"All they did in the articles was quote you. Same quote in both, that she got on your bus here at Eielson, and you're 'almost confident' she got off at the Toklat River."

Merkin nodded. "That's absolutely right. I was driving a bus at the time. They didn't include this, but I don't even *know* it was her. Based on the description of the girl, I think it was. Her mother said she'd gone to hike in Denali. Said she was in dark blue nylon pants, white shirt, gray backpack. Blond hair, ponytail. Not much over a hundred pounds. Might be carrying a large Nikon camera because she enjoyed photography and wanted to get the flowers and animals. When I heard that... Yes, I thought of the girl who got on at Eileson. And I was—am—almost confident she got off at the Toklat River, which I understand is where you're staying."

Wallace nodded.

"That's what I know," Merkin said. "It was—and I mean this in the best way possible—a memorable event. Considering how wide open this park is, we don't have the quantities of lost hikers you'd think we would. Most people play it smart. Yeah, you can get a backcountry permit and wander forever. But most people stick close to the road and don't go much beyond the beaten paths. Those who go further out tend to be the ones who know what they're doing... or they get lucky. I say all that to say this: The girl went too far, and she wasn't lucky. It doesn't happen frequently, but it *does* happen."

"You're confident she's dead."

"I didn't say that. If I had to give an *opinion*, yes, of course she's dead. But only God knows, Mr. O'Brien, and thus far, God's said absolutely nothing."

4

Even if he assumed the voice on Gunn's iPad was that of a ghost, he still had no way of establishing that it was the ghost of either of the Rawlins women. It was the stuff of classic tales, yes, but nobody even knew *for sure* that the girl was in this park, or dead, or alive, or anything else.

He'd recorded his conversation with Merkin and listened to it while he was on the bus.

It was... a memorable event.

Yes, so memorable that a whole lot of nothing had been written about it.

Because this was the wilderness, and what the wilderness takes, it consumes.

The girl went too far, and she wasn't lucky.

And so now she was singing Crowded House songs on Dolores Gunn's iPad?

Where in his book would *that* nugget be?

He did not get off the bus at the Toklat.

He rode it all the way to the main visitor center, where he purchased a bottle of Pepsi and went out to a bench in the sunshine to attempt a call.

Merkin had been right.

He needed to talk to the police.

He called the state troopers' office in Healy and asked for a man named Cormac Pearce.

"Mr. Pearce is no longer with the Alaska State Troopers," the man who answered said. "He is in Wasilla now."

"With the Wasilla police?"

"That's right."

Wallace thanked him and ended the call. He made a note of this and looked up the number to the Wasilla Police Department. But when he called, still no luck. He was told Officer Pearce was not in today.

"I'll try again tomorrow," Wallace said.

Probably for the best.

He was too exhausted for another conversation.

5

He went to drink that night. Morgan was the only bartender on this fairly quiet evening, and he told her he regretted that his new quarters were not situated along her jogging route.

She asked if he was really writing a book about the Rawlins.

He said yes.

"Good," she said, and walked off.

Wallace took out his phone. First, he sent Patricia Weaver photos of his Moleskine's first ten pages. Give her something substantial to read, he thought, so she could begin to formulate an advance.

Then, he Googled "Dolores Gunn musician."

He received far more relevant results than he'd expected.

The woman had dozens of videos on YouTube. Some she'd put there herself, and some were cell phone recordings from various live performances in clubs and bars. She had her own semi-professional website, a Twitter account, a music review blog, and several tracks for sale on Amazon and in the iTunes store.

Wallace drank his beer and scrolled through the thicket of her online presence. He came away with the opinion that Dolores Gunn (36, of Champaign, Illinois) was a straight shooting, serious woman; she was not the type to fake ghostly sing-alongs.

He looked up from his phone and saw Morgan at the other end of the bar, running a glass of Miller for her uncle and glancing his way.

"Maybe we need to talk," he said, then set about finishing his beer.

XV
A Nighttime Stroll

1

THE WRITER STUCK AROUND FOR a long time.

On his prior visits, he sat, drank, and stared, occasionally making small talk with the bartenders or whoever was sitting next to him. But tonight, after she'd asked her question, he dipped into something on his phone, and even after he emerged from it, he didn't say much. He sipped his beer and stared, until the end of the night, right before he left. That's when he asked if she knew anything about Mary or Emily Rawlins.

She'd answered vaguely, and he'd thanked her and walked out.

The bar was totally empty at 12:30. Morgan closed it down with the help of a waiter who told her to watch out for Cork. He'd come in and sat in the corner for a moment, then left.

"I didn't see him," Morgan said.

The waiter raised an eyebrow. "He probably didn't want you to."

He went outside and drove away.

Feeling more than a little uneasy, Morgan followed right behind him, stepping out into the all-night twilight that she'd never, ever get used to.

Immediately after locking the door, she heard a voice from across the highway. It was a familiar voice, faint, likely carried on the breeze. She *thought* it was her uncle... and when she heard it again, she knew it was.

There's nobody over there.

Morgan crossed the highway to the flat grassy area next to the gas station.

The night was quiet. No voices. Just the river and the wind.

Had she been mistaken? But she heard him again, and someone else.

A woman. Her voice was not familiar.

Their voices were fragmented, almost ghostly, obscured by the noise of the river.

Morgan crept toward the edge of the grass and saw them standing on the rocks near the water. Their forms were faint, but she knew her uncle's unkempt yellow and gray hair. And the woman was wearing a red shirt that was very conspicuous against the gray background. Renee, Morgan guessed, her uncle's steadily intermittent girlfriend, whom she assumed she'd never meet.

Her uncle was speaking again, very adamant about whatever it was he was saying.

The woman—Renee?—spoke loudly in return... But her uncle retaliated immediately, throwing a hand in the air and saying something blunt that Morgan was sure contained multiple expletives.

Part of her wished she could actually hear them.

Another part insisted that this argument was none of her business, and it was time to go to bed.

2

She was not within herself. That's how she felt. She saw herself, and she thought, absurdly, that she was in the mind of something not there, something that had never been.

They only saw it, she thought, if they *ever* saw it, when their minds were absent and their guards were down. During the day, when they were wide awake and the world was turning in full force, it was drowned out by light and noise, because it hardly existed, if it existed at all. In its weakest moments, it faded, and the sensation was one of near nonexistence, which was bliss. But it wanted to exist; thus, it always returned. It did not know how these things worked, did not know if there was any great entity in charge, did not know if there was a governing set of rules. It didn't matter. It was here, it was no more, and still, it was something. Welcome to my cabins, dear girl, it yearned to say. You remind me of someone I once knew. You remind me of myself. You remind me of death. I love the inside of you. Sometimes it watched. Sometimes it went into her and was beautiful. Sometimes it slept. Sometimes it woke up.

Morgan thought all of this, and maybe it came from somewhere, or maybe it came from herself. She was asleep. No?

Sleep. If sleep conjured these thoughts, to hell with sleep. If this was not sleep, she did not understand anything. She could *not*.

It was gray and bloody, and in seconds of near reality, it drifted beneath the door and seeped out of the walls, a dry and smoky vapor, there and not there. It was an exhausting effort, and for a dark and silent period, all it could do was gather itself. Blood oozed in various directions and folded on itself, faded, and dark filaments were born, ultimately rising with the gray. In minutes it was standing, and it felt as good as it had since the thunderclap jarred it awake, and dear, she was here, a warm place to be, a place to rest, a place to exist. She was asleep, and she wasn't. Silently it crossed the floor. Silently it joined her, a wisp beneath her nose, a presence settling into her body. It made itself at home because it could, there, not there, depending on her mind and certain fluctuations in the air. She was alive and warm. Her head hurt and her stomach rolled and tumbled. Her body grew tired. She felt anxious.

None of this made sense, Morgan thought, but the words came to her like a recollection of an old speech. She closed her eyes.

It settled into this warm nest like an animal on a cold night. Did it carry with it traces of old times? It had to, didn't it? It had a memory. It *was* memory. It did not care if it left images of recollections scattered on the floor of her subconscious. They could linger forever. They could dissolve. They could drain from her in sweat or blood. It did not care. It faded from existence; she was convinced, for a brief time, that it did not exist, and maybe she was right; it felt her sit up in bed. Maybe she thought it did not exist, but she was scared, uncomfortable—maybe she wasn't awake at all. She sat up in bed, sleeping. It wished for her to lie down. The effort to sustain itself in this restless environment was too great. *Lie down. Lie down.* But she sat upright and looked around the room; awake or not, it truly couldn't tell. Perhaps neither.

Morgan did not know. She knew she was upright; she could see the dim light around the door. She felt she was not alone, but she wondered if this was reality or dream stuff.

It lingered for a moment in this warm and familiar home, because it could; it felt she would soon seize on something that had flashed for a brief time somewhere deep in her brain. She might think it a piece of her imagination, but it was a drop of memory. Again, it didn't care, but curious, it lingered. It felt her as she moved her legs over the side of the bed; it moved behind her eyes and watched as she looked down at a pair of sweatpants at the foot of the bed. She took them and stepped into them. Her mind raged. It wasn't sure, precisely, what she was thinking; both her memory and imagination were fireballs in the process of crashing into one another. But it had an idea. The *thud thud thud* of her heart said a lot, as did her clammy skin and churning stomach. She was anxious. She had an idea. If she would just calm down, *please* calm down... She approached the door. It knew she would open it soon, and when she did, she would see something. It would not really be *there*, but the idea was very real. It thought it knew. And though it was very tired and already fading, it clung tightly to its existence. It wanted to see.

3

It was terrifying, then alarming, and ultimately curious, waking on her feet in the threshold of her cabin's door, dressed only in a tank top and a pair of sweatpants that she'd apparently put on backwards. For several minutes, she had no recollection of what had happened—hence, the terror and alarm. But after she'd shut the door and calmed down and removed her backwards pants, she remembered. It had been a very vivid dream, and its remnants were already solid memories.

She recalled standing at her door and watching a fire burn. It was her uncle's scrap fire, of course, and somehow standing at her door and looking out at Dragon Canyon Road made sense. What didn't make sense was the scene on the other side of the fire. This was the real curiosity, the absurdity that had become, in the center of her brain, a legitimate memory. *Yes, I remember that. I remember.* It was a dark room—a cave, maybe—and the glare of the fire made the items in that room hard to discern, but...

But nothing, except a dark, vague conclusion.

Maybe it was all the random piecing together of scattered thoughts, or maybe it was part of something else, that *something else* that had been in the room with her. *It makes me sick. It's dead.*

She shook her head to clear it, then went down to the restrooms to freshen up.

4

She almost felt like she was betraying her uncle.

He'd warned her about this, hadn't he?

But she was grown. She was aware of the danger. She would be okay.

She dressed in warmer clothes and drove out to Dragon Canyon Road, put the Frontier in four-wheel-drive, and crept slowly along the road for as long as she dared. She did not pull over and park until she was, according to the odometer, almost three and a half miles beyond the remains of the scrap fire.

She studied the terrain ahead in the glow of the headlights.

She couldn't see far, but she could see that the grade was much steeper. The rocks were getting larger. And at some point, the trail would likely disappear entirely, and then what?

And then it would be decided: she was a fool.

She had no idea where this road went, or how much longer it would take to get there, but it didn't matter.

She would go as far as she dared to go, then quit. If she didn't find anything, well... Did she *really* think she was going to find anything, anyway?

She shut off the truck. Stepped out and slung her pack over shoulders.

And started up the path.

Stay on the trail. As long as there's a trail, I'll be okay.
You're okay.
You're smart. You're in good shape. You'll be fine.

But it was three 'o clock in the morning and she was out in the woods on a road that had no business being called a road—a road that nobody knew about save her uncle and *maybe* a few others.

Who's to say she would be fine?

She stopped.

You should have never come out here. Couldn't you have at least waited till the sun was up? What in the world are you doing?

Following the path while it was there. That's what she was doing.

She pressed on.

One foot in front of the other, thumbs in belt loops, silently, steadily.

It took a few minutes, but the exercise did wonders for her mental state. She was hiking, and this was no different than her hike up the Toklat, or all those jogs along the Park Road.

The path went up and up as it grew more rugged.

About an hour after leaving the truck, it terminated abruptly at the base of a sharp, boulder-strewn slope that rose into the mouth of a narrow canyon.

She felt good. She wasn't scared anymore. And there was no way to get lost, was there? Once she was in the canyon, where else except *forward* could she possibly go?

XVI
The Missing

1

MARY RAWLINS OF NEW HAMPSHIRE.

Out of curiosity, Rawleigh did a Google search of her name and got exactly what he knew he would get: a bunch of nothing. Because Mary Rawlins was gone. And the media hadn't given a damn *then*, and she'd been gone for far too long for them to give a damn *now*.

He was sitting outside his cabin, dreading the start of today's work. Today was not about destruction and loading scraps and hauling them and setting them on fire. Today's work would require actual thought, which he thought he might be too tired to do.

Ghost or no ghost, his niece was right: it was hard to rest in this place. There was something in the air. And then, of course, there was the fact that he hadn't even attempted to go to bed till after one a.m. Mostly because of *her*.

He closed out of the phone's web browser and scrolled till he found her number.

She seldom answered. He didn't know why he was bothering.

She answered.

"Hello, Rawleigh," Renee said.

"Last night wasn't very fun."

"Not what I had in mind."

"Sorry we fought."

"There was no reason to fight."

"I agree."

"I don't come around for things like that. I didn't say anything incorrect."

"I know you didn't."

"Why did you call me?"

"To apologize for my part. I don't think you're a bitch."

"You do, and that's fine. I *am* a bitch."

"Where did you go?"

"I'm off again, and it's lovely. I'm somewhere in the neighborhood of two-hundred miles from where you are. It feels good to be away. That area is simply foul."

"Yes it is."

"I hope we agree about things, Rawleigh. I'm sorry if we don't.'

"We do."

"Good. I'm soon to lose service."

"I'll let you go then."

"I love you, even when you shout."

"I love you too," he said.

2

He supposed he did love her, even though she was the most bizarre creature he'd ever met. He'd thought that when he first met her, right over there at the bar, and he still thought so now. But she was a beautiful woman. She was quick on her feet, a pleasure to be around. And goddamn, what a life he'd lived *before* her. Back then, it was a twelve pack a day, plus however much vodka he chose to pour in his nightly glass of tomato juice. He swallowed painkillers like Skittles and had a fondness for Adderall and coke that neither his body nor his wallet could possibly sustain.

Now—and he credited this roughly forty percent to Alaska generally, fifty-five percent to Renee, and five percent to his own ability to kick himself in the ass—but now, he still drank a little too much (and probably always would), but he'd kicked the pills and the coke, and his overall disposition had, at some point in the last ten or so years, flipped completely.

When he got off the phone, he paced around the work scene and pondered how long it would take to build three new cabins and repair large portions of the others. And then he sat back down, plugged a set of earbuds into his phone, and started one of his playlists.

When he was properly motivated to start working, he took the earbuds out and approached his truck.

Okay, yes. He'd work now.

But first, coffee.

3

As he was chalking lines on one of the slabs, it occurred to him that Morgan had never emerged from her cabin. He checked his watch. Nearly eight 'o clock. It wasn't unimaginable that she was sleeping late—she *needed* the rest, yes... But she never slept late.

He chalked some more lines, scribbled a few figures, and went down to the gas station for a coffee refill, thinking she'd be outside waiting on him when he got back.

She wasn't.

And for the first time, he was truly concerned. He knocked on her door and received no answer.

He went down to the Salmon Catch when he heard Ellis Everett's truck pull in.

"Heard from Morgan today?" he said.

Ellis flicked away a cigarette and shook his head. "No. She'll be around by this afternoon I'm sure. Always is."

Rawleigh figured he was right.

She'd probably left earlier than usual for a hike or jog.

Just let me know, he'd tell her next time he saw her. *Even if it's sliding a note under my door. Let me know.*

Or would he?

Did she have to answer to him? Had she come up here to answer to anybody?

Ellis repeated his sentiments. "She'll be around soon. I'd bet my truck on it."

But if the bet were real, Ellis would have lost his truck.

XVII
Peevey Again

1

WALLACE AWOKE THAT MORNING AT nine 'o clock and let himself go back to sleep. He hadn't slept worth a damn that night. He'd indulged too much at the bar. The beer, Merkin, all of it had kept him turning and staring up into the dark till five or six 'o clock.

Nothing wrong with another hour or two, if it would actually happen.

He rolled back over.

2

He knew he might be dreaming. Hell, he *had* to be dreaming. But that didn't mean the whole thing was worthless, did it? He was a writer. Writers were supposed to dream.

At the start of it, he was exactly where he should be, in the Toklat Ranger Station, sitting at his writing table. He was trying to write, but the words weren't coming easily, and the ones he did produce weren't worth a damn. All this research, all this work, and he was stuck. The brain behind the mechanical pencil was out of brilliance.

He stood up. He couldn't remember standing up, but he stood, and he knew there was something outside. He thought, *I need to see it, because it's important.* So he went to the door and opened it and stepped into a light rain that would only get harder before it went away. Thunder to the west, somewhere over Denali. And when he looked in the other direction, he saw the approaching bear. Maybe he should be afraid, or was he dreaming?

All doubt was removed when he turned to look at what was right in front of him. Things like this just don't happen in the real world. Still, this could be important. He was here. He might as well take a look.

He crossed the street and entered Shavano's.

3

His old friend Peevey grinned as he entered and motioned him over to the bar. The room was gray and empty. The rain was beating against the windows.

"How are you, Wallace?" Peevey said.

Wallace sat down on a stool. "Why is it so quiet in here?"

"Because it's just us right now, which is a good thing. I can tell something's on your mind. Tell me about it."

"It's goddamned nuts."

Peevey walked away and returned with a glass of something stout and amber.

Wallace sipped it, then tossed it back.

"Now?" Peevey said.

Wallace told him maybe after one more.

"You'll need to start talking soon." Peevey retrieved a bottle and poured the drink. "I don't know how long this will last."

"What?"

"Any of this."

That's fair. He's right. I need to talk, like old times.

"Do you believe in ghosts?" Wallace said.

"Of course I do, since I am one."

Wallace downed the second round. "You?"

"I am. I can't say for sure what this is, actually. Are we in the past, the future, or nowhere at all? I don't know. I *do know* I'm dead."

"What was it?"

"Stroke, just like my dear old wife used to warn me about. She told me my black ass was just going to blink out one day, like my daddy did. I would say you should watch out for the nasty little bastards, but you can't, not if they're all like mine, in which you feel something *pop* in your head, and then you're on the floor mumbling through your drool, and then you're dead. There isn't much to watch out for."

"You're kidding."

"Truly I'm not."

"You don't look dead."

"Nor do I sound dead, but this is, I think, a dream."

"No, this is unbelievable."

"Don't be so dense. All the mysteries of life and the afterlife and the known and unknown universe and you're taken aback by one fucking dead guy? Liquor up."

Peevey poured another drink.

"Interesting point." Wallace approached the third round slower, just a sip, and then another. "I've heard a voice. There's a musician in the park with me. She records things on her iPad, and..." He stumbled through a poor explanation of the Table Mountain songs and his theory—his hope—about the Rawlins girl.

"It's funny," Peevey said, "because on this side, sometimes you haven't an ounce of consciousness. And then, sometimes, it's almost like you're alive again. Frequently, you're barely in control of where you are. You're just a scene from a faded old film."

"Is she trying to tell me something?"

"I would say, if she's there at all, she's just *there*, Wallace. That's how these things—all things—work. They're there, and that's all they are."

"She can't talk to me?"

"I suppose I should repeat myself. Sometimes I still come to work. Sometimes I don't exist—that's a very bizarre feeling, by the way. Sometimes I am nothing but a brief clip on the DVR of the universe. Sometimes I am conscious and sometimes I'm not. And that's just *my* experience. Who knows about the others."

"You're dead. I can't believe it."

"It's not so difficult." He poured another drink. "Pay attention to what's around you, Wallace. You're a writer, after all."

4

Wallace sat on the side of the bed, trying to decide if it were true... trying to decide if he wanted to know. Of course, right now, it didn't matter. No cell service out here. He couldn't call up and ask.

Maybe later. Maybe not.

5

He got up and went for a walk, just a mile or so up the Park Road and back. The morning was cool. The clouds were low and the air was damp with cold mist. Thunder rumbled occasionally in the west.

When he returned to the station, he dove into his work, and the experience was nothing like the one in his dream. He worked hard, he worked well, and he felt good about what he accomplished.

After a few hours, he decided to take Hemingway's advice and quit while he was ahead.

He stepped back outside.

Still gray and cool, still misting, still thundering in the direction of Denali.

And there were tracks in the mud.

He crouched down to examine the closest one. Bear tracks. And in the mud, they'd be easy to follow.

The bear had come from the east, seemingly stopped at his door, and turned around.

The animal's retreat followed a different path for the first fifty or so feet, then merged back into the path of its approach, turning the trail into a smudged mess. But still, even for a man like Wallace who'd never tracked a bear in his life, the animal's course was easy to follow.

He was not surprised at all when it led to the river and took a sharp turn to the south.

"You followed the river," he said. "Of course you did."

Lord knows how far the tracks would go; theoretically, they *could* take him all the way to the headwall of the Pendleton Glacier.

He had no intention of going that far. He had no intention, right now, of going *anywhere*—certainly not in this weather.

The distant thunderheads would break loose eventually and soak the valley.

He preferred to be inside when it happened.

6

He returned to the cabin, removed his jacket, and started a pot of coffee.

And then he returned to his writing table.

"Let's talk," he said.

He removed his phone from his pocket and opened its audio recorder.

"Are you there?" He hit the record button and set the phone on the edge of the table. "Show me."

XVIII
Darkness

1

THE LEDGE FROM WHICH SHE'D stumbled was just beyond her reach. If she sat at a certain spot, she could see it, or she thought she could... In this total darkness, it was hard to tell what was real and what was nothing.

She'd been down here what seemed like an hour—at least—but in reality, it had probably been no more than ten minutes ago she'd stumbled over the ledge.

The fall had broken her flashlight; the jury was still out on her left ankle. She prayed it was not broken, and she wished she'd ignored her dream or nightmare or ghostly experience or whatever the heck it had been; she wished she'd never driven out here and hiked up into the canyon. She'd been so sure she was going to find something, and yes! She'd spotted what looked like an old mine entrance after the sun had broken above the canyon walls.

That's it, she'd so foolishly thought. As if she knew *anything.*

And she'd entered the mine, and the tunnel had been so incredibly dark her flashlight had done little to assist her, and she *still* kept going, the curious little cat, waiting to be killed. Or waiting to fall and hurt herself and be faced with trying to crawl her way back up what was at least a ten foot wall in total darkness—with a bad ankle.

She reminded herself that a hurt ankle was not a death sentence, even considering her unfriendly circumstances. All she had to do was calm down and find a way to *stay calm.* A calm mind, hopefully, would get its bearings and find a way out of here.

A calm mind—.

My phone.

God yes! She'd been so sore and rattled and oblivious that she forgot she had her phone in her pocket—and of course there would not be service in here, but that wasn't the point. If the thing wasn't *smashed,* she would have a light.

Alas, she pulled her phone from her pocket and tried to turn on the flashlight, but no. The screen was cracked and the camera flash, which provided the flashlight function, had apparently broken with it.

The phone itself still worked, however, and the faint glow it provided was better than total darkness.

The glow revealed a strange item lying just a few feet away from her. A piece of leather? She picked it up and studied it. Real leather, a narrow, six-inch ribbon of it with a tiny hole at one end and a piece of string at the other.

A bracelet? she thought. *Possibly. But it could be anything.*

She shone her phone around and saw nothing else, just rock.

She placed the item in her back pocket, craned her neck... and again, she could just barely make out the dark ledge above her.

If her right ankle weren't on fire, it would be easy.

But I can get up there.

Or perhaps she was putting too much faith in her upper body strength.

She limped toward the wall and winced as she rose up on her toes.

No way I can jump. No way.

Indeed, her optimism that her ankle had merely been rolled over and not sprained or broken faded rapidly once she was on her toes—the pain coming from the pressure was blinding, and she dropped back down immediately.

I have to try. I can look and look, but I doubt seriously there's a step ladder or a paint bucket down here.

And if she did find a way to reach the ledge? Could she pull herself up? She thought so. *Hoped* so.

She ran her hands along the wall's surface.

It wasn't very smooth. If she could find a hold for her good foot, she wouldn't have to jump.

There had to be something, and there was. About a foot and a half above the floor, a softball-sized knob of rock protruded from a rugged outcropping, at just the right height. She could do this. She'd been up some climbing walls in the not-so-distant past... Never with a bum ankle, of course, but if she was lucky, she wouldn't *need* that ankle.

She put her good foot up on the knob and lifted herself up; she grasped at anything and everything with one hand to sustain her balance and reached for the ledge with the other. It wasn't there, it wasn't there—and just as her foot was slipping and her balance was about to go to hell... it was there.

The rest of it was mostly upper body, though her good foot did find occasional holds that offered minor reprieves.

Once she had her elbows over the ledge, she was able to pull herself up fairly easily, and then she was face down on the floor above.

She rolled over and stared up into the blackness. No time to laugh or cry. Neither reaction seemed suitable, anyway.

She still had to follow this tunnel to the exit.

She was sore. She was a fool. In a way, she deserved whatever catastrophe still might occur.

Or maybe she would be okay.

2

Damp, cold, God-blessed daylight opened the gates. It all came loose and hit her at once, as she emerged into the day's gray glow, every emotion, concern, and regret she'd ever had. She cried for just a minute, then sat down, massaged her temples, and laughed at herself. When the fit passed, she started down out of the canyon, limping heavily at first, then crying and laughing again when she realized her ankle was loosening up.

She told herself to not get *too* confident or *too* happy.

She was still out here, miles away from the truck. Thus, Fate still had a perfectly decent window of opportunity to take another shot at her.

By the time she was out of the canyon, her slow and obvious limp was a faint hobble.

An hour or so later, the truck at last came into view.

God, she nearly cried again.

And she *did* break into a jog.

3

She turned the truck around and started back through the woods. The trees and growth thickened as she descended.

Now that she was okay—or *should* be okay—her mind returned to the ribbon of leather she'd found in the mine. She reached in her back pocket and withdrew it. Surely it was some type of bracelet. That's the only possible use she could see for it.

And probably, it didn't mean a thing.

She'd been in one of Alaska's many abandoned mines.

Human beings had once worked in there.

One of them had lost his or her bracelet.

Period.

But it was still fascinating.

She set the leather on the dash and focused on the road.

The charred scrap pile came into view on the left; she bounded slowly past it, rolled over a subtle rise, and came to the highway.

Left would return her to Uncle Rawleigh and the Salmon Catch; right, and she'd be heading toward Anchorage and Wasilla. And the airport.

No chance in hell.

She knew she would turn left, but she did not immediately do it.

She was too overwhelmed.

By exhaustion. And relief.

4

According to the clock on the Frontier's radio, she was already ten minutes late for work. She sped back to civilization and found her boss out on the Catch's front steps. Upon seeing her, he animatedly wiped his brow to show his relief.

He did a fairly decent job of acting like she didn't look like hell.

"I'm sorry," she said.

"We were worried a long time ago," Everett said. "You're usually here so early, to eat and—."

"I got lost out in the park." It was a decent story. Untrue enough to be an outright lie, but it was at least *inspired by* fact, and was definitely plausible.

"You're limping. Come sit down."

She told him she was okay; it was already better. But she sat down next to him.

"You should take the night off. I've already called—."

She surprised him by saying she really *did* want to work; she just needed time to shower, and she wanted to eat.

No part of her wanted to sit in that (*smoky*) cabin all night and dwell on God knows what. Better to back brain it, stay busy.

"Your face is bleeding there," he said. "Near your chin."

She touched the place—she'd noticed it already—and told him she'd fallen. She was okay.

He looked her over. He believed her, yes. But...

"Are you sure?" he said.

"I'm sure. Just got lost."

"And fell."

"Yes."

He studied her for another moment and nodded.

"You're always welcome at work. You know that. But your uncle's out looking for you. You should try to call him."

She'd been foolish. Incredibly so. And now her uncle was out only God knew where fretting over her.

She told her boss she'd call him, reaffirmed she'd be back after she showered and changed, and she drove up to her cabin. She left the ribbon of leather in the truck and went inside.

When she checked her phone, she saw it had accumulated numerous messages and missed calls—all from Uncle Rawleigh and her boss: *Morgan? Where are you? You there?*

She called Uncle Rawleigh's number and the call immediately failed.

Damn it.

It would all be fine, she told herself. She'd try him again after she cleaned up. Or he'd be back soon. Something. But it would be fine.

As it turned out, this was true.

She called him again while she was walking down to the Salmon Catch.

"I'm okay," she said. "I'm sorry. Can we talk tonight, after work?"

"You're going to work?"

"I'm okay, I really am. I just got lost." She paused. "And fell. And rolled my ankle. But I'm okay."

He didn't pry too much.

And yes, he said, they could talk. Of course they could.

5

Uncle Rawleigh's Silverado whipped into the Salmon Catch's parking lot less than ten minutes after she'd pried open the night's first beer bottle. He rushed into the bar like a man who's just learned his wife is either dying or in labor—but when he saw her, he visibly relaxed.

She apologized again when he approached her.

"You got lost? When did you leave, and—?"

"I'll tell you everything. I promise."

He grinned and shook his head. "Your parents would have killed me."

6

Cork entered the bar at a quarter after nine. He found a quiet seat, ordered a beer, and kept both his low eye and high eye on her.

When she brought him his second beer, he said he'd heard she'd had an adventure.

She just looked at him.

He was harmless, she thought. The man just wanted to get drunk and... look at her? Maybe he just wanted to talk.

"You're looking at me funny," he said.

"Sorry." She set his beer down on a fresh napkin. "Lost in my own thoughts."

"Is that where you got lost?"

She smiled as best she could and walked off.

There was still a slight twinge in her hurt ankle.

Cork left after his third beer. She was relieved when he was gone. He'd just sat there and looked at her.

The crowd thinned.

Her uncle returned.

She set off to brew a fresh part of coffee.

XIX
Stories & Deep Secrets

1

MORGAN WISHED HER HELP A good night and closed down the bar. She left one light on and poured them both a cup of coffee.

They sat down at a little table against the far wall, and Morgan told him she'd had a very vivid dream, in which she was not alone; something was in the room with her, something was watching her, and at some point she sat up in bed and felt compelled to go to the door. Upon opening the door, she was standing on Dragon Canyon Road.

"I saw something on the other side of the fire," she said, "and it made sense, *then*. It made me think I should go there. I don't know what it was, but I went."

Up until this point, Rawleigh had found her story a bit concerning—his niece had either suffered a hell of a night terror, or something *else* was going on—but not remarkably alarming. They'd just been out to Dragon Canyon Road, and she'd had her mind on ghosts and the Rawlins ladies. Dreams consisted of what you fed them, right?

But her story continued.

She described not only going out to that location in the middle of the night, but driving all the way to the boulder field and hiking up into the canyon. At this point, his eyes went wide. Truly, he could not believe what he was hearing. She hiked into the canyon and at daybreak went into the abandoned mine.

When she was done with her story, he thought for a moment and decided that it was only right to take a brutally honest approach: "To start, I want you to spend some time in my cabin. You're grown, Morgan, but I'd prefer you not take a dream so seriously that you wander out in the middle of the night."

He thought she might get angry—walk off, argue, hit him. She did none of that.

She simply nodded.

He continued: "I assume you *do* want to stay."

"Yes."

"Fine. But for now, I want you to stay in my cabin."

Again, she nodded.

"Uncle Rawleigh," she said, "I just know there's something in that mine."

"I'd like to see that piece of leather," he said.

They dumped the remnants of their coffee, locked up, and stepped out into the night.

They trekked up the path to where the trucks were parked. She unlocked the Frontier, withdrew the ribbon of leather, and handed it to him. He leaned into the truck's cabin light and turned it over in his hands. Studied it. Smiled faintly. Shook his head.

"What is it?" Morgan asked.

"What you said it was, I guess."

2

He helped her move her things into his cabin.

She collapsed on one side of his bed and was asleep almost immediately.

Rawleigh sat down at the table, leaned into the lamp, and studied what was obviously a leather bracelet.

It was intriguing. Kind of frightening. He wondered.

He closed his eyes and thought back… He smiled.

"I'll be damned," he said softly.

And thought about going for it.

3

After an hour or so of tossing and turning, he got out of bed, put on his jeans, boots, shirt, and jacket, and went outside. He immediately noted the smell of smoke, the feeling he was not alone. The sensation sent a chill through him.

He walked out into the night, past the standing cabins to those not yet rebuilt.

The sky was cloudy and the air was damp. It was much darker than he was accustomed to.

"What are you?" he whispered. "And how?"

He did not expect a response, and he didn't get one

"You're scaring my niece. She's a nice girl. I'd rather you not do that."

Something in front of him moved. A minor shift of something darker than the cool night air.

Rawleigh's eyes continued to adjust. This again, he thought. This again.

It was rising from the ground. A thin pillar of darkness that moved and expanded until it was something close to human. Yet still entirely unnatural. When he rubbed his eyes it wasn't there. And when he rubbed them again it was. It swayed. It grew. There was a semblance of a face.

"Are you a dream?" he said.

You're asking if I am real?

Whatever it was—dream, ghost, devil—expanded to the point the black void consumed the entire area in front of him—and then it silently exploded.

Rawleigh saw the blood before it hit him. The splatters soared like dark, tiny comets through the cold night, pelting his face with foul and wet warmth. He wiped it away from his eyes with the heels of his hands and stood there, a muted fool.

For several minutes, he was incapable of movement.

And when at last he was capable of walking, he went down to the restrooms, turned on a light, and looked in the mirror. He could only curse himself, because there was no blood on him at all.

4

He left Morgan a note that explained he'd be back that afternoon, then got in his truck and drove out to Dragon Canyon Road.

The Silverado made it a respectable distance up the awful path, but it was no Jeep, and he didn't even consider trying to take it all the way to the start of the boulder field. When the rocks became as large as footballs and as sharp as glass, he stopped the truck, retrieved a flashlight and knife from the glove box, and continued on foot.

He'd follow his niece's path all the way to Dragon Canyon, try to see what she saw, see what was still there.

The canyon had fascinated him since his first trip into it.

Where does it go? he'd asked Cork that day.

I guess it's like everything else in this place. It goes forever.

No, no, it didn't.

He'd found it on an old map—it wasn't mentioned at all on newer publications—and saw that the gorge passed over the Denali National Park boundary and faded away close to Windy Creek. In another time, that would've been an appealing adventure, a week out in the wilderness, following a path that few even know exists.

Dear God, not now.

He was less than a quarter mile from where he left the Silverado, and already his knees burned and his back ached and he was breathing in bursts. Somewhere along the way, the adventurer who would've thought nothing about hiking all the way to Windy Creek had become a sore and broken down old wretch with a bad case of (ex) smoker lungs.

The terrain levels off before the boulder field, remember? There's a reprieve up here somewhere. And that's a good thing, old friend, because the boulder field is going to kick your ass.

The high canyon walls were a light shade of morning blue when he finally found himself at the top of the boulders.

There was no path along the floor, but the canyon was narrow and one could not possibly get lost.

He rested for a moment, dry swallowed an Advil that he found in his jacket pocket, and pressed forward.

The mine entrance, as he recalled, wasn't far away, and indeed, he spotted the conspicuous black portal to his left only ten or twenty minutes after entering the canyon.

He crossed the floor to it and started in.

Even with his Maglite, the darkness enveloped him. The temperature dropped considerably. He zipped his jacket.

The tunnel went on and on.

He moved slowly, keeping the flashlight beam on the floor directly in front of him. Even still, he barely saw the ledge before it was too late.

The darkness beyond it simply did not surrender easily.

Rawleigh knelt down and shone his light down into the depths.

The fall to the shelf on which Morgan had landed wasn't more than eight or ten feet, but the shelf was fairly narrow, and there was a more dramatic plummet beyond it. Morgan was lucky she'd limped out of here.

The floor down there was smooth gray rock, knobby in sections. He saw no signs of humanity. Beyond the edge of the shelf, the deeper darkness.

Rawleigh told himself he was a fool, nothing but a fool, then lowered himself over the ledge.

He paced the shelf, looking for any other signs of human life, and went to the edge.

He knew it before he looked.

And still he had to look closely.

But yes.

He knelt at the edge and stared down into the abyss.

Falling from this point would be the last thing he ever did; it was at least fifty feet to the bottom. Still, the Maglite revealed car parts scattered all over the lower floor. He could make out the steering column, a seat, a transmission, a large chunk of windshield; the back hatch clearly marked with a Kia badge was near the edge of his flashlight's reach.

Rawleigh knelt there, looking.

What would it take, he thought, for a fellow to bring all these materials up through Dragon Canyon and dump them here? A lot. It would take a lot to disassemble an SUV and bring it in here, but it wasn't impossible. If one were extremely dedicated... if one had some help... and a lot of time.

"It's here," he said. "No disputing that."

And Morgan was going to be very excited.

XX
Pendleton Borealis

1

THAT MORNING, WALLACE LISTENED TO the empty white noise of his phone recordings. He set the phone on his table and played it while he wrote—or tried to write. Last night's silence was very distracting. Minute after minute and hour after hour passed, and it was all grainy silence, broken occasionally by a snore or the faint creak of the bed. Yet it captivated him. He did not know what he was listening for; it probably didn't matter. The white noise alone seemed to signal that something was there, which was madness. And what did this mean for his book? Was he unknowingly wading into a ghost story? As intriguing as it sounded, he *hoped not*. He'd come up here to write a *serious book*. And how could any *serious book* be truly *serious* if it were only one step removed from belonging in the HORROR section alongside the likes of Bentley Little and Stephen King? Not that there was anything *wrong* with those authors—Wallace respected King and would, without doubt, love to be cashing Stephen King's checks, but the horror field was not where he belonged. It wasn't his thing. He didn't stand a chance in it. He was here to be *serious*, not to (halfheartedly) announce his allegiance to the horror genre.

Yes, of course. He wasn't here to talk to ghosts. He was here to be SERIOUS. That's why he was staring down at his notebook while listening to a five-hour recording of *ghost* noise and nocturnal farts.

If she's here, she's here.

"She's not here."

What was he doing to himself, to his book? Was he really going to turn his New Journalism Masterpiece into the stream of conscious ramblings of a lonely man being led astray by a ghost that surely did not truly exist?

Then came a *new* sound amongst the white noise.

He set down his pencil and paused the recording, backed it up a few seconds, and listened again: heavy footsteps, and something that sounded like breathing, but surely not *human* breathing.

Not a ghost, the goddamned bear.

The noise lasted four full seconds: three heavy footsteps, followed by a loud *sneeze*-type noise that could not possibly have come from him.

The bear tracks had been real, hadn't they?

One of the beasts—for whatever reason—had developed an affinity for him, and had (apparently?) come to visit him last night. And on other occasions, too.

He listened again.

It was *not* him. If he'd made a noise like that, he'd have woken up. And besides, there were footsteps, and that's almost certainly what those three muffled *thuds* were, footsteps.

Outside.

Considering the bear tracks he'd seen and followed, it made sense.

"All right, you pretty blond thing," he said. "Is it you?"

2

He wrote furiously, drilling deeper into the first quarter of the post-New Hampshire Alaska narrative, in which the Rawlins women arrived in Anchorage and spent five weeks living in a rented room behind an Outback Steakhouse (this, according to Ellis Everett and the manager of the Outback), and Mary and Emily waited tables, and Mary's health, already in decline, dipped even further, and Mary decided to bring them closer to Denali so Emily could see the Alaskan Range; he proceeded into a brief history of the Salmon Catch and the surrounding community, introducing readers to marginally fictionalized avatars of Ellis and Cork Everett and Rawleigh McCown, among others… For now, he ignored any ideas about ghosts and bears and stopped only to rest his hand and check his notes.

Morning became afternoon, and afternoon became evening, and that is when a cold blast of wind sent the station door crashing inward.

Wallace—comically, he thought, even as it was happening—simultaneously jerked his head up and fell back in his chair. He landed hard; the back of his skull cracked the floor with a brilliant flash of light.

He thought he was okay. It seemed likely, but the door had crashed open, and wasn't that strange? And when he looked toward it, he saw a visitor (*Death*?) had crossed the threshold, but it wasn't a cloaked figure clutching a scythe, it was her.

Nobody's there. Except this was not altogether true. She was not *entirely* there, sometimes she was nothing more than a faint mist, but she wore dark blue nylon pants. The glimmer of her white shirt, a wisp of blond hair.

Yes, the shape that occupied the space between his conked head and the open door was that of a female. Her. She looked down at him, there, not there, nearly solid, nothing more than mist, and the voice in his head was female, too: *Follow me.*

She turned and started away and stepped outside.

She was gone.

The pain in his head persisted, though as he grabbed the edge of the table and picked himself up, the sharp bolts faded to a dull throb, and he was not dizzy.

The door was still open—he hadn't dreamed *that*—and he knew good and well that he'd shut it and locked it, just like always.

He reached around and felt the tender, marble-sized knot on the back of his head.

You bumped your head, you VERY SERIOUS WRITER. *Toppled over in your chair like a fool.*

But he'd never lost consciousness, and he'd seen her clearly.

3

Or, perhaps one sometimes saw ghosts and heard voices upon getting one's bell rung; that sounded more plausible than certain other explanations. But doors that were latched and locked couldn't open by themselves, could they? Well then, the door hadn't been latched and locked. Wasn't that *more possible* than the door being blown open by the mysterious and misty dead?

Bullshit. He'd shut the door. And locked it.

He approached the door. Shut it, threw the lock, and pulled on it.

The door did not move.

He opened it again and went outside. The first thing he noticed was the fresh line of tracks leading off toward the Toklat; the second thing was the bear itself, small and distant, moving south toward the mountains.

He could follow it, if he wanted to, though it was surely too late in the day for such an excursion, even if he *did* believe in a connection between this bear and his recent trip to the madhouse.

Nonetheless, he started walking.

Before he knew it, he was looking down at the Toklat Station, which was almost lost in the dark glow of the nighttime sun.

This was a bad idea. He should not continue. He did not have his jacket; he did not have any supplies…

So he continued.

This VERY SERIOUS WRITER had a knot on his head and was out of his mind. So be it.

By the time he reached the west shore of the Toklat, the beast he was theoretically trailing was nowhere to be found. But that inconvenient fact did not stop him, because he knew where the bear had gone. He recalled the previous set of tracks. Same thing here; yet again, south along the river, toward Pendleton.

He did not allow himself to think too much.

When a VERY SERIOUS WRITER is in in pursuit of something serious, he mustn't allow himself to hesitate, even for things worthy of hesitation; he must choose his course and follow it to its end. Especially when he has a bump on his head and is for whatever reason following a bear up a Denali National Park riverbed, even when there is no logical reason at all to conclude the bear *went* up the riverbed. Fuck such hesitations. They only interfere with VERY SERIOUS WORK.

He stopped.

He was crazy.

He continued.

4

He could not be sure how far he walked.

Far enough for the river to become wider and stronger. Far enough for the terrain to steepen and the mountains, Pendleton specifically, to loom directly overhead.

Up and up he trekked.

The evening wore on, dim to the point now that he realized what he was doing.

Straight ahead, he could make out Pendleton Glacier. The beginning of the river was his destination.

I need to turn around.

His feet hurt. His lungs burned. How long had he been——?

He sat down on the bank and rubbed the bump on his head.

No way to rationalize this.

The moon crept out from behind a distant summit.

Pendleton Glacier became a glowing, ghostly, coiled mass. It called to him—no, it had *been* calling to him, and he only just now realized it.

Yes, it was still far away, but he was so close. Had the bear really gone all the way up there? If so, why?

I don't know.

But the truth was, he did know.

Or, he had a very good idea.

The sky over the glacier was glowing so brightly now it nearly blinded him, a hypnotizing aurora of pink and yellow and green, revealing, below, the ice and the flowers growing out of it.

Come on, Wallace, the colors said. *We have things to show you.*

He got up and pressed on.

He did not have a choice.

XXI
Reflections

1

MORGAN WOKE THAT MORNING FROM a sleep so deep it temporarily blocked her memory of the previous day. She sat on the side of the bed trying to identify what was different (this wasn't her cabin, was it?), trying to decide why there was a black hole in the center of her memory.

It all returned to her while she was in the shower. The whole frightening, miserable day unveiled itself.

She returned to his cabin and found a note from him: *Left early, be back this afternoon. Love, UR.*

Odd, though she couldn't actually say *why*.

She was still looking at the note several minutes later when a knock came at the door.

She put down the note, opened the door, and Cork was there.

He was wearing jeans and an unbuttoned denim uniform short. His hair was unkempt; his eyes were red. The sagging eye seemed to study her, while the normal one gazed past her into the cabin.

His smile was slight and awkward.

"Skipped work today," he said. "Will you take a walk with me?"

"Down to the gas station?" she said.

He agreed, and she stepped out with him. She *almost* dove right into an apology—*Sorry for being kind of rude last night. I was just tired and sore and I hate the weird look that's always on your face*—but she refrained at the last second.

"I didn't sleep last night," he said. "Couldn't stand the thought of going to work today. I called in."

"Are you sick?"

"I don't think so." But he wiped his nose with the back of his hand as if to prove otherwise. "Headache. And I worried about you, too."

"About me?"

"You looked like a ghost last night. Acted like one, too."

"Yesterday..." She didn't want to go into it with him. Truly she didn't. "Yesterday was a long day."

"So what's wrong?"

They reached the highway, checked for cars, and crossed to the gas station. Cork paid for his coffee and her Sprite.

"Nothing's wrong now," she said, after they stepped back out. "I just had a terrible day. I probably shouldn't have worked last night, but I did, because I didn't want to spend all night in bed thinking about it. I got lost, way out in the middle of nowhere."

He leaned back against the front window and sipped his coffee. "That would suck. I'd be a ghost too." He grinned, and it didn't help his cause. "I wish you trusted me, you know. I don't like it when people don't trust me. I know how I look. I don't like that either. But that's got nothing to do with *trust*, you know. It's just one of those things."

His words were unnerving, and now she *did* apologize—not with a big long speech, just a simple apology.

He continued: "I'll be the first to tell you, you know, that I'm not always nice. But you *looked* at me like I was a piece of shit, and I hated that. I didn't hate you. I hated *that*. I come in and ask about you, because I was worried, and I get looked at like that. My feelings weren't hurt, I just didn't like it."

She apologized again.

They crossed the highway.

"Is there anything else?" Cork said as they walked back up to her uncle's cabin.

Anything else?

"Shouldn't I ask you that?" Morgan said. "You're the one who knocked on my door."

He stopped. He wasn't grinning anymore.

"I don't have anything else," he said.

2

He walked away silently.

Morgan continued on past the cabins. She walked up the forested hillside behind them, to the approximate location of the tracks she'd seen in the dirt. They were gone, of course, having been washed or blown away.

But she liked this spot. It was quiet, out of sight of the cabins, and there was a large boulder there that was perfect for sitting... and she sat down.

Cork's message had been clear: *I know I look weird, but you shouldn't treat people like dirt.*

Kudos to him for showing up and being out with it, she thought.

She'd gotten the drift.

But she still didn't like him.

If that made her shallow, well then...

She pulled her phone from her pocket and saw her uncle's number on the screen.

There was service up here. One bar's worth.

She answered the phone, making sure not to move—she might step out of the service cloud.

"I've been trying to call," Uncle Rawleigh said. "I need you to meet me."

She asked him what was going on—then asked where.

"The start of Dragon Canyon Road. When you get here, I'll tell you everything."

"Are you okay?"

"I'm perfectly fine. I found something."

3

She covered the ten or so miles between the Salmon Catch and the inconspicuous turnoff for Dragon Canyon Road in less than five minutes.

Uncle Rawleigh was indeed waiting on her.

His Silverado was perched atop the rise that shielded his burn pile from the highway. He had the tailgate down and was sitting on it.

After she pulled in and parked next to him, he invited her to have a seat.

They were waiting on somebody else, he said.

She hopped up on his tailgate and asked him what he'd found.

"I wish I had a cigarette," he said. "I really do."

And then he told her how close she'd come to falling to her death on top of what was almost certainly Mary Rawlins's vanished rental.

4

An older 4x4 Chevrolet with a Honda ATV in the bed pulled in about half an hour later, and a short, stout man of about fifty approached them and confirmed that he was Officer Pearce of the Wasilla Police Department. Uncle Rawleigh had explained that he'd called Pearce's personal number first, as Pearce had been just about the only one back then who'd gone above and beyond what he was required to do—he'd argued extensively with the Alaska Bureau of Investigations, specifically the Missing Persons Unit, and had continued to personally search for Mary and Emily long after all organized efforts were called off; if this were indeed a new lead in the case, he wanted Pearce to be the first one on it.

"If what you think you have is true," Pearce said, "we're gonna have to bring the cavalry here. But let's see it first."

They piled in his truck and began the slow, cumbersome journey up Dragon Canyon Road.

When they reached the boulder field, Pearce shut off the truck and used two metal ramps to unload the ATV from its bed.

Before they climbed on, Pearce and Uncle Rawleigh walked up to the base of the field and studied the terrain.

"That'll get us over halfway," Uncle Rawleigh said, "but even that thing won't make it all the way to the canyon. Or I don't think it will."

"We'll see." Pearce went to the ATV and started it.

Rawleigh and Morgan piled on behind him.

Pearce had a keen eye for monitoring the terrain. With his driving, it almost seemed that there *was* a path, however faint, up through the rocks. But her uncle proved to be right; about forty yards shy of the crest, the rocks became so large there was simply no way the machine could pass over them.

Pearce shut it off and they footed the rest of the journey.

Once they were inside the mine, all three of them aiming powerful flashlights into the thick darkness of the mountain's interior, Pearce said: "Tell me again how you found this? Are you folks crazy?"

Uncle Rawleigh had already discussed this with her: You don't tell cops about bad dreams and late night wanderings into the wilderness *based on* those dreams. It just doesn't sound believable. So they gave a much more nuts and bolts account that wasn't quite lying by omission. It was more like straight-up lying.

"I've been hiking," Morgan said. "Mainly in Denali, but all over the place. I came out here to hike, and I found this mine. Up here, there's a ledge that's hard to see. So after I came in here, I tripped over it."

Uncle Rawleigh picked up the narrative: "We were all worried about her, by *we* I mean myself and her boss at the Salmon Catch. We figured she'd gone hiking out in the park, but anyway, when she got back, she showed me a piece of leather, like a bracelet, and she admitted she found it in here. Why is that significant? I'll explain that in a minute."

"And so you came up here to look."

"It's right up here. Be careful."

They reached the first ledge.

Staring down into the darkness, Pearce said: "How in God's name could anybody get a car in here? Forgive me for being a skeptic when I'm supposedly a minute away from seeing things for myself."

"You'll see."

And, as if to prove they weren't trying to con Pearce into a deathtrap, Uncle Rawleigh tucked his light into his back pocket and lowered himself over the ledge.

Morgan next.

Pearce followed them.

And when Pearce shone his light over the next ledge, he dropped down on one knee and leaned as far out as he dared. He said softly: "It's in pieces. That must have…" More silence. "Kia. I'll be damned."

5

The next discovery came almost an hour later.

They went deeper into the mine after Pearce found a break in the wall at the end of the shelf. Morgan and Uncle Rawleigh followed the cop down a low and narrow corridor that ended in a vast chamber that had obviously, at one time, been well trampled by miners. The floor was strewn with old soda cans; the air hung heavy with soured sweat and ancient tobacco… and something else. Something much fouler that was, perhaps, not a smell at all, but a presence.

Morgan felt it.

She was fairly sure they *all* did.

Pearce and Uncle Rawleigh pressed forward into the chamber.

Morgan followed.

Their flashlight beams struggled to penetrate the darkness, but the opposite wall, and the corpse leaned against it, eventually came into view.

Morgan put a hand over her mouth.

He'd been there a long time, this man, this formerly *large* man who was now a skeleton wrapped in leather and dusty clothes, with his skull slumped over on his left shoulder and his hands in his lap. His legs were splayed in a wide V.

Pearce motioned for the two of them to stay back, and he knelt before the dead man. He stayed there for a minute or more, totally still, with his flashlight tucked under his arm.

Morgan reached for her uncle when the cop grasped the dead man's jacket and reached into a pocket.

He withdrew a wallet.

"I already know who it is." Uncle Rawleigh tossed Pearce the leather bracelet. "Look at his wrists. He's the reason I got the idea to come out here."

"Friend of yours?"

"His name's Devin. And no, he never was a friend. Thank God."

XXII
Drink Pictures

1

AS USUAL, CORK RETURNED TO booze.

There was a bottle of Pinnacle gin in the cabinet by his refrigerator. The gin went slowly because he usually preferred vodka or Irish whiskey, had on many occasions drank from those bottles like they were water, but, you know, as a result, those two bottles were nearly empty, and he couldn't stand the thought of burning through the last of his Irish whiskey for an occasion like this, in which he only wanted to look at the fucking wall and lose himself in it, and so gin on crushed ice it was, a big goddamned plastic cup full of it—like it was water.

Gin wasn't so bad for a time like this.

He carried the cup into the living room of his collapsing shoebox, which sat about a mile and a half down a dirt road that cut off the highway just past the

Salmon Catch. He'd walked it before, on those nights when he didn't trust himself not to smash his miserable old Ford into a tree and finish it off; he'd walked it before, walked his drinks right off. On cold nights, when it was too cold to walk. But oh hell. For sure, he wouldn't be walking his drink off now. He was right here where he needed to be. He figured he'd stay. Come at me, wall. Come on at me now.

He took a drink. The gin was good. It was okay. He sloshed it around like Listerine, but it was a hell of a lot better than Listerine.

"You better wash your mouth out," Mom used to say, and this was when? All the time, but there was *one* instance he specifically recalled, though he couldn't recall the specific year. He couldn't remember. He'd been a kid, and she'd been doing her typical drunken patrol, one room of the house to another, and he'd known it, but sometimes it gets to you and you don't care, so he'd taken Macy into the closet off the spare bedroom. She'd been related, second cousin maybe, he didn't know at the time and it didn't matter, it was all the same. It just gets to you. He'd poured her the remainder of one of his mother's bottles of rum, and of course she'd been unable to handle it, and when Mom opened the closet door, well, it had almost been funny. After all, she hadn't yelled at him or yanked his face out from between Macy's legs. Mom had just stood there with her arms crossed, and then she'd kicked him in his ribs. Cracked one, too; it had hurt to roll over in bed for the next three weeks. Then, *You better wash your mouth out.*

"You're all fucking worthless," Daddy had said later that day, and what a statement that had been, because Ellis Everett was a decent man who didn't form opinions about people until he had to, and he had the strength to speak the truth. "You and your mother are both sorrier than the fires of hell."

Macy, Cork later preferred to think, didn't know a thing about it. She'd been out of her mind. If there was a memory in there, it was painted over and half dead. Sometimes he was sure she *thought* she remembered something. But not really, probably. Time passed, and Macy stumbled into the road and got killed, and that's what mattered.

The gin made him wonder about the world. He wasn't sure he understood. What he *did* understand was that certain things could not be done about certain things. He couldn't make himself not consider certain things. This was complicated, and it wasn't. But he knew things could not be done about it. It was not his fault, was it, that placing his hands around his mother's neck and squeezing it like a stress ball when he was thirteen years old had made him tremble with pleasure just like any number of other things. That wasn't his fault. It happened, and it was a good thing, he supposed, that *he* hadn't actually finished her off: that had been the aneurism a week or two later, though Daddy was still sure it had been Cork's fault. And oh well. They were all sorrier than the fires of hell.

This is why he drank. This was why he liked to drink at the Salmon Catch. But it was another of those *oh well* type of things, and it was short lived. There were more pressing matters, like Morgan, going numb, like Morgan again. Like he could look at her and indulge himself in her curves. These things he understood, and the beer and vodka helped him appreciate them without going too far, without treating her like a stress ball. He was better when he was right on the edge of being totally fucking hammered; when he was there, he could admit that he looked forward to saying something to her, so she would respond, and he *would* talk to her, and he did not ponder those few things that wanted so badly to preoccupy him and make him tremble.

Morgan could be so very bad for him. He needed to sit here and get drunk and consider the images in his head and on the walls. He liked her and liked talking to her, but she could be so bad for him. She was this new thing, this new pretty thing who seemed so exotic and actually spoke with him and walked with him, and things like this were rare.

Maybe he would be okay when the gin took hold.

He hoped so. She was bad for him, and he didn't want her to be.

2

It occurred to him later, after most of the ice was gone. Just some diluted gin, a large gulp, and on his way toward the back porch to piss, he heard his dad, he of the Salmon Catch, best goddamned fish in Alaska, and it was his voice from all those years back, after the boy took his hands off his mother's neck: "You know, it isn't right, Cork. You know it isn't. I know it isn't. You're sorry, but at times, I don't blame you." And then dear old Ellis Everett had started crying 'cause he couldn't believe he said it, and when she was dead, it *really* happened. Crying, like Cork had never seen from him.

Thanks Daddy, he thought, back door in sight, and thank God, because his bladder hurt; the gin went down and out just like water or coffee or beer, worse really; it always made him piss and piss. Thanks Daddy, don't blame me, he knew it wasn't right, knew it, but there's only so much a man can do with his own self, right? Maybe he was sorry as the fires of hell, maybe there was so much wrong with him he probably shouldn't even be around, but what kind of bitch just stands there and watches and then her first real action is to kick you in your fucking ribs. What about that? And then: *You better wash your mouth out.* She'd *needed* a good strangling, really, the drunken and hypocritical belittling bitch, and it's not like he'd finished her off. The thing in her brain went *boom* and *splat*, and that was that.

He opened the back door. He needed to drain it so badly. He unfastened his jeans as he stumbled out onto the back porch, but with his bladder so full and his head so numb, he didn't immediately realize that he wasn't on his back porch; he was standing in a city on a bridge and there were snow flurries in the air. He began to piss. It didn't even matter. At first the piss went down his leg, but then he took something close to proper aim and sent it into the dark water below. He felt better; his brain wasn't swirling as much anymore, either, but why was he here? Where was his back porch? How did this happen?

A slight noise from below, ripples in the water, and something burst from it, and fingers wrapped themselves around two of the posts in the rail, and she pulled herself out. The woman who clambered over the rail and landed on the wet concrete was very much dead. What remained of her was blue and gray and decayed, and the opening of her mouth was too big, revealing the rotted remains of most of the left side of her jaw, teeth, and gums, because something had been eating on her. Surely this was a nightmare. Surely. But it didn't feel like a nightmare.

She put her hands on the ground and pushed herself to her feet. She started toward him, initially hesitant to move, then with increased confidence, and she told him she would have him dead, and even though she couldn't chew so good, she was going to chew it before she killed him. Finish up, Cork, finish up, and them I'm going to chew it up, and I'm going to kill you.

Kill you when you finish.

XXIII
Photo Album

1

FIRST, WALLACE TRIED TO CONVINCE himself it hadn't been real. It was almost easy to do and actually somewhat logical. There'd been a bear. There'd been bear tracks. Maybe he'd followed them. But at some point, and this is where the issue became confusing, he *hadn't* followed them. Because he'd never reached Pendleton Glacier; Lord knows he'd *never* walk so far so late in the day, and he'd certainly not seen those lights or seen the flowers growing out of the ice, a memory he had for which there was no logical explanation. It was the stuff of Beatles music—"Wallace on the Ice with Flowers"—inexplicable, psychedelic, not possible. He'd surely been here, in the old Toklat Station, *asleep*, with a hell of a knot on his head.

Next, he told himself it didn't matter. It was just, as they'd say, *one of those things*. Just because the dream had been vivid and had partially lodged itself in his memory, that didn't mean it was substantial.

All this sounded good when he considered it, or when he spoke it aloud. It almost made sense. But as he went about his morning, he realized that he could not possibly believe it. The girl had been in his cabin. The bear had been outside. The riverbed that had, for some reason, been a part of his life since he'd been knocked on his ass by that grizzly had led him up to the glacier and it had been glowing like the northern lights, and whether or not it had *really* happened was irrelevant. The image *itself* was the important part.

Thus, he could not write. He tried. He wrote a few lines and erased them. He drummed his fingers against his notes, stared out the window, stared at the table.

"I want to help you," he said to nothing at all. "I hope you understand that. But this sucks. Do you realize what you're doing to me? You're turning my brain to mush. Who am I talking to? Who? And what the hell is wrong with me? Hey, don't dream it's over."

He looked up, shook his head, and flipped his mechanical pencil in the air.

2

Next, he accepted that he might have actually made the hike. And maybe he'd hiked further than he thought, though he still refused to believe he'd made it to the glacier.

There were recent human footprints in the riverbed, about the size of his. And in the mushier parts of the bed, he had to admit, the pattern matched his boots.

Not to mention, the backs of his legs felt like…

Yes. Some things he had to accept.

He looked back at the station, and something hit him—a thought, a memory?

You dropped something.

"What?" he said. "What did I drop?"

The question was soon answered.

Less than twenty feet up the river, he found a faded purple book embedded in the mud between two tendrils of water.

Wallace stepped over the closest of the frigid streams and picked it up.

Not really a book, no—a photo album.

It was as thick as *Lonesome Dove* or *War and Peace,* and most of its pictures were ruined.

She had a camera. She liked taking pictures.

Did I drop this? Really?

More likely, it had spent God knows how long being washed down the river. Or maybe not? Surely it would have been full-fledged FUBAR if it had been hitching a ride down this riverbed for several days, not to mention months or years.

So how long had it been here? And how had it gotten to this location?

You dropped something.

For now, he thought, how it got here was irrelevant. It was here, he had it, and it could be important.

3

There were twenty-two photos in the album, tucked into plastic sleeves, and most of the pictures were ruined beyond recognition.

But this did not stop him from sitting at his writing table and flipping through them.

Of the pictures that actually contained discernible traces of their former selves, there seemed to be a common theme: nature. Judging by the smudged colors and patterns, he concluded that most of the photos were close ups of wildflowers.

So, a nature photographer had lost her work.

And given the color of the album, he assumed the owner was, or had been, female.

You know what you're thinking.

Female nature photographer, out along the Toklat River.

It was a thought. Just a thought. But an intriguing one.

4

He was halfway to Eielson before he waved down a bus.

When he arrived, he went to the Pepsi machine and bought a Sierra Mist. He downed a large portion of it in a single gulp, suppressed a belch, and took to sipping it. His head hurt. His stomach, too. The drink helped, but it was no magic cure. One more drink, and he tossed the bottle into a trash can and approached the counter.

"Ed Merkin around?" he said to the ranger who'd just finished helping three young hikers plot a route on their map.

"He is. I think he's busy."

"Tell him it's Wallace O'Brien. The writer. And tell him it might be important."

The ranger nodded and set off on the task.

Wallace pondered a large scale model of the Alaska Range. Denali rose high from its center, a sentinel; lesser peaks tapered off to the northeast and southwest. The range was vast, and the massiveness of Denali rendered the entire region impossible to measure for inexperienced eyes.

One could *easily* set about on a hike, lured by the apparent closeness of any particular feature in the park, and become hopelessly lost. But Merkin had said that didn't usually happen, right?

The ranger returned and said Merkin was at his desk.

Wallace found him kicked back in his chair.

He took a quick look at Wallace, leaned forward, and asked him how he was doing, in such a way that suggested he had a good idea of the answer.

"Fine." Wallace reached into his jacket and withdrew the photo album. "I found this."

The look on Merkin's face as Wallace passed over the album was amusing.

It became less amusing after he turned it over a few times and flipped through it.

"Flowers, wouldn't you say?"

"Most of them. You can make out wildlife in a couple."

Merkin set the album down. "Where did you find it?"

"The Toklat. I was following bear tracks. They came all the way up to my cabin door. I followed them toward Pendleton."

Merkin frowned. "It was in the riverbed? People hike that river frequently."

"So I've heard."

"You found it in the middle of the Toklat? Close to the station—close to the road?"

"Yes. I know what you're thinking, that if it had been there a while, for *years*, say, somebody would have seen it by now."

"One would think, yes. That's what I'm getting at."

"But there are ways around that."

"Sure there are, I guess. You're thinking of the girl, aren't you? Emily Rawlins."

Wallace said, "Maybe."

5

As best he could, without making himself sound totally insane, Wallace described his dream that wasn't a dream. Including the vision of the glacier. The lights, the flowers.

When he was finished, Merkin leaned back in his chair and shook his head.

"I appreciate your honesty. I don't think you're crazy, and I don't think you're full of... stuff. But there is no way you hiked all the way to Pendleton Glacier last night. Way too far. It's *at least* a full day's hike from the Park Road, and that's for the mountain goats. It sounds to me like you had a very vivid dream, Wallace. That said, there's no denying the photo album."

"It could have washed down the river."

"Absolutely, and you found it close to where I strongly believe Emily Rawlins got off my bus. It could be hers. It's a shot in the dark, but it could be. We need to take this seriously. I want somebody to go up that way. Painter, probably, and one of those mountain goats, Makayla." He paused. "Feel free to join them."

Wallace didn't have to think about it. He said he would.

6

Merkin said they should leave tomorrow morning.

Painter and Makayla arrived and joined in around his desk. Painter leaned against a nearby wall and Makayla sat down in an empty chair next to Wallace's. She leaned forward and folded her hands in her lap; several locks of dark brown hair hung over her eyes.

"It's eight to ten hours out to the glacier, if we're going that far," Painter said. "So if by 'tomorrow morning' you mean three or four 'o clock, yes, I agree."

"Are we actually looking for a *body*?" Makayla said.

"We have a photo album and a far-out theory *based* on that photo album," Merkin said. "I intend to hand the album to the authorities. It's probably nothing at all, but if it is, they'll find out. But first, I want you to go out there, and so... Yes, I suppose you are looking for a body."

"We looked up and down the Toklat years ago, Ed," Painter said.

"Things have changed," Merkin said. "And we sure as hell didn't go all the way to the glacier."

"Because mountaineers bound for Pendleton are the only ones who go up there. Hell, you're *supposed* to get a permit before you go that far. Emily Rawlins didn't get a permit."

Ed Merkin nodded and was about to speak when his phone rang.

He picked it up and said hello.

"Pearce?" He leaned into his desk and put a thumb in his open ear. "*Cormac* Pearce? This is unexpected. It's been a while."

He listened and looked up at Wallace with his eyes wide.

"You're kidding," he said into the phone. "I just told one of my rangers that things have changed. I didn't know I was right."

XXIV
Lady in the Road

1

THAT EVENING WAS *ALMOST* LIKE so many others. They were at the Salmon Catch. But Morgan was not working. She was sitting at a window booth with her uncle and Officer Pearce.

They hadn't talked much.

Yet.

Ellis Everett was behind the bar. He stepped out occasionally to check on them.

"Sit here and talk all night," he'd said shortly after they arrived. "I'll take care of you."

But thus far, Uncle Rawleigh and Pearce were silently making their way through a pitcher of Alaskan Amber, and Morgan was sipping on a glass of spiked Sprite, thinking about dark mines, dead men, and a torn apart Kia.

It was Pearce who started the talk.

He asked Uncle Rawleigh about the dead man, Devin.

"Devin lived up the road from here, in Healy," her uncle said, "He lived alone. As far as I know, his only family was a twin brother who died back in the late nineties. Never worked—that I know of. I'll be honest with you: I didn't even know he was missing. If I heard about that, I forgot. That sounds terrible, I know, because I did *know* him. We hung out some after I moved up here, beat around on the back roads, got drunk together a few times. I don't know when the last time I saw him was. I truly can't say."

"So he was a recluse. Other than that, what type of fellow would you say he was?"

"Quiet. Lonely." Uncle Rawleigh thought for a moment. "He could be fun to be around, but at the end of the day, he always said he didn't want any friends, and he never had any."

Pearce tipped a couple of inches of beer into his glass. "Dangerous? Perverted?"

Her uncle's eyes widened a bit. "I couldn't say. If you're asking if *I* ever saw anything like that, no. If you put a couple of drinks in him he'd…" He seemed to note Morgan's presence. "He'd make a few cracks. But shit, so did I. No, I never saw anything like that."

"Fair enough." Pearce returned his focus to his beer.

"Do you think it's a coincidence that we found the car at the same time that writer in Denali found her photo album?" Morgan said.

Both men looked at her.

Pearce politely said: "We don't *know* it's Emily Rawlin's album."

And we didn't know *it was Mary's Kia, either*, Morgan didn't say. *But it* was.

"Would you bet on it?" Uncle Rawleigh said.

Pearce started to say *no*—but then he smiled. "I'd have to think about it."

And then Wallace O'Brien entered the room.

2

When Pearce learned who the long haired man was, he stood and waved him over. Wallace pulled up a chair at the end of the table and told Ellis he'd like to buy a fresh pitcher of whatever it was they were drinking.

"I thought I'd find the people of the hour in here." Then the writer placed his gaze on Morgan. "Tell me the truth. Have strange things been happening?"

She didn't hesitate, didn't ask him to define or clarify his key phrase. She simply said yes.

It was Pearce who wanted clarification. "I don't recall 'strange things' being mentioned."

Ellis returned with a fresh pitcher.

"I don't know about Morgan." Wallace set about filling their glasses. "But when I start to question my sanity, I don't immediately converse about it a lot with strangers, though I will now. To be clear, I have heard things, seen things, and followed bear tracks—I think—into a kind of fucked up dreamland. Pardon my language. I would think myself totally crazy, but I'm not crazy, and I'm *almost* convinced that Emily Rawlins' voice has popped up on a singer's iPad. I'm serious. Keep in mind, I came up here to write this book. It was supposed to be a story about a crime, about a mystery being solved. I didn't come up here to hunt spooks. But look at me. Do I believe Emily, and maybe Mary, too, might be lurking around? I think I do. The photo album has all but convinced me. And now we have the Kia and a dead guy. I think I believe it."

Pearce raised his open hands—*didn't mean any offense*—and let the ghost issue die.

"According to Merkin, you're going out to the glacier," Pearce said.

Wallace said he was.

"Mind if I join you?"

"It's a long hike, Officer Pearce. I mean nothing by that. I have no idea if *I* can make it."

"Understandable."

"I can't tell you no, and I wouldn't. Two Denali rangers will be with us."

Pearce said: "I wonder if there is any *real* hope of finding her. If that area is hiked often, and it is, and if Pendleton is climbed often… wouldn't somebody have found her after all these years?"

"And wouldn't they have found the photo album?" Wallace said. "You're from around here, Officer Pearce. You know how huge this place is. No way we can say with any faith something *should* have happened or will or won't happen. No way."

"Let's go back to Devin."

"The guy in the mine, right?" Wallace said.

Pearce nodded.

Uncle Rawleigh said: "What about him?"

"Was he a strong guy? A determined guy? The kind of person who could, and would, haul an SUV up into a canyon and chunk it piece by piece into a mine? Or hike all the way up the Toklat River, to whatever end?"

Silence.

"He was out of shape," Uncle Rawleigh said. "Who knows?"

"Or is it also possible he's a damned good scapegoat?"

Uncle Rawleigh nodded. "That's a possibility, but I think it'd be a mistake to write him off. That he had some *help* is probably a greater possibility, don't you think?"

"He'd have needed help," Ellis suddenly said.

Morgan jumped at the sound of his voice.

The old man was standing right behind Wallace.

"Devin was fat as hell, and I've been to the head wall of Pendleton Glacier," Ellis Everett said. "I have, years ago, and it's an experience I won't ever forget. It was beautiful. And maybe it's because I'm no mountaineer, but just following the river is exhausting. And to climb up on the glacier you'd need some help, probably some spikes and an ice axe, too. It's not something you do on a whim. Certainly not if you're as big as a gorilla."

"I suspect I'll agree with your assessment if I make it up there," Pearce said.

"Summer of '84, I think it was. Shortly before that damned boy of mine was born." Everett's voice faded off as he finished: "It was beautiful. I felt like I'd made it up to Everest Base Camp. Anyway. Sorry to intrude."

He walked away, and after a silent period, Pearce turned again to the writer: "I assume it's an early start tomorrow?"

"Three a.m."

"Do you mind if I stay at your place tonight?"

Wallace checked his phone. "Last bus into the park departs in half an hour. Just let me finish off this drink and we'll go that way."

3

After the festivities, Morgan returned to her old cabin.

She did not tell her uncle what she was doing; she told him she was going to the toilet and then to the shower.

She turned on the lights and shut the door behind her.

Immediately, she regretted coming in here.

The cabin was empty, but it didn't feel empty. It felt heavy. She thought she heard somebody breathing.

She felt cold.

Before she could register what she was doing, she said: "There's a dead man in an old mine in Dragon Canyon, along with the remains of your car, or I guess it's your car. Are you there?"

Something.

She knew *something* was in here with her.

But would the spirit of this woman feel so malevolent?

"Were we supposed to find that car?" she said. "Is that guy—Devin—did he do something to you? Are you nice, whoever you are?"

Smoke. Only for a second, only...

She'd only been in here a minute and she already felt sick.

She turned off the light and pulled the door shut as she stepped outside.

I'm not alone.

This realization may or may not have been separated from the unnerving presence inside; she couldn't say what triggered it. Had she heard something? Or was it just another vague idea?

She stepped around to the back of the cabin.

The entire scene was lit in charcoal gray.

If somebody were out here...

"Ms. Rawlins?"

My God, Morgan. Stop it.

No answer, of course. Not even a twig snapping.

But a *voice* came out of the trees: "Morgan."

A dry, hoarse whisper. It didn't sound familiar, except it *did*.

She squinted up the hillside.

But there was nothing to see in the dark gray.

"Hello?" she said.

Nothing.

She pulled out her phone and used the screen's dim glow for a makeshift flashlight.

She'd heard something, she knew it, and if it were Rawlins, maybe she could learn something. Never mind that Rawlins was dead and these thoughts were insane. Death didn't have to mean much.

She took a few steps up the slope. A few more. Before she knew it, she was above the cabins, near that certain rock that was good for sitting, near where she'd seen the tracks. She hadn't heard her name again. She probably never *had*. She shone her phone around the area, and *now* she heard a twig snap.

She realized the horror was real a split second too late.

Hands closed on both sides of her neck and squeezed.

She felt her phone drop. She thrashed and sent her right elbow into her attacker's chest. The squeeze slackened just enough for her to pull away, but the attacker pounced again, sending her to the ground. She couldn't see him, not really, but she saw his shape and smelled his breath, and she felt sure—she *knew*—it was Cork.

It disgusted her how unsurprised she was.

Just like a bar exam question. Go with your gut. Don't *switch* it up or you'll *fuck* it up.

Hands on her neck again and he knelt between her legs.

He pulled one hand away from her neck and placed it on her left breast. He squeezed and lowered himself onto her. She could feel his heat; she could feel *him*, right there in the last place she *ever* wanted to feel any part of him, and his breaths on her neck were rapid, hot, and sickening.

He released her breast and sent his hand down to the button of her jeans. He pawed at it as he panted into the hollow of her right shoulder, shoved the button back through its hole, and sent the zipper down, along with several of his fingers. And in all his blind determination, he somehow forgot that she might still be able to use her arms to resist him.

With both hands, she reached for something, anything, and her attacker (*Cork,* she reminded herself) either did not notice or was too oblivious to care.

A low grunt escaped his throat when she brought the jagged end of a broken tree limb into the side of his head; he let go of her neck and withdrew his hand from her jeans, and in a precious gasp of air, she screamed as loudly as she could—and then brought the weapon up again. This time it caught him in what she assumed was his cheek, as the landing point was soft, and the attack was not nearly as effective.

He rose up a bit and slung his right fist into her face.

The blow was solid, just behind her left cheek bone. Her vision went white, and a few details of the murky charcoal scene returned slowly as he lowered himself again, returning both hands to her neck. Again, he neglected to account for her outstretched arms.

She clenched the limb tightly and brought it up and around, delivering a solid blow to an upper region of his face, somewhere around his left eye. She sucked in another gasp of air as he again loosened his grip on her neck, screamed again, hit him again, and when the attacker—*Cork*—attempted to rise up and compose himself, she took advantage of her momentary access to that fragile area between his legs: she immediately introduced it to her right knee.

He fell over her face with a muted *oomph,* and Morgan worked her way out from under him.

She screamed for help and made a split-second decision to kick him once more—this time in the side of the head—before taking off down the hillside.

If she'd just killed him or knocked him into a coma, so be it.

She ran and stumbled down through the woods, avoiding the ghost-like shadows of the trees in the near darkness, not thinking of anything except getting away and that awful stiff heat against her, and thank God— thank *God*—she still had her jeans on. She cried out again, probably *"Help!"* or maybe just a random noise, and thought she heard him behind her; she knew very well there was *something*—and somebody caught her.

The cabins were in sight and he emerged from the shadows and she fell into his grip.

Panic—but only for a split second, only until he said her name and she realized it was her uncle.

"It was him," she said. "I know it."

She started to babble and caught herself.

Uncle Rawleigh asked her what was going on, and she gathered her senses as he led her down into the supposed safety of the common area at the center of the cabins. They sat down on a bench outside the bathrooms. Morgan touched the red welt on her cheek and tried to describe the attack. She did a poor job. Her voice trailed off.

Uncle Rawleigh looked straight ahead. Hand on her back.

The wind in the trees.

A car passed on the highway.

Somewhere, an engine started.

Morgan bit her lip and told herself that if she wanted to cry, it would be okay to do it. Truly it would. She did, a little. And then she stressed it again: it was Cork. She *knew* it was Cork. Not only had it sounded and looked like him—for whatever that was worth—she'd smelled his breath.

Something from law school, she thought. *You can't trust these things. You can't trust yourself. Not on this.*

She sent the thought off to hell.

Uncle Rawleigh stood and began to pace.

Really, she thought, he did not seem very surprised.

4

There was lightning over Mount Healy. The clouds began to spit cold rain and sleet.

Uncle Rawleigh took her to his cabin, locked the door, and turned his back while she changed into a pair of pajama pants and a sweatshirt.

He tried to call the authorities. Then Pearce. But the already spotty phone service was made worse by the weather.

"Damn it," he said. "I want you to keep trying, okay? Pearce is out in the park so you probably won't get him. But keep trying."

She nodded and asked what he was about to do.

He opened the night stand next to the bed and withdrew a flashlight. When she again questioned him, he told her he wasn't going far, and he had a rifle in his truck.

"I'm going up there. I won't shoot anybody. Hopefully. Lock the door. Keep trying the phone."

He stepped out.

Morgan locked the door and sat down on the bed and stared at nothing. A minute passed, maybe two, and all was quiet. She felt hands on her neck and felt that *nasty* presence down there; she couldn't help imagining him going much further than he did. She grimaced and took her uncle's phone and tried both of his recent calls again, but no. The damned thing wouldn't do anything. And why was she surprised? Several times a month there wasn't even decent cell service in *Little Rock*. She was honestly surprised there was service up here at all.

And hadn't she come here for solitude, for mountains, for flowers?

Not for cell phones.

She saw lightning in the cracks around the door. Time and silence passed on by.

And there was a whisper in her head.

Just a whisper.

Its origin was hard to discern, and it didn't matter. Lightning around the door, whispers in her head, and sure enough, the bastard was back on top of her with one hand around her neck and the other right there—he was about to mess all over her jeans if he didn't hurry—and the whisper returned.

A low rumble of thunder. The cabin walls trembled.

No, she was alone. Then came the light knocking at the door—or was it just the thunder? Not just the thunder, she thought. It was the lady in the road. Mary Rawlins. Some other unknown victim, this one without a face, it didn't matter. She was there, knocking on the door to the rhythm of every clap of thunder, and she bore wisdom in the sound of Morgan's voice.

Check his house, girl. Check his house. You want to find me, don't you? You want to find us, don't you? Check his house.

XXV
Again in the Lightning

1

PEARCE FOUND A POCKET OF cellular service while he and Wallace were at the gas station stocking up on snacks, toiletries, and other supplies. He called his wife and the Wasilla Police Department. Neither call went well. But he was so enthralled by the resurgence of the Rawlins case he barely cared. He would be fine, he told his wife. It wasn't like he was going out there alone.

Later, he stretched out in the floor of the old Toklat ranger station and rested his head on his jacket. He stared up into a dark, blank ceiling, and his imagination filled that blank space with a variety of concerning images. He was no longer confident he would be *fine*.

He was not young anymore. He hadn't done a good job of keeping himself in shape. Who was he to think he could make this trek? And what would he do if he couldn't? Turn around and shamefully stumble back to the Park Road on his own? Ask a ranger to go with him? God, how humiliating that would be.

Maybe he could summon his youth again. Or maybe there was nothing to worry about. As the bird flew, they weren't going *that* far; nor would they be in a hurry. If there was a dead girl out there who'd been gone for a decade, she wasn't going anywhere now.

But what about everything else?

His wife had made a comment about *some maniac still being around* and, like a jackass, he'd laughed aloud. There probably never was a maniac, he'd said, and even if there was, he wouldn't still be hanging around out in the wilderness.

But what if?

The car and the dead man in the mine. The photo album in the riverbed.

What if?

What if I'm with a maniac now?

Wallace O'Brien seemed all right, but he was a quiet fellow, kind of strange, and… And hell, he was a writer. Mister Artsy Fartsy. Mister I Don't Own A Razor Or A Comb. They were all *kind of strange*.

Still, the dark ceiling was full of dark thoughts.

He eventually accepted his fate: he was here and he was going out to the glacier, and with this acceptance, he drifted off into a shallow sleep, which was a stew of reality and dream stuff. He had no idea how long it went on before he heard Wallace crossing the floor to the door.

He sat up and briefly imagined the writer coming at him with a knife, then asked what was wrong.

"It's out there again," Wallace whispered.

"What?"

"The bear."

"Bear?"

The writer ignored him, opened the door, and stepped outside.

Pearce followed.

There was no bear, and Pearce indeed wondered about this man's sanity. But then the beast lumbered in the distance through a dim, eerie flash of lightning to the top of a high area somewhere close to the river.

Empty darkness returned as quickly as it had departed.

2

At three 'o clock in the morning, the writer and the Wasilla police officer sat on a low ledge of stone on the shore of the Toklat River, less than thirty yards from the Park Road. Two stuffed backpacks were on the ground behind them.

They talked some, not much, and occasionally glanced up at the road. Close to three thirty, they saw headlights, and a few minutes after that, two park rangers were descending the slope toward them.

But it wasn't the park rangers who reached them first.

A thin, dark, and damned near frail-looking woman was about thirty seconds ahead of them. Wallace clearly knew her and asked her what she was doing here.

"The rangers saw me on the side of the road. I was coming to meet up with you, Mr. O'Brien." She turned to Pearce, shook his hand, and told him her name was Dolores Gunn. Musician, she said, and a little bit crazy, very curious. She'd heard through the grapevine—via talk between rangers at Eielson—about this venture.

Pearce introduced himself and said it was nice to meet her.

The rangers stepped up behind Gunn.

The musician locked eyes with the writer: "Did you see Mount Pendleton earlier?"

"What about it?"

"The mountaintop was covered in lights. Like the aurora borealis. The glacier reflected them. It was beautiful."

"Is that normal?" Pearce turned to the rangers for his answer.

Both shook their heads.

"We generally don't see the aurora this time of year," the short, dark-haired girl named Makayla said.

"Did *you* see it?" Wallace asked.

"I saw it," Painter said. "It was scary as hell."

XXVI
The Aftermath

1

MORGAN WAS GONE.

Rawleigh stood in the doorway of his cabin, rifle in hand, cursing himself for being gone so long. He'd intended merely to search the immediate area, but he'd found her (ruined) phone and thought he heard something, and...

Now, she was gone.

"Not gone," he said.

He almost called out to her, but when in doubt, he thought, best not to make a lot of noise.

He went to her old cabin. She wasn't there, and the scene inside was anything but normal.

Blood was splattered and smeared everywhere. The epicenter of the mess, based on the amount and density of the blood, appeared to be to his right, near the table in the corner. The room stunk of what he thought of as dank smoke.

He told himself to breathe. Think.

All around him, the blood splatters began to twitch and expand. Subtle at first, then more and more pronounced.

He blinked rapidly and wished it away.

But it didn't go away.

You should find your niece, Rawleigh. I kind of like her.

"Go away," he said.

He felt his heart thudding haphazardly—lethally.

He stumbled out and vomited.

Cork. The bloody cabin. Morgan. What the hell is going on?

2

The Nissan was gone.

This gave him hope, but it did nothing to alleviate his concern.

He threw his rifle into his Silverado's back seat and drove down to the Salmon Catch, wondering if the Good Lord would allow him to find her sitting on the steps, perhaps talking to Ellis Everett. Anything at all, as long as she was okay.

But his niece was nowhere around, and neither was Everett.

A brilliant flash of blue lightning over Healy.

Sleet pelted the windshield and hood.

Rawleigh drove past the Salmon Catch and turned right onto the highway.

When he finally found cell service, he dialed the authorities. But after the second ring, another flash of lightning, and the signal vanished. He cursed and threw his phone into the passenger floorboard.

Two miles north of the Salmon Catch, he made a right onto a dirt road he'd only driven once before. If he recalled correctly, Cork's four-room box was less than a mile off the highway, tucked into a cirque of low mountains.

The road rose and fell. For at least a full minute, the sleet mixed with rain and became a driving downpour that rendered the truck's headlights all but pointless. When the downpour eased, he hit the button for the truck's traction control and pressed on as fast as he dared go. The truck wasn't a 4x4, but it managed to creep slowly up a steep stretch of the road that had all but washed away.

At the top of this crux, the terrain leveled out and he saw the drunken young man's house dead ahead, just beyond the effective reach of his headlights.

He eased up a short ways and shut off the truck.

"Damn it."

Cork's Cherokee was parked at the end of the house.

And the Frontier was less than twenty feet away from it.

He didn't understand how or why. Had he brought her here? Had she come on her own? But it didn't matter. The scene before him was very real, and he had to deal with it.

He got out of the truck, retrieved his gun from the back seat, shut the doors as lightly as possible, and approached the house.

Morgan was sitting in the mud just to the right of the front door.

Her hands were buried in the muck at her sides. Her wet hair partially concealed her face. Her expression was lifeless.

"Morgan." He knelt down and nudged her.

She simply stared past him.

"Morgan, tell me what happened." He waved a hand in front of her face. Nudged her left shoulder. "*Morgan.*"

We're getting you out of here, he thought. *I don't care what it takes.*

He put one arm under her knees, the other around her back, and he picked her up. The strain he felt in his back and chest suggested he was way too old to be dead lifting adult human beings—heavy or not.

Fuck it. He carried her to the Chevy. She did not move or object; she barely acknowledged him at all as he placed her in the passenger seat.

He locked her in the truck, and for the fourth or fifth time, checked to make sure there were a few rounds in his rifle.

Then he turned back to the house.

The front door was ajar, he needed to know.

He was not afraid of Cork, but he did fear the unknown.

He aimed the gun straight ahead, imagining he looked something like the poor unfortunate fool that he was.

He stepped up onto the stack of concrete blocks that served as a step, pushed the door open with the toe of his right boot, and entered the house.

It stunk. Badly.

There was a light on in the room to his right. It was a bedroom, as evidenced by the unkempt twin bed in the corner. But also crammed into this room were a dated washer and dryer and a desk covered in beer bottles and pornography. The floor was strewn with years and years of grime, trash, and laundry, including a few scattered feminine items, such as the bra at the foot of his bed—though Cork had *never*, so long as Rawleigh could remember, had a girlfriend. Rawleigh pictured the scenes, and his chest tightened.

He turned away from the room. To hell with it.

To his left was a bathroom. There was a gun rack above the toilet that did not contain a gun.

He proceeded into the next room and turned on a light.

The kitchen.

The foul, cluttered, unwashed kitchen.

Straight ahead was a door that led out onto the deck. It stood ajar.

He nudged it open, hoping he was wrong about what he would find.

But he wasn't.

The exterior light to the right of the doorway was broken, but the glow from the kitchen was more than enough to illuminate the scene: the deck was splattered with gore, and at the center of it all was Cork's corpse, face down, still oozing and bubbling.

Rawleigh had always been a bit too left of center to overly familiarize himself with firearms and their various capabilities, but he'd fired a few shotguns in his time, and he could clearly see that this poor bastard's head had just been obliterated by buckshot.

My God, Morgan.

But *surely* it hadn't been Morgan.

A creaking noise, very brief, very slight. It was the front door, and it wasn't being pushed, just nudged.

Rawleigh felt his hands quiver.

He couldn't raise the gun right now if he needed to.

It's just Morgan, he told himself.

Except it wasn't.

3

Ellis Everett entered the kitchen looking older and frailer than Rawleigh had ever seen him. He lingered in the doorway and Rawleigh stood before the back door. They looked at each other for an indefinite period, until Everett broke the silence:

"Is that Cork?"

Rawleigh told him it was.

Everett's gaze went to the rifle in Rawleigh's hands. "You?"

"This gun couldn't do what's out there, Ellis."

"Then what happened?" The old man reached to his right and grasped the countertop.

"I can't say what happened. I don't know."

Ellis moved along the counter, past Rawleigh, until he could see clearly what was beyond the back door. He looked out at his son's remains, then turned and settled himself into a chair at the small round table in the corner.

"I have some ideas," Rawleigh said. "Do you feel like talking?"

Color rushed into the old man's cheeks as he locked eyes with Rawleigh.

"My kid's dead. What do you think?" He slowly, maddeningly lit a Kool and continued: "And if it wasn't you, what are you doing here? I'm not saying anything. Just, you might as well shoot me with that .22 or whatever it is, because..."

His burst of energy vanished. He looked down at the table.

Rawleigh felt much calmer than he ever thought he could in such a situation. He did not want to talk to the man. He needed to go check on his niece, he needed to see if there was a working phone in here, but of course there wouldn't be... so he had to find some cellular signal—but not just yet.

What if it kills him?

He must tread lightly and be ready to retreat.

"Was your boy dangerous, Ellis?"

Another flash of red in the old man's cheeks. "He's dead."

"*Was* he dangerous?"

"He was a drunk." A pause as the old man's tongue went over his lips. "I don't know. Why?"

Tread lightly.

But how could he?

"Why?" Ellis repeated.

Out with it, Rawleigh. Right now, it's just as bad not to say it.

"Morgan got attacked by somebody tonight. She thinks it was Cork."

Everett's head bobbled slightly; his hands shook.

"I wouldn't rule it out," he said.

4

He did not tell Everett that Morgan was in his truck.

Right now, the old man didn't need to know.

He left Everett at the table, stepped outside, and wandered into the shadows beyond his truck, where he paced till he found a trace of signal. He dialed 911 and briefly explained the situation. Then returned to his truck.

Morgan was not there.

He panicked, cursed, turned on the Chevy's headlights and circled the truck—and found her on the front step. She was a zombie, just standing there before the door, like she'd forgotten how to open it.

"Morgan." He squeezed her shoulder.

She did not acknowledge him.

"Morgan!" He tightened his grip and turned her around, moved his hand from her shoulder to her chin, and turned her face slightly as he repeated her name.

Her blank gaze evaporated and she squinted at the truck's headlights.

"Sorry," she said.

He wrapped an arm around her and they sat down on the step.

"Nothing to be sorry for," he said, wondering if that were true.

Surely it was. Surely she didn't do what he supposed there was a *chance* she did.

She stared blankly ahead.

"I shouldn't be here," she said. "I know I shouldn't."

He squeezed and told her she'd be all right, hoping he was correct.

XXVII
Ice

1

THROUGH THE SMALL HOURS OF the morning they followed the river. For the first few hours, they ascended toward a brilliant display of lightning, but as dawn approached, the clouds broke, and by seven, Pendleton's summit was reaching toward a clear blue sky.

They pressed on, stopping only occasionally to prop their feet on rocks, nibble on granola bars, and sip water. The writer was an adequate hiker. The two rangers and the musician were gazelles.

Pearce joked that since he was still moving forward, he was handling it better than he thought he would. But the closer they got to the river's origins, the more frequently he had to rest.

"Go on ahead," he frequently told them. "I'm a grown man. I'll be all right."

But there was no hurry.

The glacier slowly unveiled itself as the riverbed rose and the coiling, narrow streams merged and widened. Their path became a field of wet boulders and pockets of colorful wildflowers. Dead ahead loomed the rising wall of ice.

They picked their way up and up. Pearce slowed them down, yes, but his hiking partners insisted they didn't care.

The morning grew old.

Pendleton's shadow fell over them.

And damn that ice wall, Pearce thought. *Why is it not closer? Why?*

The writer had spent most of the trek enjoying his companions. He seemed to be in a pleasant mood—better than he'd been the previous evening. Presently, he approached while Pearce was hunched over his hiking pole sucking the cool, thin air.

He put a hand on his back and told him he was just glad to be out here. Maybe they were about to find out something.

"It's right there." The writer aimed his hiking pole toward the glacier. "I'd say we're within a mile."

Again, Pearce nodded. "I hope you're right."

2

They reached the headwall shortly before noon. It rose some forty feet overhead, though with the steep frozen river of ice rising up into the mountains beyond, it looked much higher. Part of the headwall was nearly vertical, but a vast portion of it to their right was a much more forgiving slope of perhaps thirty or forty degrees.

The rangers, Painter and Makayla, tossed down their massive packs and distributed traction spikes and ice axes. The rangers made sure the party's spikes were fitted properly, and Makayla performed a demonstration on how to use (and not use) an ice axe.

"I've seen worse in the Sierras," Dolores Gunn said. "This doesn't appear too steep or dangerous."

And with Makayla and Gunn in the lead and Painter in the back, they started up the headwall. The going was not particularly difficult, not even for the two souls who were scaling an icy slope for the very first time. Indeed, less than fifteen minutes after digging in and beginning the climb, they were standing on the glacier and gazing up at the frozen river's course toward the saddle between Pendleton and the unnamed eight-thousand-foot snowy hump to its east.

From here, the trek appeared smooth and generally undramatic, but then, looking back over the valley, the Park Road looked maybe half an hour away, too.

They sat down, ate snacks, and shared a bottle of Gatorade.

"The glacier's surface gets more steep and rugged as we go up," Painter said. "Just a warning: some dangers you won't see till you're *there*. If you get nervous, slam down the axe, stop, and wait."

The slope was gentle for the first few hundred feet, and they barely needed the spikes, much less the axes. Beyond that, as Painter warned, the course steepened dramatically, and the glacier's surface was like a crumpled blanket.

They dug in with the axes.

Pearce couldn't help it. He began to mumble about being in over his head, about how he should stop, but really, he didn't want to.

And then Dolores Gunn stopped.

"Look." She pointed up ahead. "Right there."

She scampered to the top of a high fold in the ice.

Through his labored breaths, Pearce called up to her: "What is it?"

"Something. I think."

3

She was right. It was something.

They came to a fissure that stretched nearly all the way across the glacier. At its widest, the break was almost twenty feet across; it narrowed to little more than a thin line toward the west.

A common thought lingered amongst them, practically visible it was so conspicuous.

In some way, it made sense. Yet it didn't.

"No way Devin or anybody else dragged a body up here," Pearce said. "Even if he *were* a mountaineer. No way."

They stood quietly. The air was cold and still, as if the mountains were trying to hear their thoughts.

Painter said: "You could make it without spikes, if you're stupid enough to try it."

Makayla knelt down and began to dig various materials—rope, an ice screw, carabiners—out of her pack. Both Pearce and Wallace's eyes grew wide when they realized what she had in mind.

Dolores squatted down to help her; the musician began to twist the ice screw into the ice at a moderate angle.

"How deep is it?" Pearce said.

Both rangers shrugged.

"We have a hundred feet of rope," Makayla said. "So we'll see."

4

When Makayla revealed a trace of nervousness about lowering herself into the fissure, Gunn stepped up immediately.

"Let me," she said. "I've done this before. It doesn't bother me."

Makayla looked up at Painter.

Painter shrugged.

I'm too damned old, his expression said. *If you're nervous, let her do it.*

So Gunn clipped on the Kenwood radio that Makayla handed her; she put on Makayla's helmet, stepped into the harness, lowered herself over the edge, and rappelled down into the darkness with amazing confidence. The light on her helmet illuminated the depths substantially, but as she went deeper, the light grew dimmer… smaller.

And by the time she called up on the radio that she was at the bottom, it was gone entirely.

"Can't see your light anymore," Wallace said. "Stay in contact with us."

Gunn said: "Stepping out of the harness. I feel like I'm on the moon. Or in the moon. There's a narrow band of daylight. I think I see you."

"What do you see?" Painter said.

"Nothing. Just ice."

Of course it's just ice, Pearce thought. *What else would be down there?*

But he knew what she was looking for, and honestly, he was afraid she might actually find it. Somewhere along the way, he'd changed his mind.

If the Rawlins girl were dead, he thought, truly down in the ice, maybe they should just let her be.

"Going to the right," Gunn said. "Twenty steps. I can't see you. I can still see the rope."

Painter leaned out over the abyss.

"Think I see your light," he said.

"Fifty steps. I'm about to turn around. There's nothing down here."

Pearce didn't know how in God's name the music lady was down there. What an awful, claustrophobic, ominous place to be. She had to be a little bit crazy to hook herself to that rope. To be walking around down there, to—.

Gunn said: "Returning to the rope. Then I'll go the other way."

"The walls swell down here," the writer suddenly said. He'd been pacing a hundred or so feet to their left.

Pearce and the two rangers walked over to him.

The writer was right. Here, the fissure's walls closed in on each other, forming an extremely tight squeeze about halfway down.

"Going the other way," Gunn said.

"The walls close in on each other," Pearce said.

"Not down here."

Silence.

Pearce's heart was racing.

"Twenty-five steps to the left of the rope," Gunn said. "The walls are nearly sealed up above me, must be like an hourglass. Still nothing. Going a little further."

This update was followed by an extended period of silence.

"Still there?" Painter said. "I can't see your light."

"I'm here."

"She needs to get out of there." The writer was pacing again.

"I went ten more steps," Gunn said.

"What is it? Are you okay?"

"I'm okay. I thought I saw something." She paused. "I *do* see something. I'm going back to the rope."

"What is it? What do you see?"

"She's here. I'm almost to the rope."

XXVIII
The Unexplored

1

AT SIX 'O CLOCK THAT morning, while Wallace, Pearce, and the others were still footing it up the Toklat River, Rawleigh pulled his Silverado into the gas station across from the Salmon Catch. Morgan was in the passenger seat, head back, eyes closed.

They'd left the Frontier at Cork's house.

A state trooper had combed through it after acquiring Rawleigh's permission, and when he was satisfied there weren't any bodies, drugs, or murder weapons in it, he'd told Rawleigh somebody would drive it down to the Salmon Catch for him.

The night had been miserably long.

All Rawleigh wanted to do was collapse.

But not yet.

"I'm going inside," he said, not expecting a response, and not getting one.

His knees hurt. His back hurt. His head hurt.

And he had to make this dreaded call.

He'd rehearsed the script over and over again, but that did not—could not—alleviate the dread he felt when he thought about talking to Morgan's parents. And it was past time; he'd toyed with the idea of not telling them, but his conscience always thumped his skull. He had to make the call.

Tell them the truth.

The truth was, he was tired.

He went inside and bought a cup of coffee, then stepped back out and walked to the end of the building. From here, he could keep an eye on the truck and not be heard should Morgan wake up.

He stared down at his phone, wishing he could tell his conscience to fuck off.

She's a grown woman. She chose to come up here. Go to hell and leave me alone.

But he dialed his brother's number, hoping *he* would answer, not her.

Thankfully, he did, and he remained amazingly calm as Rawleigh summarized Morgan's time in Alaska… Specifically, last night's events. Rawleigh concluded by saying that, yes, absolutely, she was okay. She was currently asleep in his truck.

"What if there's something wrong with her, Rawleigh?" his brother said. "God be good, I'm not saying that, and I'm not blaming you, but if she's been going into trances, hearing things—."

Rawleigh's response was truthful bullshit: "I think she's had very restless sleep, being in a new environment, in thinner air. That might sound lame to you, but it gets to you. It took me weeks to get used to this place and get a good night's sleep."

"Trance. You said she went into a trance."

"She described it as that, she felt like she needed to go look. She'd just been attacked. We'd all be a little out of our minds."

"And so she *drove* to her attacker's house, and when she got there, she watched him kill himself? Do you know how that sounds! Even if she was fine before, who's to say she's fine now?"

"I know. I'm going to talk to her."

"The police have accepted all this? That she got attacked, went into a trance, got the bright idea to go over there, and he just happened to kill himself?"

"What are you suggesting?"

But he knew.

"I just want my kid to be okay. And I sure as hell don't want her caught up in... a *murder* investigation! This guy attacks her and winds up splattered all over his deck a few hours later, and she's there! She's there, and she's catatonic—in a *trance*, I guess."

"It's obvious he killed himself. His shoe was off. Hell, there was still an indention in his toe."

Silence.

"I'll see her home as soon as I can," Rawleigh said.

Maybe.

If she wants to go.

"She loves the hell out of you, Rawleigh. She trusts you more than either of us, more than anybody she went to school with."

Rawleigh closed his eyes. He didn't say anything.

"Call me back," his brother said. "Soon."

Rawleigh didn't say anything to that, either.

2

They both slept till noon.

Rawleigh's sleep was broken by nightmares and a sick stomach.

When he awoke, Morgan was sitting up on the side of the bed. Her back was to him, her head down.

"I thought there might be something there," she said. "I thought *I* had killed him. His door was open, and I went inside. He was on the deck. He had the gun. It was standing up, and his toe was on the trigger. I saw his face. It was twisted up, and he told me it was his fault, not mine. He told me he was dead. Go away, because he's dead. And he did it. It's like I was watching a TV screen, like it was in the distance." She turned around. "Do you believe me?"

He told her he did—of course he did.

3

Rawleigh walked down to the Salmon Catch just in time to see Ellis Everett's Tundra pull in and park up next to the door. Rawleigh hung back and watched the old man clamber up the front steps, go inside, and step back out less than a minute later. He looked dead, or close to it.

Everett stood at the top of the steps and stared blankly across the highway.

Until Rawleigh approached him.

"Three people in there," Everett said. "When they're gone, I'm closing. Probably won't reopen till I get my kid in the ground. Tell Morgan she's welcome to stay here, if she wants to. Can't imagine why she would. But if she wants to."

"I will."

"Awful thing." These words were barely audible, just a hoarse whisper. But he regained some volume as he continued: "If he tried to hurt her, I'm sorry." There was a long pause after this, and then he said something that Rawleigh wasn't entirely surprised to hear. "I can't say it's uncharacteristic of him. We both know that. I told you, he got his hands on his mother's neck once. He wasn't a good boy. I thought he calmed down some when he went to work for Chugach Timber, then he came up here, got to drinking, and I always told myself it was better to be drunk than violent. If it happened…" He shook his head. "I guess it happened."

"I think I'm going to take her up to my place," Rawleigh said. "It's not that far. It'll be good for her."

"Don't blame you."

"I won't forget about your cabins, Ellis."

"I'm not worried about those cabins. Get her out of here, and if she wants to go home, get her there as soon as you can. You're doing what you should do."

4

When he returned to the cabin, Morgan was sorting and packing her things.

He stood in the doorway and watched her, thinking about what Ellis Everett had said.

Morgan looked up and noticed him, and she asked if something was wrong.

"Not at all. I just thought of something."

"What?"

"I'm not sure yet. Let me help you."

5

They loaded their things into the Silverado's back seat, and Rawleigh briefly described what Ellis Everett had said to him.

Morgan did not show much emotion about it. She simply asked what it was he'd thought of.

Again, he did not answer.

He pulled up to the highway. If he turned right, they'd go north, through the town of Healy, and eventually to his home in Fairbanks. If he turned left, Anchorage.

"I'll explain," he said, "but first, are you okay? Do you feel like you could hold up if we drove into Anchorage?"

"Yes. But why?"

He turned left, then explained.

6

They arrived in Anchorage just in time to catch after-work traffic, and it took over twenty minutes to make it across the city to the hospital.

"I don't like this place," Morgan said as they crossed the lot. "Remember when I first got here? I thought you were dead."

He told her he didn't like it much, either.

They proceeded through the front doors and took a left to enter the emergency room, where they approached a kind looking old nurse at the front desk. Rawleigh told her he was looking for an item, not a person.

The nurse waited for him to explain.

He said: "I was here not long ago, unfortunately, and there was a magazine in my room, on the table by my bed. A local thing, *The Unexplored* or something like that. It was old. 2004, '05 maybe."

"Published here in Anchorage. This place is full of them. They bring them here in bulk for advertising. Would you like to have it?"

"If I could, if it's still here. I was in that room… right there over your shoulder."

She told them to hold on just a minute and walked back to the room, knocked lightly before entering, and emerged a few seconds later with a magazine in hand.

"Is this it?"

Rawleigh told her that was the one and asked if he owed her anything.

"They walk out of here all the time, sir. I suppose that's what they're here for."

7

They drove down the street to the 10th Avenue Mall and settled down at a table in the attached Chili's. Rawleigh ordered a round of chips and salsa and two frozen margaritas.

And then he handed the magazine over to his niece.

The story he'd read during his hospital visit was on page seven, below a large heading that read: GOING ON AROUND ANCHORAGE. It occupied an entire column:

SHIP CREEK FISHING LOCATION RE-OPENS

A popular fishing location on Ship Creek has re-opened after being closed and set off with crime scene tape for the last three weeks.

Readers will recall that the body of 28-year-old Julie Vanbrite was discovered at the location on July 19.

Police initially thought her death a murder due to the markings on her neck and lack of clothing. Their latest theory is that Vanbrite jumped from the Ship Creek Bridge following a violent confrontation with her boyfriend, Seth Newton, 29.

Newton, a student at the University of Alaska in Anchorage, who also lived in the Ship Creek Apartments, where Vanbrite lived, said he fought with Vanbrite on numerous occasions, but denied any of the arguments were ever physical…

The article proceeded to discuss Julie and Seth's relationship, how Julie and Seth had "engaged in sexual relations" that night and then gotten into a very "heated, hateful argument." It concluded by discussing the location as a popular fishing spot where "thousands of locals and tourists fish for salmon…"

By the time Morgan finished reading, their food and margaritas had arrived. Morgan took a moment to eat some chips and take a few relaxing pulls from the margarita… And then she went to her phone to look up the story.

"Not much," she concluded. "There's a blurb here from the local newspaper. Nothing different."

"Local woman, local boyfriend," Rawleigh said. "Why make a big deal about it, why push for a different conclusion? Not saying I agree, but that kind of thing goes on. Back in Tennessee, a little girl disappeared, supposedly just walked away from her parents' house. That story got hyped for about a week, and then… nothing. Real journalism is dead. Now it's all about headlines and short attention spans."

"You think there's a link between the Rawlins women and this?"

She knew there was more. She just didn't want to say it.

So Rawleigh said it for her: "I think it's *possible* there is a link between this woman, the Rawlins women, and *you*, Morgan. It's ridiculous to think the Vanbrite girl killed herself. There were marks on her, and they found her in her underwear. It's just they couldn't easily damn the boyfriend. And Cork was *there,* honey. He was working out of Anchorage at the time and *living in the Ship Creek Apartments*. The police even questioned him, not about possible guilt, just the usual—did you know them, did you hear anything, etcetera."

"It sounds like it was her boyfriend."

"Sure. But they couldn't prove it. They'd been together for months. They had sex that night, they argued, and yeah, there were marks on her neck. But who's to say the argument didn't get a little bit physical, or they didn't get a little... *kinky* during their festivities. They argue, it's really bad, and she wanders out and dives in the creek."

"You said you don't believe that."

"I don't. I think it was either Seth Newtorn or... *your guy*. And isn't it interesting the Rawlins women disappear shortly after he's out of Anchorage and up north with his daddy?"

Morgan sat still, looking past her margarita to the magazine. It took her a moment to reply. "So what do you want to do now?"

"Walk off these margaritas in the mall, buy you some good stuff, whatever you want, my treat. Then we'll go back up north and see if our buddies are back from their hike. Sound good?"

She smiled, an honest, beaming smile. It apparently sounded like a fine plan to her.

XXIX
Story

1

WALLACE O'BRIEN DID NOT WANT to think about it. He certainly did not want to talk to anyone about it. Even if it hadn't been the most unbelievable moment of his life, and that's exactly what it had been, he was too tired to function, and only God knew what he would say.

He imagined the cop, Pearce, felt the same way, and here the poor bastard was, in front of the Denali National Park Visitor Center, and he had to talk.

Wallace felt for him, but he wasn't about to join in. He hung back with Dolores and the rangers.

There were only eight reporters. Three holding microphones, five holding notepads and voice recorders. But there might as well have been twenty, and that wasn't counting the crowd right behind them, their cameras raised, curious faces honed in atop straining necks, and really, truly, fuck them all, because Wallace was too tired and out of his mind and old for this shit.

Thank God he wasn't the cop.

He was just the writer, the guy who found the photo album, yes... but he wasn't the cop.

The park superintendent had already spoken about the sobering day, that certain suspicions were now unfortunately confirmed, but maybe closure was in sight, and Mr. Pearce was a Wasilla police officer who was a State Trooper back when this first occurred, and he volunteered to go the extra mile today, just as he had back then, and now it was Pearce's turn.

The cop stepped up and looked out at the faces.

Not their fault, Wallace thought. *It's natural to be curious. Curiosity is why I get paid to write, isn't it?*

The media drones thrust their microphones and recorders into Pearce's face.

"I'll start from the beginning." Pearce cleared his throat, likely because it's all he knew to do to buy himself another second to think. "I'm too tired and rattled to take another approach." Camera flashes. "Wallace O'Brien, a writer who's been staying in the park, discovered a photo album in the bed of the Toklat River. There wasn't much left of the pictures in it, but a few of them were clearly pictures of flowers and wildlife. Because of the location and subject matter, this album triggered ideas of the Rawlins—the mother and daughter who disappeared here six years ago.

"Early yesterday morning, I joined Mr. O'Brien, Ms. Dolores Gunn, and two park rangers..." They were standing to his left; he motioned to them. "I joined them on a hike up the Toklat River. We made it to the

Pendleton Glacier earlier today, at about noon. We climbed up onto the ice and found a deep crevice, which Ms. Gunn rappelled down into. She can tell you about that. In short, we seem to have found the body of Emily Rawlins… The sight of her remains being pulled from the Pendleton Glacier is something I'll obviously never forget. Ms. Gunn can say the rest."

He stepped away and dipped back into a recess near the visitor center's front entrance. Wallace joined him, cast him a sympathetic glance, and they listened as Dolores Gunn spoke:

"The fissure's walls close to where I landed squeezed in on each other, and that's where she was. She was caught in the narrowest point. My headlamp caught some of the green on one of her shoes, and that's how I noticed her. I climbed back up, set up another anchor, and went back down. I knew we could get her out of there. I attached a rope to her backpack and looped another one around her waist." Somebody asked a question. "No, we didn't drag her back. We got her out of the ice, that's all."

2

Rawleigh and his niece were standing at the back of the crowd. Wallace noticed them after the thicket thinned.

They approached each other in the middle of the lot. The evening was waning—the sky was nearly as dark as it was going to get—but their blank faces could not be any clearer.

No one spoke for several minutes, until Gunn said she had to rest.

"I'm not going back in the park," she said. "I think I'm going to the Mountaintop Lodge."

"That's near the Salmon Catch," Wallace said, "and I need a drink. I'll join you."

"The Salmon Catch is closed," Rawleigh said.

But Morgan said they could talk there; she had a key.

3

Gunn's car was parked near Wallace's, but she had no problem letting him drive her up to the lodge.

She sat in the passenger seat of his rented Escape with her head propped against the window.

The Mountaintop Lodge sat on top of a hill that was by no definition a mountain. Its turn-in was less than a quarter of a mile down the road from the Salmon Catch.

Wallace made the turn, navigated the Ford up and around the hillside, and walked with her inside

They approached the desk and Gunn told the young man she needed a room for the night. Two adults, she said.

"And do you have a place to do laundry?" she asked. "I'll need a toothbrush, too. I'm sorry for being needy."

The clerk told her it was no problem. He provided her with a toothbrush and pointed her down the hall to the laundry room.

Wallace followed her back away from the counter.

"It's just a place to sleep," she said with a smile. "We won't have to worry about the bus schedule."

"Can I bring you anything?"

"No. I'm going to put on a robe and wash these clothes. If the washer will hurry up, I'll be dead to the world when you get back. I don't know how you're still going."

But he knew how he was still going. It was a very simple matter.

"Story," he said.

That's all it was.

XXX
End of Discussion

1

MORGAN UNLOCKED THE SALMON CATCH'S back door. They went upstairs and sat down at a table at the end of the bar. Morgan turned on only the light behind the cash register and got drinks. As she was doing so, there was a knock on the door at the bottom of the stairs. Pearce went down and returned with the writer.

They sat in silence for several minutes as they came to terms with their exhaustion.

"I don't see any way," Wallace O'Brien said, finally breaking the silence after downing half his beer, "that Devin, or whoever you all found in the mine, acted alone. There is simply no way."

"I agree," Pearce said.

The writer continued: "Furthermore, and I sincerely believe this, I think Devin could have been a plant. I don't know that we should assume he had much at all to do with it, if anything."

"Could Devin have thrown Emily Rawlins in the glacier, disassembled a car and dragged it into that mine all by himself?" Pearce paused. "Probably not. Seems like Devin might have taken a bullet just to distract from the real actor. It's a plausible theory. It'd be easy enough to leave him there."

Wallace nodded. "Why, exactly, would a man go to all that trouble just to sit down against the wall and shoot himself in the head when he's done? Who would fucking do that?"

"So let's say Devin wasn't the primary actor. Let's say he was killed by somebody else, maybe for money, or maybe as a distraction. There is the scenario in which Devin acted alone, did all these feats solo, and celebrated by committing suicide. But it doesn't seem likely. Maybe his corpse is not related at all. It just happened to be in there, or he stumbled upon the actor in the midst of his crime and got a bullet for being in the wrong place at the wrong time."

"It could have been Cork," Morgan said.

Her companions turned to her, and she explained that she'd been attacked in the woods behind the cabins. She did not use the word *rape*, though it was clear to Pearce that this is what Cork had attempted. She then described feeling ill and making the bizarre decision to seek out her alleged attacker's residence.

When she was done, Pearce leaned in and said: "He attacks you. And then you seek him out. And you watched him... do what he did."

"I didn't think he'd be there."

He wanted to ask her to repeat her reasons for going over there, but he didn't care to hand her a shovel and ask her to start digging into her ghost story, or whatever it was. So he merely stared at her over the top of his glass.

"What you did was foolish," he said.

"I talked to her," her uncle said. "So did the police. She obviously wasn't in her right mind. You wouldn't have been, either."

"So she's suggesting Cork did it—raped, killed them, whatever—and then Cork killed Devin," the writer said.

"Years ago," Pearce said, "I know Cork worked for Chugach Timber, before Ellis insisted he come up here closer to home. I don't know how all that works out, I'd have to look into it. I do know Cork had his problems. Of that, no doubt." He waited for somebody else to jump in. Nobody else did. "It's plausible, but for now, that's all it is."

"Let's suppose it was Cork," Rawleigh said. "And let's say there's more."

The expression that came over Pearce's face gave away his thoughts.

What now?

Rawleigh withdrew what looked like a folded up magazine from his jacket and tossed it on the table.

Pearce picked it up, unfolded it, and saw that it was already opened to the relevant page: one article was circled in red gel ink.

"The Vanbrite girl," he said. "So?"

Rawleigh said. "It fits when Cork worked for Chugach, down in Anchorage. Keep in mind he *lived* there, in those apartments. Then the Rawlins, *after* he came here, and now Morgan."

Pearce sighed. "Yes, I think she was murdered and tossed in the creek, but that was never proven." He stared down at the magazine. Had Nancy Drew and her hippy uncle honestly stumbled upon a narrative? Vanbrite, the Rawlins women, and now Morgan. Was it truly all the work of lonely and drunken Cork Everett?

"The Vanbrite girl was '05. The Rawlins women disappeared in the summer of…"

"2008," Morgan said.

Pearce nodded. "And when did Cork quit Chugach and come up here?"

Rawleigh and Morgan exchanged glances.

"It fits," Rawleigh said. "He came up here in 2007 or 2008, because it was after I moved up here. I remember Ellis saying he wanted to keep a closer eye on him."

Pearce shook his head. "It's all speculation right now."

2

I have to sleep.

Pearce thought it, said it, knew it, and when they were done with their drinks and silence returned to their table, he told them he was leaving.

He was ready to see his wife, ready for bed… Very much ready for his own bed.

Morgan had brewed a pot of coffee. He filled a foam cup and went out to his truck. For several minutes, he simply sat still with the heater running, gazing out at the dim, murky sky, thinking about nothing, then thinking about the dead girl. That poor, frozen dead girl.

Damned right it's all speculation, he thought, *because something doesn't fit.*

He wasn't brilliant. He was not the kind of guy detective novels or crime shows were inspired by. But he was an intelligent person, and he was a cop, and Alaska was a much more violent state than many folks thought it was. Yes, it was a vast land of mountainous wilderness, and millions came up here to hike and fish and see the mountains and glaciers. But Pearce had always, in his heart, been of the opinion that people were, for the most part, worthless fucking creatures, and given too much freedom, too much room to roam, the Lord of the Flies would ultimately surface, every time.

He'd seen this sort of thing before. He'd worked rape cases, murder cases. Several, unfortunately. He'd seen the work of the Lord of the Flies, and by God, he trusted his instincts.

And his instincts called bullshit. Devin, Cork, all of it.

I need to go to bed.

But that was irrelevant.

He was tired, but there wasn't a thing wrong with this thought process.

Go home.

He pulled out of the Salmon Catch and made a left on the empty highway.

He played music from his phone, but he barely heard it.

He heard only the silence beyond the music, and he saw the dead girl.

Her shoes. The remains of her hiking pants. That frozen backpack.

The Vanbrite girl had washed up dressed in nothing but her underwear. She'd likely been raped and murdered. The Anchorage authorities and media only *suggested* suicide (suicide, yes, of course) because her dorm was close to the bridge, and they'd found her bath robe a few days later further up the creek where it narrowed to a fine stream; she was getting ready for bed, they figured, and decided to wander out for a suicide stroll after a nasty argument.

Pearce admitted it was possible. But that's *all* it was.

Morgan, too, had been attacked, and though she hadn't divulged many details, it had been clear in her narrative that the Everett boy had attempted to have his way with her. Had he succeeded, Morgan probably would have turned up somewhere in a condition much like Vanbrite's.

He clenched the steering wheel and sent those images away.

The Rawlins girl was gray. She'd looked inhuman, alien. An alien with her clothes on.

Was it *possible* an attacker (Cork, he thought, for the sake of self-discussion) would indulge himself, then make sure Emily was tidied back up before hurling her into the ice? What kind of sense would that make, when the odds of the body *ever* being found were so slim?

And if Cork had attacked Vanbrite, he hadn't bothered to put her back in *her* robe. True, he thought, the creek or something in it *could* have removed it, (that was the story everybody wanted to believe, anyway) but if Cork *was* going to go to the trouble of re-dressing his victim, wouldn't he have also tied the belt snug around her waist before throwing her in, so that the chances of this were significantly reduced?

Lack of deep thought, he thought, from the people paid to engage in it. When given an out, all too often they take it. The Vanbrite girl, they said, had wandered out in her robe and jumped into Ship Creek. Yes, of course, she was so distraught from one of her many arguments with her boyfriend that she hadn't bothered tying the robe, just stepped out into the night to air some things out, yes, sure. And hell, Ship Creek wasn't the most convincing way to commit suicide, but it was so Shakespearean, wasn't it? The *boyfriend* had an alibi, so it simply *couldn't* have been rape or murder, or both.

It was the same thing here, with the Rawlins women. Daughter loses herself in the wilderness, goes a few steps too far in her quest to take flower pictures... Yeah, we'll look for her. We'll look pretty damned hard, but not for too long. Oh, the mother disappeared? Hmmm, see, the Kia is *also* gone, so she must have gotten upset and driven off. To where? Doesn't matter. Nothing indicates murder, so fuck it. God *damn* how Pearce had fought and yelled. There were noble men amongst the Alaska State Troopers and the Bureau of Investigations. But few of them showed up for the Rawlins case.

He pulled over on the highway and went to a picture on his phone.

It was Emily Rawlins in all her gray and blue and frozen misery.

He'd taken it while kneeling next to her, for the sake of close study. Particularly of the gruesome, broken indention on the right side of her skull, where he assumed she'd hit the ice.

No, he didn't think the girl had been raped.

If not for her mother's disappearance and their Kia appearing in the bottom of a fucking mine, he'd think it likely she'd simply stumbled into the break during an ill-advised climb.

"Your shirt's still tucked in," he said.

Nobody had messed with her, not like *that*. And nobody in their little group had mentioned it because the case was ethereal, and the girl's body had been *right there* in front of them.

He sent the picture to the writer with a brief message: *Thoughts? I have one.*

Maybe that was a mistake. Or hell, maybe not.

"Go home," he said.

He closed out of the picture and pulled back onto the road.

The silhouettes of one of central Alaska's many mountain ranges loomed straight ahead. To his left, a vertical rock wall, dotted with the ghostly shapes of evergreens.

He crossed the Nenana River, and then came to the frozen dead girl, right in front of him, standing in the road.

No, his tired eyes realized, that wasn't her. That was a person, but *who*—.

He slammed the brakes, but the damage was done; he had no control of the truck, not a bit, and he skidded toward the steep slope beyond the highway's right shoulder.

He made one last effort to halt the truck's momentum—cutting the wheel to the left and pumping the brakes—and it worked, somehow. The Chevy came to a dramatic halt with the passenger wheels barely finding purchase atop the grassy slope that plummeted down to the river.

He sat, clenching the wheel, motionless.

When a small noise sounded from somewhere behind him, the cab's back window splintered into millions of fragments of broken glass, and he knew what was happening.

A great weight hit him in the back of his right shoulder, flinging him forward and slightly to the left. His chest hit the steering wheel, his head hit the window, and he saw a pulse of light, but that wasn't so bad. Nor was the numbness in his arm. It was the disturbing realization that somebody was *shooting* at him—that was bad.

He hit the unlock button and pawed at the door handle, flung open the door, and fell out onto the road. Bad idea? He didn't know. But if he was going to live, he had to go somewhere.

He'd thought he could stand up and take off, but his head was in a fog, probably because his arm wasn't numb anymore, and pain was shooting in sharp bolts from his shoulder to his wrist and back up again.

Never mind that. Move.

He picked himself up.

The shot had come from behind him, so—.

The figure approached from the darkness on the other side of the road.

Pearce's head spun as wet warmth expanded over his back.

"Time to move on," the figure said.

Pearce saw the pistol's glint. A faint flash when it went off.

Kind of bright.

Not like he thought it'd be.

XXXI
The Bar & Box

1

WALLACE O'BRIEN STUCK AROUND FOR one more drink. He had a decent conversation with Morgan; there was a kinship between them, since they both, in recent memory, had questioned their own sanity. And both of them wanted to find Mary, because the mother surely deserved to be found, too. Wallace did not mention that his fascination with the case had very little to do with justice or closure; it was all about his book. He needed facts—preferably *solid* ones.

Rawleigh was clearly getting tired and did not say much.

Eventually, it hit Wallace, too—the effects of hiking and climbing and two tall beers. He thanked Morgan and her uncle for the drinks and discussion and explained he didn't have far to go, just up to the lodge.

He was pulling into a parking space outside the front entrance when his phone sounded in his pocket.

He shut off the vehicle, dug out his phone, and immediately saw that he'd received a picture and an attached text message from Officer Pearce: *Thoughts? I have one.*

"I don't know if I have any thoughts," he said.

He already knew what the picture was before he enlarged it.

He didn't know Pearce had taken any pictures of the frozen, snow-dusted corpse, and for a few minutes, he had no idea what he was getting at. She was dead, obviously. The picture was a grotesque thing that he did not care to look at, but Pearce *wanted* him to, and why?

Sit for a minute, he thought, *and think, because Pearce has obviously thought of something.*

The night was totally silent. He stared at the screen, though perhaps he did not stare at what was *on* the screen.

"He put her clothes back on," he said. "Or he never took them off."

Yes, well... Maybe that was it?

Wallace figured there were three common reasons for murder: anger, money, and sex. Had Cork been angry with her? According to everything he'd seen and heard, there was little or no connection between them, so that seemed unlikely. Money? Maybe Mary and Emily Rawlins had been blessed with more money than the facts suggested, but no part of the circumstances indicated he'd been after her money (even if she *did* have enough to justify murder). Sex? That was the assumed motive. But Emily's body certainly didn't suggest it.

Wallace was too tired to know if their narrative, if there had ever been one, had truly been flipped on its head.

He decided to get some rest and return to it in the morning.

2

Gunn was under the covers and in a deep sleep when he entered the room.

He used the bathroom and changed into a pair of athletic shorts, then eased quietly into the other bed.

He thought he would fall asleep immediately, but instead he simply stared up into the darkness, head still numb from exhaustion and alcohol, and he wished he were sitting at the bar in Shavano's; he could talk some things through with his old friend and…

Well, look! Damnation! He closed his eyes and that's exactly where he went. He stepped through the front door and the whole place was empty, except for Peevey. His old friend was standing behind the bar, exactly where he should be. He grinned as Wallace crossed the floor, asked him how it felt to be back in New York so suddenly. How were things going?

"They're going well," Wallace said. "That's one side of the coin. On the other, they're not going well at all."

Peevey decided Wallace needed some whiskey and Evian. He poured it up and handed it over.

Wallace took a large drink and nodded his approval.

"Now you're better," Peevey said. "And remember, Wallace: you *could* be dead like me."

"I'm tired and confused, Peevey. My career is all but dead, and I *have* to write this book. But every single time I think I've figured it out, it evades me."

"Did you expect to go up there and have the whole story fall into your lap?"

"Part of me thought I'd come up here and it would just... happen."

"A foolish part of you. I'll tell you, realistically, what you went up there to do, aside from simply getting out of New York. You went up there to investigate your story, to make contact with the ground on which it occurred and the people who saw it happen—to the *extent* they saw it happen. You went up there to *begin*."

"I know."

Peevey poured another splash of whiskey, another splash of Evian. "So what's the problem?"

"Originally, in the event there *is* no resolution, the *mystery* was going to be the point of it all! The possibilities were as vast as the landscape! I intended to write a book about the Rawlins and their disappearances, and the kernel at the center of it all would be the mystery, Alaska; the land itself would be a character. The *theme* of the book would be the wild blue yonder. That changed almost immediately. I realized something was happening. And we found Emily."

"Intriguing."

"Plenty intriguing. And a potential deathblow to my idea, if we can't find Mary."

"Come now, how many pieces of writing actually turn out as you intend them to?"

"Not one. But listen, Peevey: if this book is going to put me back where I need to be, it has to tell the truth. My wide open theme is no longer wide open. The mother is still missing. Is her body in the river? Is it in the glacier, too? We have perhaps two dead suspects, a fat slob and a perverted drunk who just blew his brains out." He inhaled over half of the whiskey and water and studied the glass. "I tell you, Peevey, I don't think Devin had a thing to do with it, and I *think* I feel the same way about that boy, Cork."

"Feelings are good. Follow them."

"To where?"

"To wherever you need to go." Peevey leaned into the bar. "Take it from somebody who's on the other side of this thing: keep your eyes open. You'll be all right."

3

"You talked in your sleep last night," Gunn said.

She was standing in front of the room's floor-to-ceiling mirror, already dressed, running a brush through her shiny dark hair.

Wallace had just woken up, rolled over, checked the clock between the beds.

It was five a.m.

His dreams had gotten the best of him.

"I don't doubt it," he said.

"What are your plans?"

He threw his legs over the side of the bed and sat there and tried to determine if he was all right.

"I guess we'll see," he said.

Gunn said she was going back into the park.

After he showered and put on fresh clothes, he drove Gunn to the park entrance and waited with her till the day's first bus arrived. She told him to be in touch, and he told her he'd see her soon.

When she was gone, he drove to the Salmon Catch.

He pulled in behind the restaurant and walked the rest of the way up to the cabins.

Two still stood.

One was in the early stages of being rebuilt.

The rest were either flattened or in various stages of disrepair.

Wallace wondered if the old owner would bother proceeding with the repairs. His son was dead. Wallace had never married, never cared to have a kid... He had no way of knowing what such a loss felt like.

I call myself a writer. I don't know anything.

But he'd always been pretty good at faking it, hadn't he?

Until it caught up with me.

This time, he'd tell the truth.

He steered clear of the two standing cabins. Rawleigh had mentioned taking his niece up to Fairbanks, but Wallace assumed he hadn't done so last night.

They were resting. He was not. Because he was afflicted by the insanity that infects men who have something to say and are incapable of saying it. He wanted to believe his cynicism was the result of exhaustion. But, cynical or not, could he argue with it? Could he say what he needed to say?

Keep my eyes open.

He stopped amidst an empty foundation and tried to let it come to him, whatever it was that needed to come his way. The only thing he received was the faint caress of a wisp of smoke.

Not that of the fire that had ruined so many of these cabins. No. More like…

Hell, he'd been a smoker once. He could still identify the smell of a menthol cigarette.

He inhaled deeply, trying to determine if it was real, and yes, it was.

It was also quickly gone, carried off by a breeze. And the breeze reminded him there was a full day ahead, and he needed to get on with it.

He walked down to the station for breakfast: coffee and a Milky Way. As he paid, his gaze fell on the cigarette rack behind the counter. Immediately, he spotted the row of Kools.

The clerk could see what he was looking at and asked him if he wanted a pack.

"No," Wallace said. "Thank you."

He took his change and stepped out.

Okay, he thought, so he'd caught a whiff of a cigarette, and yes, come to think of it, Ellis Everett smoked Kools—he'd seen them behind the bar in the Salmon Catch, and he'd noticed them in the old man's shirt pocket.

This meant nothing.

Except that he'd smelled cigarette smoke when there was nobody around, and unless he was reaching for something that wasn't there, it had probably been a Kool.

He stood outside the station and ate his Milky Way.

Ellis Everett had known for years that his boy was a fuckup. And about ten years ago—shortly after a girl named Vanbrite turned up dead in Anchorage—he'd called up his boy and told him to quit Chugach Timber, get out of Big City Anchorage, and come up here where it's peaceful.

Wallace's brain was cooking up something, he just didn't know if it was worth a damn.

He was tempted to go back inside and buy his own pack of Kools. Because, he thought: *Cigarette smoke, which yielded Ellis Everett, which yielded Cork and Cork's return home to Daddy, which yielded... The Rawlins disappearances and...?*

And what the hell *was* he thinking?

He thought of that picture of Emily Rawlins that Pearce had sent him. Something triggered. He tried to call Pearce, perhaps to expand on a theory, but the cop didn't answer.

He stuffed the Milky Way wrapper in his pocket and crossed the highway.

He tried the Salmon Catch's front door and found it, as it should be, locked. But that didn't matter. There was another way; he'd spotted it on his way to the gas station.

He went around to the side of the building to a window near the back. It was cracked open; he'd noticed it on his way down to the road.

The window faced both the driveway and a slight bend in the highway. He could get through the window, yes, but he preferred not to be seen clambering up the side of the Salmon Catch.

Nobody was coming.

It was still early; the lighting was poor.

The whole damned process would take, what? Twenty seconds? Ten?

What am I looking for when I get in there?

Anything. He was looking for anything.

He checked the highway again.

Confident that he wasn't being watched, he reached up, using a ledge at the bottom of the wall for a boost. He nudged the window up several more inches, then gripped the windowsill and pulled himself up; he shoved the window up the rest of the way, squeezed through... and landed awkwardly in the floor beside the desk in what he assumed was Ellis Everett's office.

So his illegal entrance had gone smoothly. He was where he needed to be, though he had no idea why, but if he wanted to pursue this sad and hopefully crazy idea about old man Everett, where else better to look? His house? He had to draw a line somewhere with the illegal activity.

Now, was there anything worth his time?

There was nothing obvious on Everett's desk, just a calendar, computer, coffee cup, and a legal pad that contained what appeared to be a few perfectly normal notes. Nor was there anything substantial in the desk's only drawer... pens, pencils, paperclips, a cigarette lighter, a can of snuff...

There was a cheap bookcase in the corner behind the desk. Its top two shelves were sagging beneath the weight of a dictionary, a partial set of encyclopedias, a thick volume about Denali's wildlife, and a few paperback novels. On the next shelf down was a model of a classic Mustang and a miniature globe. And on the bottom shelf were some computer items—a USB mouse and a box of Memorex CD-Rs, probably business records. There was also a Nike shoebox that Wallace assumed did not contain shoes.

He was reaching for the box when he heard the considerable rumble of an engine, almost certainly that of a pickup. It sounded close.

Wallace pulled the window down to its former position and stepped out of the office. He locked the door back and pulled it closed, and as he stepped out into the short corridor that led to the dining room, he saw Ellis's red Tundra pull up outside. The old man parked in front of the dining room's front window. He did not get out, just sat behind the wheel with the engine running.

This, Wallace thought, was an unfortunate turn of events.

He could not go back; like a fool, he'd locked the door behind him.

Forward, then.

He kept low, following along the far wall behind the tables and chairs, hoping Ellis Everett was distracted and the window tint was adequately dark. He arrived at the stairs leading up to the bar confident he'd not been caught. And if his memory was correct, there was a back door at the top, right before the bar entrance.

He sprinted up the stairs, and yes, at the top was a door clearly marked EXIT. He passed through it, shut it back, and proceeded down a set of wooden steps.

He stopped at the bottom, listened.

No sound at all except for the low rumble of Everett's truck—which shut off several seconds later.

The truck door opened, shut, and Wallace heard the old man making his way up the front steps.

Wallace waited until he thought the old man was inside, then moved back around to the office window. He pressed himself against the wall below it and listened.

Ellis was in there. He was talking, but his voice was barely above a whisper, and Wallace couldn't make out any of it.

As quietly as possible, he moved out away from the window and did a wide circle out into the driveway that eventually led him back to the front of the Salmon Catch.

He was approaching the front steps when Ellis Everett stepped out the door.

"Will you open today?" Wallace said.

"No. I won't. I need your help." He sat down on the top step. "I came to call the police. I have a little flip phone. I couldn't get it to work, not out there. I couldn't sleep. So I went out this morning. I came here and walked around some, and then I started driving. Part of me actually thought I was going to Anchorage. And I don't know what I was going to do there. Catch a plane I guess. But I can't leave this place, I couldn't ever. Oh hell."

The old man was legitimately unraveled. He was shaking, his voice cracking.

Wallace knelt down and asked him what had happened.

"I thought I saw something," the old man said, "near the river. I need your help, Wallace, to make sure I'm not crazy. I talked to the police, but it'll take an hour for them to get here. Will you give me a ride?"

4

At Ellis Everett's request, Wallace drove them south.

The old man started rambling again as soon as they pulled away from the Salmon Catch, and he only stopped when they were several miles beyond the entrance to Denali and coming upon a crossing of the Nenana River.

"Right here," Everett said. "Pull over right here."

Wallace did so, and Everett led him a few feet down the embankment and pointed down at the roaring, rushing gray water.

Wallace did not initially see it.

But there it was, half-submerged in the river, toppled on its side.

"I didn't go down," Everett said. "Don't think I could've. But if I'm not mistaken, I've seen that truck before. You see it too, don't you?"

Wallace nodded. "I'll go."

5

The hundred-foot trek down to the river was much more treacherous than it looked. The grass was damp and slick, many of the rocks embedded shallowly into the slope.

At the bottom, he discovered that the half-submerged, toppled pickup was indeed Pearce's Chevy. Their Wasilla friend was afloat in the cabin with a crusted, gory hole just above his left eye.

Wallace's stomach lurched, and he turned his back to the river and the death.

Then he started back up the slope.

XXXII
In the Box

1

MORGAN AWOKE AT SEVEN TO the sound of rustling paper.

She sat up in bed and found her uncle sitting at the table. He was studying something intently by the gray light in the window.

"I've got an idea," Uncle Rawleigh said. "I'll dwell on it while you get ready."

She gathered her things and kissed him on the top of the head before going down to the showers.

The phenomenon from the previous cabin had followed her to this one. She'd slept okay, yes, but frequently it had been shallow, her head invaded by a faint, numbing paranoia and dreams of blood and smoke and bizarre, hollow voices. All night, her stomach had rolled and cramped... But all this withdrew as she stood under the hot water and let herself relax.

She told herself she should go home. Then decided she couldn't.

And she didn't want to.

By the time she was dressed, she felt healthy again, and sane.

Uncle Rawleigh was standing over the table when she returned. He'd apparently just gone across the street to the station, because he was sipping coffee, and there was a hot chocolate waiting for her on the bedside stand.

On the table was a large and apparently very *old* map of Alaska.

"My favorite," he said. "It's outdated, but I love how it shows the roads and the geography. I didn't have a vision last night. I'm not a prophet. But I *did* have an epiphany."

She sipped her hot chocolate and asked what he was talking about.

He motioned for her to come closer, put a fingertip on the map, and traced it along a faint gray line.

"Dragon Canyon Road," he said.

"Yes."

The gray line ended abruptly between two ridges.

He tapped the area. "And here is our mine."

"Yes."

Again he traced his fingertip along Dragon Canyon Road. "We all know this road is awful. No way in hell any vehicle, not even Pearce's ATV, could make it all the way to the mine."

"Right."

"So it would have required nearly *ungodly* dedication, and a hell of a lot of time, for anybody to drag a vehicle up there, right? And who do we have as 'suspects?' Devin. No way Devin did it. Cork. More feasible, yes, but you'd think he would have needed help. Which brings me to my epiphany. The range containing the mine is part of a narrow ridge. I thought, isn't there another way in?"

"Wouldn't the police or the media have already found it?"

"I don't know. But if my theory is right, I doubt it. What I'm thinking isn't on a map, not even this one. It might not even exist."

She was growing a little impatient. "Are you going to tell me about it?"

Fingertip back on the map. "Right before you get to Cantwell, right after the highway swings to the southwest, there's an old logging road that goes north into the mountains. It's not used or maintained anymore. I've been on it once, a long time ago. Conventional wisdom, I think, is that it ends long before it would ever reach the backside of our mine. But maybe?"

"And nobody knows about this road?"

"Loggers *did*. Some of them."

"If it's so old and gone, would it be any better than Dragon Canyon Road?"

"We need to see, right?"

2

They took the Frontier, Uncle Rawleigh driving, but they did not make it far.

They were crossing the Nenana when Morgan spotted the silver Escape on the side of the road. Her boss was standing next to it.

Uncle Rawleigh pulled over, and Ellis Everett approached them as they climbed out of the truck.

The old man said: "There's a truck down there. I've called the police. Your writer friend went down."

The three of them approached the edge of the slope. Wallace O'Brien was picking his way up the grass and rocks. Beyond him, there was an older pickup half-submerged in the river. When Wallace reached the shoulder of the highway, he jabbed a finger in the air— *One minute, just give me a minute*—and looked up at the sky as he caught his breath.

"It's Pearce." He went to the Escape and leaned back against the front grill. "Shot. Definitely dead."

Morgan and her uncle remained at the edge and gazed down at the pickup.

"I'm nervous for us," Everett said. "Old skeletons are being exhumed, and somebody doesn't like it."

After that, none of them spoke until the state troopers arrived in marked Explorers. One was a younger male, the other a middle-aged female.

Everett spoke the most; he relayed his story about not being able to sleep. He said he paced around his cabins, chain smoking and trying to calm down, and that didn't work so he went for a drive, and he didn't know how he saw it, his headlights just fell on it the right way as he was crossing the river, but he saw the truck, and he got out and looked. He went back to the Catch and called the police. There, he met up with "the writer" and asked for a ride.

The old man nodded at Morgan and Uncle Rawleigh. "These two got here just before you did."

Wallace took over from there. He described going down to the river and what he saw afloat in the truck.

When he finished, one of the troopers descended to the river.

The other said things sure were going to hell.

3

The male trooper took their statements and asked Ellis half a dozen times if the old man needed to go to the hospital. Ellis insisted he was fine. Nerves, he said. Probably related to losing a son and finding a dead guy in a river.

The trooper frowned and told them to keep an eye on him.

"And stick around." He fixed his eye on Morgan. "Including you, Southern girl."

When it was over, they drove back to the Salmon Catch. Ellis did not care to go inside. He insisted on driving himself home and going to bed.

"Hang around in there all you want. I'll be fine. If I don't make it, that's fine too."

Morgan watched her boss's truck disappear around a bend, and then she unlocked the restaurant.

Wallace immediately said: "Can you unlock his office?"

Morgan thought for a moment and said she didn't have a key... but there was *likely* an extra one upstairs.

"Why?" she said.

"I have an idea. I won't hurt anything."

Uncle Rawleigh suggested she get the key.

She thought she remembered him keeping one under the bar's cash register, an emergency key that only existed because he'd gone through a spell of locking himself out of his truck, house, and office.

It was still there.

She unlocked the office, feeling more than a little guilty, and the writer went straight to a shoebox on the bottom shelf of the bookcase behind his desk. He placed the box on the desk and lifted the lid.

Inside was a collection of foreign money—change and bills from all over the world—and a pistol.

Morgan didn't know guns very well. She only knew that it was a small revolver.

None of them touched it.

Satisfied, Wallace put everything back as it was.

They went up to the bar, sat down at a table, and Uncle Rawleigh said: "Ellis Everett? Really?"

The writer spoke with confidence: "It has its flaws, but it's possible and maybe plausible. Think about it: Father knows his son is a creep, suspects or *knows* his son assaulted, raped, and/or killed the Vanbrite girl, and Father gets his kid to quit his job and come up here so Son can drink himself into permanent stupors and Father can keep an eye on him. Son does it again, this time to the Rawlins girl. Maybe it's even Father who kills the mother, because he's helping Son cover it up. Son pulls another stunt, this time against Morgan here... Father knows some of the locals, and not-so-locals, are getting suspicious, and what do you know? Doesn't take long for one of them to turn up dead.

"It works, but there are flaws. We still don't know where Mary Rawlins is. That's not necessarily an issue, but it's a huge question mark. Then we have what I consider to be *clear* differences in each set of facts:

"The Vanbrite girl met her demise in the middle of Anchorage and turned up dead in a creek, wearing nothing but her underwear. Not to sound too cruel, but in the world of violent crime, that's not altogether an unusual set of facts. Neither—and forgive me—is what happened to our friend Morgan. She was attacked in those trees just right out there, and we all know what her attacker—Cork—apparently wanted to do with her."

He paused. Morgan had gone behind the bar; she returned with a pitcher of water and some glasses. She'd hung on every word Wallace O'Brien said. She'd already developed respect for him. The man sounded as if he were picking apart an essay question on the bar exam.

After Wallace wetted his throat, he continued: "Emily Rawlins, however... Whatever happened to her, it happened in Denali National Park. We *still* don't know what happened. We do know she turned up just now, dead and frozen, in a glacier; she's fully clothed, still wearing her backpack, and her hiking boots are still laced up. Does this sound like it was a rape, to anybody at this table? Really? Sure, it's possible to do such a thing only for us to find her with her clothes on, but really? And it sure doesn't sound like the other two, does it?

"The mother is still missing. An entire automobile is dissembled and tossed in a mine that, much like the glacier, is *very close to inaccessible* under ordinary circumstances, for ordinary people. Ellis Everett is, what? Seventy-four? Seventy-five? Granted, this happened several years ago, but he would still have been an old man. If we assume Cork did most of this, there is no way Ellis would've been a worthy assistant to such a task. And now, we have Pearce, dead. *That* wasn't Cork."

Uncle Rawleigh went behind the bar for a lemon wedge for his water, then excused himself, he said, to go downstairs to the restroom.

When he returned, he said: "There was a time when I'd argue that Ellis Everett was incapable of such a thing. But I won't pretend to know anything. Before all this, if Morgan had asked me if Cork were dangerous, I'd have said probably not. So what do I know?" He paused and turned to Morgan. Then looked back at the writer. "About the Kia, and the road, I've been thinking about that. Morgan and I were going somewhere earlier, and it might be important. Want to go for a ride?"

XXXIII
The Dark Side of the Massif

1

THEY TOOK RAWLEIGH'S FRONTIER, AS it was the most rugged 4x4 they had. Rawleigh drove, and Morgan volunteered herself to the irrelevant bench that was supposedly a back seat.

As he drove, Rawleigh elaborated on his idea that there was a logging road—or the remains of a logging road—that might provide another way into the mine. No, he wasn't saying it was a smooth road, but maybe it was *smoother*, with no boulder fields.

Or maybe it didn't exist at all.

And then he changed the subject to Devin: "I was never friends with Devin. No, that might be unfair. I was never *close* friends with Devin. He might've been a serial killer for all I know, but I doubt it. He was too worthless to do any serial killing."

Wallace stared out the Frontier's passenger window, the trees and mountains and the Nenana River passing by. But he was taking it all in. He was recording Rawleigh on his cell phone and taking notes on the notepad he kept stashed in the back of his brain.

Approximately two miles north of the Cantwell community, Rawleigh slowed the truck to a crawl and turned off at a seemingly random location that required them to cross two muddy creek beds. The Frontier handled the obstacles with ease.

After they started up a modest slope and into the trees, Wallace noted that Rawleigh indeed knew what he was doing. They were on a road—or something *resembling* a road. It was dirt, rock, and root, but it was, at least, passable.

Rawleigh said he was surprised he was right, but they'd still be lucky if it actually went all the way to the mine.

For its first few miles, the road ascended and unwound through dense forest in a general northwesterly direction, until it broke dramatically out of the trees and leveled off on the floor of a vast, rocky tundra and cut sharply toward the snowy mountains to the north.

As they bounded along with no conversation, Wallace forgot all about death and books and bears and—.

"Losing it," Rawleigh said.

The road now was not so much a road as a faint footpath, and if it continued like this, proceeding any further in the Frontier would become impossible.

But it returned shortly after it disappeared.

Rawleigh, seemingly thinking aloud, said: "Make it past the mud at the start of it, and I think you could get any decent SUV up here, assuming it continues long enough. You just need to take it slow, need decent ground clearance. I don't think we've even spun tires since the mud. I don't think so."

"How did you know where to turn?" Wallace said. "There was nothing there."

"I'm a long term local."

The road turned gradually and began another march toward the northwest.

"Cross your fingers," Rawleigh said.

2

The road faded to nothing along the lower slopes of the peaks, but the terrain was grassy and fairly smooth, and so Rawleigh kept going. Wallace and Morgan looked for any sign of an entrance into the side of the massif.

The terrain dipped. A boulder scraped the bottom of the truck.

Rawleigh muttered that they weren't going much further. Fuck this.

And then, Morgan tapped the window.

Rawleigh pressed the brakes, and his niece said: "Up there, at the edge of the grass."

There *was* a cave up there, Wallace saw. The girl was absolutely right.

Rawleigh shut off the truck.

They climbed out

This was isolation, Wallace thought. Out here, there was no theoretical safety net of being in a national park. This was nowhere.

"Let's go see," Rawleigh said.

The portal into the mountain was a wide break in the massif's sheer rock face. They ascended to where the face shot abruptly out of the grassy slope and followed the wall down to the cave.

Rawleigh turned on the flashlight he'd taken from the truck and entered the darkness. Wallace and Morgan followed.

The cave was a winding, uneven corridor that descended into the guts of the mountain.

Wallace hated it.

Especially after all traces of daylight were gone.

After no more than a hundred or so yards, the corridor ended. And thank God Rawleigh *noticed* the end of it, or they'd have likely walked one, two, three over the ledge like pigs into a lake.

It was a deep plunge that Rawleigh's flashlight struggled to reveal.

But there at the bottom, they saw a few glimmers of light bouncing off what were almost certainly the remaining, scattered pieces of Mary Rawlins' rented Kia.

Rawleigh raised the flashlight beam, attempting to reveal the ledge on the other side of the gulf, but the darkness was too thick.

"I think we've found what we're looking for," Rawleigh said.

"Yes, and this route is much more feasible," Wallace said. "I agree with you, the Kia could have made it up the road. It would still be work, of course, *tons* of work..."

And, he thought, the authorities likely did not know of this route; nor would they have much chance of finding it. From the highway, all traces of the road were washed away. So maybe this *did* explain how they—*whoever* they *were*, he reminded himself—managed to get the Kia down in the depths of the mine.

"It took days," Rawleigh said.

For a second, or it might have been closer to a minute, Wallace assumed he'd misheard him.

But the look on Morgan's face indicated he'd heard correctly.

"What?" Wallace said.

"I said *it took days.*" Rawleigh withdrew a revolver—*the* revolver, Wallace thought—from the inside of his jacket. "But I was willing, and poor old Devin was nice enough to drive the second vehicle for me. That helped."

Morgan's mouth was wide open.

Wallace could not speak, either. His brain could not produce a coherent thought.

Except one: He'd been dragged in here to be killed.

XXXIV
Alone

1

MORGAN BACKED AWAY.

"Stay where you are, honey." Uncle Rawleigh put his hands in the air, aiming the gun and flashlight at the ceiling as if to now proclaim his innocence. "I didn't bring you in here to hurt you."

"Uncle Rawleigh..." Her words were barely more than a broken squeak.

Rawleigh lowered his hands and placed a finger over his lips. "Not right now. I do *not* intend to hurt you. I love you. You know I do." He slightly shifted his gaze, the gun, and the flashlight toward Wallace. "But there have been some unfortunate occurrences take place. You found this mine, Morgan. That was unfortunate enough. And then Pearce and Norman Mailer here weren't buying what I was selling."

Morgan realized what was happening a split second too late. She thought her uncle was about to delve into a corny movie monologue about how wicked he was and how he intended to get by with his brilliant plan... But the gun went off immediately after his Norman Mailer remark.

Morgan lunged.

The bullet, she thought, likely landed somewhere in the middle of the writer's brain. And Uncle Rawleigh went over.

His plunge into the pit was remarkably silent.

She barely heard the faint *thud* of his landing.

No scream. Nothing else.

For a long time, she just lay there... Her head hanging out into the darkness. Still. Listening to her breaths.

The flashlight, along with everything else, was dead and gone.

It was totally dark.

She scooted away from the ledge and used one of the walls to climb to her feet.

She was disoriented by the thick blackness, and she didn't have her phone—it had fallen victim to Cork Everett—but...

"Mr. O'Brien?" she said.

No answer from the man who'd been shot at point blank range (and she could have stopped that, she knew she could have stopped it, had she reacted a fraction of a second faster), but she knelt down and reached for him. It should have disgusted her, feeling around on his motionless body for the bulk of his cell phone, but she was too desperate to be disgusted.

She pulled his phone from a pocket and hit the home button. It was an iPhone, one generation older than hers, but the flashlight app worked just the same. For a split second she saw the blood on the side of the writer's head.

She almost cried. She almost vomited.

She almost called for her uncle.

But if she'd done any of those, she might have lost it, and she couldn't do that. Not now. Not in here.

I have to get out.

I have to get help.

She told herself to go, then. Just start walking.

2

She kept one hand on the left wall. She listened to her intermittent sobs, and she pressed forward.

The journey was, by proper measurements, fairly short, but it was long, miserable, and haunted, and she did not feel much better when she finally stepped out into the daylight.

She walked down the slope and sat down against the Frontier's front passenger tire. She stared straight ahead, not blinking, trying to gather herself so she could think straight and her heart would slow down.

And then she heard herself speak: "Uncle Rawleigh has the keys."

The thought didn't even strike her as that bad.

Right now, what *was* bad? What did that mean?

She stood up and tried the passenger door.

It opened. She found two water bottles and a large pocketknife in the console between the seats. She stuffed the knife and bottles in various pockets and spent a moment looking for a key she knew she wouldn't find.

After she accepted her fate, she looked out across the tundra... The edge of the forest, way down there, that was her first destination.

Once she was in the trees, the highway couldn't be more than a few miles away.

Then quit thinking.
Get to the trees.

Again, she started walking.

XXXV
Nightmare Fodder

1

TRULY, IT WAS NOTHING HE could understand; he knew because he'd tired, many times, dozens of times, infinite times. When he wasn't walking its edge, he could look at it objectively, as if it were nothing but a passage in a book, but it was not meant to be understood, and it didn't matter. Certain things had been done, they were his memories and his problems, if they *were* problems, and whatever the case, they could not very well be undone.

Damn this rambling. His brain always rambled when he was in the midst of making a decision he could not quite make.

Your problems don't leave when you cross state lines, no matter how far away the state is, even if you have to take a plane to get there. Distance is not a cleanser. Temporary relief, sure, because you get away from some of the things that upset you and drive you to certain things, true enough, and the scenery's a hell of a lot different, and these changes are decent distractions, but a faulty device will eventually fail, and if there ever was a *faulty device,* it was the clump of gray matter tucked between his ears. What a fuckup that thing was. Hence, this snapshot, this memory, this nightmare, this fuckery:

It's two 'o clock in the morning and it should just be a pleasant sort of buzz, but he went and crunched a few bits, bits is what he always called them, crunched them between his teeth thinking it'd be kinda pleasant, maybe fun, to wash them down with that big glass of Jack and Dr. Pepper—buzz my ass, this thing is going to be a fucking killer, and all that. So it's two 'o clock in the morning and that's why he's sprawled out by the Nenana soaking wet and cold and staring up at the sky, a bastard dope in a bastard situation.

He's still buzzing. It's pleasant. The stars are moving in slow and steady circles, and he's only vaguely aware of his teeth chattering, and if he closes his eyes it feels like he's on a carnival ride, going up and down and round and round. But pleasant effects aside, he's coming back to his right mind, and that's not pleasant at all, because he knows, hell, he knew it when he was out, he knows it's been a long time since he's been this low, and he's probably going to still be shaking and fucking himself long after this shit is out of his system. Better to not be in his right mind. But that's a matter for the future, should it ever come, and he's halfway in the water and staring up at the stars right now, feeling good yet wallowing in his own misery.

A voice comes to him. It's not his voice, and he knows this cause he's pretty sure it's female. Regardless, it's not his voice, and it comes out of the sky or the water, or something. It's not a real voice, not like he usually thinks of *real* stuff, but it's not altogether in his mind, either. The voice tells him he's one sad, sad man, and he needs help. Really, he does. And then the voice asks him a question, and he doesn't know the answer to it. Something about death.

He's scared. He came up here to get away from his family and get away from all the reminders about how worthless he is; he came up here to get to work and enjoy the change of scenery and make himself better, and now he's here. But he hasn't been here long. There is no instant fix. Distance doesn't in and of itself make you better, and all that. The voice tells him again he needs help.

It's a kind voice. The kindest voice he's heard in a long time.

He thinks he'd like to meet the face behind that voice.

2

Now a warm dampness between his legs. In the end, we always piss ourselves. He almost recalled it happening, was just now thinking clearly, if he truly *was* thinking clearly. No matter, the piss was real. This was reality.

He was here. Almost ten years down the road from that night in which he wallowed on the side of the Nenana and looked up at the stars, and now he was looking up into a deep subterranean darkness. He was somewhere close to Hell. Death might be preferable to this.

He moved one foot. Then the other. That was good. If he wasn't going to die, he had a ray of hope; this was better than certain alternatives.

He tried to collect himself.

The memory of the Nenana had been so clear. Where had *that* come from? From the piss between his legs?

He tried to sit up.

Too much. Sharp pain radiated throughout his ribcage, and he cried out.

The noise echoed in the darkness.

He was on the outskirts of Hell.

Morgan.

He called for her. She did not respond. Nor did the writer.

It was dark, and he was alone, and he was all but guaranteed to die and rot in here. He'd let it be and tell himself he deserved it, and he partially believed that.

Death was probably better than this, anyway.

I think I got the writer.

He hadn't wanted to do it. But what was he supposed to do?

He closed his eyes.

If he closed his eyes, the darkness wouldn't drive him mad.

Yes, he got the writer, he was almost sure of it, but his niece, the poor girl, had tried to do the noble thing, and now he was here, and death just about had to better.

He was sorry and broken down, no doubt about it. No doubt, too, that death was better. Fine. But where was the gun? It could be anywhere, and if he thought about the gun, he got excited, got his hopes up—but he shouldn't think about it. It was somewhere far off in this thick blackness that had consumed him.

Or, it was around here somewhere.

He felt around his immediate vicinity and found nothing but the cold rock floor. Wincing, he moved a few inches to the right. He flailed with both hands in a variety of directions, feeling nothing and more nothing.

I'm tired. I'm hurt. I'm probably dying.

Where was the goddamned gun?

It would only take a split second of bravery to send himself off.

And then, he wouldn't have to face his niece. She was hurt. Of *course* she was hurt.

At first, he thought she would probably come visit for two or three weeks, then go home. But something had rekindled that old fire. The storm. The aurora in the storm. Her arrival. The writer's arrival. All of the above? None of the above? And she'd gotten nosy. And the writer had gotten nosy. And the thing about it was, he'd planned for all of this. *If* the girl was found, *if* the vehicle was found, there'd been a plan for all that, right? He'd known of Cork's problems; Ellis had confided in him many times, usually over drinks.

But no explanation was perfect, except the real one.

He yearned for Renee. It was time to move on. Why not? He supposed this thing could still work out, but he would need to get out of here, and his niece would have to forgive him. Both of these were long shots.

A non-issue.

You're not going to get out of here.

He shifted again. The pain was immense. But he could deal with it, if he could find the gun. But finding the gun would require him to move again, and...

He needed to rest, just for a minute.

3

The worst part came after he pushed her.

Because he did not leave. He should have—it would have spared him more than a few nightmares—but the moment had its arms around him. The blue sky. The glacier. The moment did not look like murder. And it wasn't yet.

Her voice emerged from the depths: "Please."

It would have been better if it were a scream. But she sounded like a school kid asking for another day to finish an assignment.

It was probably her backpack, he thought, that kept her from sliding through the squeeze in the ice and dying a fairly painless death at the bottom.

And she *wasn't screaming*. She was so calm and resigned!

And yet, she was in need of something. What?

"Please."

That's all she said. It was maddening, and part of him actually wanted to call down to her and apologize—because he *was* sorry... or, he wasn't. None of this was her fault, and it wasn't fair. But none of it was *his* fault, either, and he hadn't done anything wrong, except push her.

That was supposed to be it. She would be dead. She would never be found, just a hiker who went missing in the wild. Anything could have happened, anything. It was, in a way, exhilarating, despite how depressing it was, but this… was ruining it.

All he could do—because he could not leave it like this—was sit here with his back to her eventual tomb and listen to her say it, over and over again, "Please." That word, every time it crept up out of the dark ice like a tiny acid bubble from an upset stomach, was torturous. She was as good as dead, they both knew it, and she knew he wouldn't help her, if that's what she wanted, even if he could.

Nor would he speak to her.

I'm sorry. I don't know how this happened.

He should have paid more attention to the ice. But dear Jesus! Certain things were out of his control, weren't they?

"Please."

It echoed.

He focused on the river. Its fine threads coiling across the valley floor.

Several silent minutes passed by.

She'd either fallen through, or her heart had stopped, or she'd given up.

One of those. Hopefully.

Still, the river.

At least none of this looked like murder.

4

Where was the goddamned gun?

5

He arrived at Mary Rawlins's cabin late that night, knocked on the door, and stepped inside.
She was at the table drinking whiskey from a foam cup. He sat down and she poured him a splash.
Neither of them spoke. They didn't need to.
He remembered the smell of the whiskey, her face in the lamplight.
He remembered the sad smile that was barely discernible in one corner of her mouth.
The faint smell of smoke, and somehow he knew it was already happening.

6

He found the gun not all that far away.
He held it for a moment, so grateful and terrified.
He missed the days of emailing his niece and recommending music to her. He missed asking her about school and encouraging her to do with her life whatever it was she wanted to do. To hell with everything else because you only have one life, and you're the only one in control of it, and... Oh Lord, look at his own. Who was he to give such advice?

He missed the past. He certainly did.

He regretted nothing, because regret was a waste.

This thing was over.

He imagined one last email, an email from the dead lands, in which he would not try to explain the inexplicable. He would merely tell Morgan that her days in Alaska with her favorite uncle had been appreciated, just ill-timed, and he hoped somehow, in some way, he was *still* her favorite uncle. A fine example of his undying, utter selfishness, to hope for such a thing.

He placed the barrel of the pistol up under his chin.

He did not need but a second of bravery. No, less.

But this wasn't about *bravery*.

Abandon this idea, Rawleigh. Don't be a fool.

Morgan was still alive.

There was hope.

And he'd given the keeper of the universe an eternity's worth of nightmare fodder.

XXXVI
Virus

1

HER FEET AND KNEES BURNED and ached and were threatening to fail her entirely by the time she reached the highway. Morgan stumbled the last mile in something close to a catatonic state. One foot in front of the other, again and again; the dry mechanics were all that kept her moving forward.

The path had been nothing but mud for the last quarter mile, and her feet were cold and wet and close to numb by the time she ascended the last slope to the highway's shoulder.

The highway was quiet. All she heard was the wind.

She needed to return to civilization, but not just yet. She was weak and sore.

She let herself collapse and leaned back against the grass below the road.

If she could cry, she'd feel better, but she'd choked back the urge while she was in the mine, and now she was too tired. Rest. For now, rest was all.

When she felt like she could walk again, she got up and started toward the north.

It didn't take long for someone—a young couple from Indiana—to pull over and ask if she needed help.

Morgan told them she'd be very grateful for a ride back to the Salmon Catch; she'd gotten lost and was very sore. She did not tell them anything about what had happened inside the mountain.

She'd have drifted off if the ride hadn't been so brief.

As it was, almost as soon as she was settled into the back seat, the driver was pulling into the Salmon Catch's empty parking lot.

Morgan thanked them and got out.

She told them yes, she'd be fine, she just needed to go to bed.

2

She stood in the middle of the Salmon Catch's parking lot, a trace of civilization with a trace of cellular service, and called 911 from the writer's cell phone. She did not give her name. She only stated that something had happened in a cave at the end of a logging road that you can't see from the highway. Her brain was a stew of incoherent thoughts. She struggled for what to say—she had to provide a detail, something—and then she thought of Cantwell. The community was Cantwell.

"You'll need to cross a muddy creek," she concluded.

This had to be enough. It's all she knew.

She ended the call, snapped herself out of yet another catatonic state, and went back to her uncle's cabin

If a ghost wanted to use and abuse her, if a smoky demon wanted to rise up and drag her down to hell, if any of these things were real—if any of them were *here*—so be it.

She could not find the ability to care.

She went inside and locked the door and collapsed on the bed.

She dreamed she was somewhere in the woods, sitting on a boulder, looking down at her phone, which magically worked again. She was reading an email she'd never received: *I am your Uncle Rawleigh. I love you. I will never hurt you. Just the opposite. I've enjoyed seeing you, and I hope to see you again.* She stood and walked through the forest. Looking for Mary Rawlins. What had happened to Mary Rawlins? If he'd killed Emily, and she knew that's what he'd done, what had he done with her mother?

She wandered amidst the trees.

He would never hurt her; she believed that. He'd never given *her* one tiny reason to ever believe otherwise.

She loved her uncle. She *still* loved her uncle. She'd always had more in common with him than either of her parents. What did this mean? Anything? She did not want to go back to her parents, but what had happened, and why? *And where was Mary Rawlins?*

At the top of the slope, she looked north, toward his home in Fairbanks.

I hate you, Uncle Rawleigh.

Why would you do such a thing?

I had to.

And where is Mary?

Come on, honey. I'll show you.

3

She awoke, and the first thing she saw was Wallace O'Brien's cell phone on the pillow beside her head. She wanted it in case she needed it, but that was all. She would not be accepting any of Mr. O'Brien's calls; she would not be talking again to the authorities. Not right now. She checked the time—nine p.m.—and turned the device off.

It took days.

The words haunted her, his tone, his blank expression in the flashlight glow.

Come on, honey. I'll show you.

She didn't know what this meant. Most of her dream was gone, and what she could remember now seemed like nothing but nonsense. Her uncle had fallen God knows how far into a dark abyss in the bowels of a mountain. He was not going to show her anything. And even if he *could*, did she want to see it?

Yes, if she could find closure for Mary and Emily Rawlins. Dead, alive, frozen, whatever: they were human beings and deserved peace and finality. She could not undo Uncle Rawleigh's actions, but maybe she could give them *that*.

Uncle Rawleigh.

She now wondered why she was so shocked. That her uncle had treated her with kindness and respect carried very little weight. Really, she hadn't known him all that well. He'd fled his family because he was a loser. Was it such a shock that he was a *violent* loser?

She got out of bed.

And collapsed.

She thought she'd had a stroke—the pain in her head was abrupt, blinding, and thankfully short lived—and when she picked herself up off the floor, she felt her stomach roll over and cramp. Vomit surged into her throat, which she released in the nearest corner.

She reached up for the bedside stand and used it to pick herself up.

Another bolt of pain in her head. She barely made it to her feet, and she had to cling to the wall to maintain her stance.

Blood, she felt it but barely noticed.

She only wanted out of here.

In another blast of pain, she saw the smoky, bloody, human-shaped figure standing in front of the door, those dark and coiling crook-shaped streaks of black rising throughout, dancing absurdly to a breeze that wasn't there. Come on, dear girl, come closer. You won't make it to the door, and you shouldn't. You're such a warm, inviting place—why would I want you to leave? I am dead. I am a ghost. I am the remains of a virus, I'll haunt you, warm girl, I'll destroy you, and I'll move on.

Virus.

The word came to her and she didn't know why.

But again, it didn't matter. She needed out, and…

The figure faded with the pain, but its absence was mere illusion—it was there.

Get back in bed, dear Morgan.

You're ill.

Get back in bed. We'll be together. I'll show you more.

"Go away," she said. She begged it, despite the growing throb in the front of her skull, despite the apparition's strengthening presence, which was more physical, more constant—and clearer. Indeed, as she felt herself slowly and steadily losing grasp of what was real and what wasn't, she discerned a face, not an altogether unpleasant one, a face of blood and smoke and something else that was dark and foul and tarry, a cancerous substance that was growing and spreading, and if she would just *give up* and *get back in bed,* they could relax together. Nothing mattered now except rest. That was all.

She was numb, thinking it was probably a good idea, going back to sleep, it's not like things could get any worse, or maybe she was about to shout one last time for it to *Get out!*—when somebody knocked on the cabin door, and Morgan almost cried, because only God knew what it was—she assumed it was something dead or malicious.

A familiar voice called through the door: "Morgan, can I come in? Is it locked?"

Dolores Gunn.

Morgan started to speak—she couldn't—and the door opened.

Dim, cool nighttime rushed into the cabin, and the virus dissipated like smoke from a dead firework.

"Morgan?" Gunn said.

The musician crossed the floor and wrapped an arm around her and helped her outside, asking her if she was okay. Why was she just standing there?

Morgan told her she needed to sit down. That was all.

Somewhere else.

Could she just sit down?

4

They went down to Gunn's rental, which she'd parked alongside the Salmon Catch. Gunn helped her into the Toyota's passenger seat and handed her a thermos of coffee. Then she climbed in behind the wheel.

But she did not start the car.

She'd been looking for Wallace, she explained, but he wasn't in the park, nor at the lodge; nor was he at the gas station or anywhere else, and he wouldn't answer his phone.

Morgan pulled his phone out of her back pocket and handed it to her.

Gunn turned it over a few times in her hand and asked her what was going on.

Morgan handled the story as best she could. She wasn't sure it was clear, and much of it she had a hard time speaking aloud. But after ten minutes or so of her broken, choked up rambling, Gunn seemed to have the gist of it.

The musician was quiet for several moments. Maybe she wiped a tear or two of her own. It was dark and Morgan couldn't tell.

"Did you call for help?" Gunn said.

Morgan said yes.

Gunn said softly: "I heard sirens earlier. They were in the distance. I didn't think they mattered."

They'll be up here soon, Morgan thought. *They'll ask questions I don't want to answer.*

"Will you drive me somewhere?" Morgan said.

It took Gunn a minute, but she said yes. Absolutely.

Morgan said: "I want to go to his house. I want to find Mary Rawlins."

5

Uncle Rawleigh's house was in a sparsely populated area south of Fairbanks. It was a simple two-story structure that sat by itself on a dirt road half a mile off the highway.

There was another house across the road. Morgan had noticed it during her weekend stay. It looked empty and gutted.

Gunn pulled into his driveway at a little after eleven 'o clock. She drove up into the shadows at the end of the house. Beyond his back yard, the land fell away rather abruptly, and the lights of the city were spread out below them to the north and east.

They got out and walked a lap around the house, finding both the front and back doors locked.

At the back door, Gunn brought up her phone's flashlight and said: "You really think we might find something?"

Morgan said she didn't know. She hoped so.

Gunn went back to the Toyota and returned with her driver's license. She had the door open in less than a minute.

They proceeded into the darkness.

Morgan turned on a lamp near the door.

Her uncle's living room was drab and perfectly acceptable. There was a flat screen television on one wall with a recliner and sofa positioned before it. A round glass table was in the middle of the floor. On it was a laptop and a Bible. They looked quietly around the room, and then Gunn said she was going to look around and set off into the shadowy depths of the remainder of the first floor.

Morgan knelt before the computer, raised the screen, and pressed the power button.

After displaying TOSHIBA in bright red letters, the computer went to a login screen.

She gave up after her third password attempt... and noticed a framed picture of herself on the table beside the recliner. In it, she stood in ridiculous garb, beaming, her arms around her dad's shoulders. For that brief time, during and right after her law school graduation, she'd been so incredibly happy.

She'd sent her uncle the picture just a couple of months ago.

It was bizarre, she thought, that *she* was the girl in that picture.

Why did she feel this way? Why did it matter?

Gunn reentered the room.

"Nothing that I can see," she said. "His bedroom is messy. Nothing unusual. Upstairs?"

Morgan nodded.

The second floor was almost entirely empty except for a room that appeared to be used for storage. Two entire walls were lined with shelves, which were stocked messily with books and various other items. The floor, too, was strewn with clutter: a weight bench, two old televisions, bottles, cans, papers, stacks of books and magazines, DVDs, VHS tapes, an old dot matrix printer...

Morgan was picking through a pile by the light of Wallace's phone when Gunn called to her.

She looked up and saw the musician standing near the room's only window.

"There's a light on over there," Gunn said, "in that house across the street."

Morgan approached the window. The sight was eerie, she thought, a single lamp in a downstairs room... She couldn't imagine anybody actually *living* in such a dilapidated old—.

The light went out.

Morgan's heart jumped.

Gunn pulled the curtain over the window and suggested Morgan go back to what she was doing; best to lay low up here anyway.

Morgan tried to focus on the junk pile she'd been sifting through.

Most of the items were mundane, but there were a few oddities and treasures: a love poem titled CONTRACT OF SALVATION written in black ink on what looked like genuine leather, a signed copy of Hemingway's *A Farewell to Arms*, and a box that contained what could only be drug paraphernalia: pipes, pills, bottles, the remnants of various powders.

She studied the CONTRACT OF SALVATION and noted that the messy, smeared signature at the bottom—the poet's, she assumed—started with an R... Renee.

Morgan sat on the floor and read:

The low cannot be raised until he knows
The one who loves regardless of his faults,
Someone who loves when love she cannot show,
Someone who loves when love's not seen at all.
This love is me no matter what might change.
This love is me no matter what my name.

Gunn knelt beside her. "Lovely words."

Poor Renee, Morgan thought. Yes, the woman had been stringing her uncle along for years, and maybe he liked it or maybe he didn't. But no woman deserved to love a... She hated the thought of calling her uncle a killer.

Gunn took the poem, shone her phone light on it, and read it again.

"Someone was very fond of him," she said.

Downstairs, the back door opened and closed.

Morgan and the musician momentarily stopped breathing, looked up, and waited.

A woman's voice came from below: "Who is in here?"

Gunn squeezed Morgan's shoulder, motioned for her to stay still and be quiet, then moved toward the door.

The voice came again from downstairs: "I'm about to come up there. You might as well come on out."

Gunn stepped out into the hallway and took a few steps toward the stairs.

Total silence for a moment. Morgan heard only her own breathing, the faint scurrying of a mouse... and then, footsteps.

The stranger's voice came again: "Who are you?"

A few faint thuds. She was coming up the stairs.

"My name is Dolores Gunn. I don't think that's necessary."

"You're in Rawleigh's house. You're not Rawleigh."

"We're not here to threaten anybody," Gunn said.

"*We*'re? Who's with you? The girl?"

Gunn did not respond.

The stranger said: "It's Morgan, isn't it? Come on out, Morgan. I've been hearing about you. I want to see you."

XXXVII
Memory of a Second Drink

1

"I CAN HELP YOU."

He did not immediately realize she was talking to him. He probably should have, since he'd made eye contact with the woman less than a minute ago, and the seemingly innocent acknowledgment of each other had lasted at least a split second longer than it probably should have. I've seen you before, the contact said, and then it was over.

But now she was at the bar on the stool next to him, this forty-something woman with straight, mid-length brown hair and sharp features. He certainly did not mind her taking the seat next to him. Nor did he mind the occasional opportunity to look at her and take her in. A modest woman, he thought. Jeans, plain red button-up blouse, sleeves rolled up to her elbows. She ordered a beer.

When he asked her what she meant, saying she could help, she turned toward him and looked him over, said he looked alone; she simply meant she could be somebody to talk to. She probably meant more than this, he thought, but that was irrelevant for now.

"Unless you don't care to talk," she said. "If so, I get that."

"I wouldn't mind the company," he said.

So they talked.

He told her he'd moved to Alaska less than a year ago. From where? Tennessee—hence, the accent. She'd noticed but wasn't going to say anything. Where did he live? Fairbanks, he said, up near the edge of nowhere. "But I'm down here a lot. I work for a construction company, and they send me up and down the highway. I'm saving my money. I want to live peacefully and be my own boss."

"Don't we all."

"I moved here to actually do it."

She stared at him and said he was tense and should relax. No need to be tense, she said, as her expression changed. She was suddenly very concerned, apparently about something on or around his face. He couldn't imagine, truly he couldn't, and she leaned toward him, gravely concerned—about what? *Why don't you let me get that for you?*

She reached behind his ear and withdrew a ten-dollar bill.

"A second drink?" she said.

Yes, a second drink, and that second drink led to one of the most pleasing nights of his life.

2

Another memory.

Almost two weeks later.

They were in a hotel room in Anchorage, and he was in bed under the covers, and she was standing in the bathroom doorway in jeans and a navy blue bra; this was his first time to see her in such a way, and he realized how little he knew about her. He only knew that she had a daughter and they'd been living in New Hampshire.

That was, literally, it.

Fleeting thoughts. None of it mattered.

She unfastened her jeans and lowered them, came to the bed, and climbed in next to him.

"I need somebody like you." She moved on top of him. "I need somebody who needs me."

He thought this was likely true for both of them.

He unclasped her bra, removed it, set it aside.

"Do you need me?" she said.

He didn't have to think about it. The thought, he admitted to himself, had come to him several times over the past few days. He'd realized not so long ago that he not only looked forward to seeing her, he didn't know what he'd do with himself *without* her, even though, like a couple of kids, they only got together at night, not even every night. Only once had they met each other in the afternoon; only once had they met for breakfast…

But yes, he needed her. Even when she wasn't around, he wanted to know she was there.

She leaned down and pressed her breasts against him and kissed him. She smelled like bourbon. Her hair fell in his eyes and she spoke nonsensically into his right ear. He had no idea what she was saying. It didn't matter. He reached for her panties, found them, and her nonsense shifted into a plain statement: she was sorry, just move it out of the way. He did so and she let him in, telling him to roll over, it would be better that way.

Somewhere, in the deepest depths of his mind, he wondered if he'd been reeled in.

It was a fleeting thought, one that truly didn't matter.

3

He awoke first.

It was almost four a.m., and she was still asleep.

When she awoke, she raised her head a few inches as if to confirm where she was, then asked if he was awake. He told her he was.

"Did you know my daughter was unexpected?" she said. "Like a miracle."

"I don't know very much about you."

"I was nineteen. She was very unexpected."

"Where is she?"

She leaned in and kissed him. "She's a few rooms down."

4

They met again the next night, and the next. Then she brought her daughter up to the Salmon Catch. They got a cabin. So did he.

She came down to his cabin and told him her daughter had gone to bed early.

They made love.

Afterward, she rolled over to face him and said: "You know I'm from here. After her dad died, I took her to New England to get her away. I thought we could escape a fate I'd very much like to escape. But there is no escaping. So I brought her back. It's better up here. I wasn't supposed to have children, but I prayed for a daughter, and a miracle happened... Except it wasn't."

"You sound upset."

"I am. I told you I could help you, and I think I have. Do you agree?"

It was a foolish question; they both knew it.

"Now I need your help," she said.

"With what?"

"My little girl." She barely said it. "I'm dying, Rawleigh."

He told her he didn't know what she was talking about.

"Call it a virus, or cancer, it's been in me since she was born. Now I'm sick every day, weak, and I'm dying." Her voice cracked, and she forced a very pathetic smile. "If she doesn't die, I will."

He turned away from her, looked at the wall, and tried to determine what this was, and when he turned around again, the room was floating in a dream, and in the dream, she was just a woman. They might even get married and be happy, because she was *just a woman*.

She kissed him again and the dream ended.

5

Finger on the trigger. He returned to the past. He recalled the two times she truly talked to him about the past: before he left for the park, and when he returned.

Before he went into the park, she told him she'd been around a long time, in various forms with similar faces. She vaguely remembered childhood, growing up in a mining valley between two high ranges, an American girl, born in Alaska, parents from the faraway lands of Montana and South Dakota; she remembered being a young woman and being ill, gravely ill, and following the minister, her father's best friend, to the dark place beneath his church. You're not well, he said, but you can still do this. She let him have her, and she journeyed off when she began to show.

She remembered going elsewhere, and on the night of the day she gave birth and disposed of the child (because if she couldn't live, *it* wouldn't, either) she met a shaman who took her face in his hands and told her she was very beautiful, but she was also, obviously, tormented. He said, *You must talk to your god and be at peace.* When she told him she did not know how, he took her to the river where she'd disposed of the baby and pointed up into a distant range where a river of ice swept between two mountains and met the valley floor.

He said, *There is a place up there, girl, where spirits dance in the sky. There, you can talk to your god.*

"I went up there, Rawleigh, all the way to the ice. I was weak and it took hours, or days. I don't think the shaman intended to punish me. I think he just delivered me to fate. I went to sleep on the ice, and when I woke up..." The demon that crawled up out of the ice was smoky, frail, and tiny; any physical attributes it might have had were nothing more than bits and pieces of hair and flesh and teeth. It came to her and she let it. It called her a poor, weak girl, and it settled into her lap, felt her where she was ashamed to be felt, and mockingly asked where her daughter was. And she cried. Of course she did. The demon laughed. *Like a weak one, you came to talk to your god. Dear girl, your god's sent you to me.*

When Rawleigh returned from Denali, she was at the table in her cabin, not a trace of color in her face, her jeans dark with blood. Her head had been back against the wall, her eyes closed, and when he opened the door, her eyes opened, she raised her head, and his expression said everything that needed to be said. It was done. Mary's body had been trying in vain to rid itself of the disease for over twenty years. Now it would actually happen.

She was drinking whiskey from a foam cup. She poured him a splash and said: "Enough ancient history. Before Mary Rawlins, I called myself Desiree Knight. Desiree specialized in sex and parlor tricks." She grinned. "I'm not joking. Desiree didn't need a job. She—I—went from town to town and developed a reputation. She'd enter a bar, sit down next to you while you're trying to relax, and she'd turn your beer into lemonade or vanish your money, then she'd go upstairs with you. This was the most fun I've had, in the shallowest possible way..." Her voice trailed off. Something dark and tarry seeped from her nose, from between her lips. In fine trickles it ran down her chin. For several minutes, she sat quietly. "But deep down," she continued, "I am just a woman, and sometimes I think about what it would be like to... be a woman and have a second chance, to be a mother. Desiree—*I*—wanted to try again, truly try. But I've never been able to experience that. So she went into the mountains and prayed and looked for the lights in the sky that look like dancing spirits, and it came back. It crawled up out of the ice, and she begged. It answered her prayer, *yes*. She made it back to civilization, and she was a few years younger and not *quite* as good at parlor magic." She managed a weak grin. "She gave herself a new name and went straight into Anchorage and got a driver's license and a job. She met a man named Joseph Paul Hillward. And she had a baby... I loved her, Rawleigh. I truly did. I loved my Emily. But there is always a price. We couldn't go to New Hampshire and live normally and escape fate. I'm back to where I started. This is me."

Rawleigh's finger was still on the trigger, trying to find a way to squeeze it. *I did it for you, and this is how it ends.*

"You're okay, Rawleigh."

He lowered the gun and turned his head, and she was kneeling beside him, faintly luminescent. He wondered if she was real. Or if it mattered.

"They're coming," he said. "Morgan called the police, I know it."

"That doesn't matter." She rubbed her hands together, as if she were rolling a ball of clay. But it was not clay between her hands. It was light. And when the light was a proper ball, she took a piece of that glow, set the rest of it down beside him, and applied it like lotion to his face, down his neck, eventually over the rest of him.

Her hands were warm, almost scalding.

"Stay very still, Rawleigh. Close your eyes. Rest."

XXXVIII
Black Magic

1

THE WOMAN—MORGAN ASSUMED THIS was Renee—stood at the top of the stairs with her arms crossed below her breasts. She wore jeans and a flannel shirt with the top two buttons undone. There was a rifle tucked under her left arm, aimed generally at the floor.

"You're the niece," the woman said. "I'm glad to meet you."

"Are you Renee?"

"I am. And I wonder why you two are here."

"Rawleigh is—was—a dangerous man," Gunn said. "Did you know that? And no matter your answer, can we talk about it?"

A disturbing, subtle smile crept up from the corners of Renee's mouth.

"Let's go downstairs," she said, "and we'll talk as much as you like."

2

Gunn had turned off the lamp.

Renee turned it back on.

She propped the rifle against the wall and sat down in Uncle Rawleigh's recliner; Morgan and Gunn took seats on the couch.

Renee's eyes glanced back and forth from the graduation picture to the girl on the couch, then she folded her hands in her lap, leaned forward, and said: "Rawleigh is dead?"

"We think so," Gunn said.

"I suspect you're right."

Gunn said: "We'd like to talk. We think he killed a young lady named Emily Rawlins, and earlier today, he killed somebody I considered a friend. He's *your* friend. Does any of this surprise you? Did you know he was such a man?"

"'Such a man.' He kills, so he's wicked."

"In this situation, I think so."

"What if a certain death was necessary?"

"Talk to us about it."

"I don't know much about you, Dolores Gunn. Maybe I've seen you before? Maybe not. You independent artists spring up like dandelions all over the place. The 'friend' you claim he killed, I'd guess, was Wallace O'Brien, the plagiarist. It's regrettable he's dead, but I'm devastated to hear about Rawleigh."

"We're also looking for Emily's mother," Gunn said.

"I know what you're looking for." Rennee leaned back into the dim lamp light.

Something about the woman had been nagging at Morgan ever since she first saw her. Now, as Renee sat back in the recliner, that *something* hit the light at just the right angle. An old newspaper photo splashed all over her face.

Be out with it, Morgan, Renee's eyes suddenly said. *I know you know.*

"You're Mary Rawlins," Morgan said.

Gunn turned to Morgan, obviously confused.

Renee let herself smile sincerely.

"No, I *was* Mary."

Gunn shook her head and started to stand.

Renee told her to sit down.

"You're fortunate, Dolores. I would do anything in the world for Rawleigh, including cover up his so-called crimes. But he's dead, you say, and I don't see the need for further bloodshed. Still, I think you could use some enlightenment. You're naïve and uninspired."

The woman in the recliner nonchalantly twirled a finger in the air, and almost immediately there was something in her hand—a green guitar pick.

Renee studied it as if she'd never seen one before.

Gunn's eyes were as large as quarters. Unblinking.

"Neil Finn, right?" Renee said. "Front row, and Mr. Finn reached down and flashed you a sweet smile and handed it to you. If I'm not mistaken, it occurred right after 'I Feel Possessed.'"

Gunn did not—could not—respond. She reached into her pocket, perhaps expecting to find a certain guitar pick, but alas, this impossible display was authentic.

"My daughter was fond of 'Don't Dream It's Over,' but I don't think she delved much further than that into the Crowded House canon. Here." Renee flicked the guitar pick like a coin. Gunn caught it.

But she didn't. What she caught was an egg, which she immediately dropped.

The egg hit the floor and shattered—and its yolk was crimson, lumpy, and horrid. A network of flailing black filaments emerged immediately from the mess, enveloped by a thickening cloud of smoke.

And Renee was gone.

Initially, the filaments flailed blindly in the air, until they became aware of the women in the room and shifted their focus.

Morgan grabbed the musician's arm and yanked her away from the couch.

Black smoke billowed upward, and the cloud's source, that nasty yolk in front of the couch, was expanding. The filaments reached for the outer edges of the cloud, curling, wavering, predatory shepherd's crooks. The front door was locked, and Morgan, for several seconds, could not recall the simple process of flipping the deadbolt and turning the knob.

"Morgan," Gunn said.

The smoke was strong.

Gunn squeezed her arm and Morgan looked up, looked back, and the floor around the yolk was black and the black was expanding. It occurred to her—and it was somehow common knowledge, though it should have been anything but that—but it occurred to her that the black must be rot and the rot must be very fragile.

The filaments were much closer now. Morgan could see them, even though she couldn't see much of anything at all.

Morgan.

She felt light headed, sick; her lungs and stomach burned.

Gunn flung open the door and gave her a hard shove.

The cold night air cleared her mind immediately, but she did not stop to breathe it in.

Gunn was dragging her far out into the front yard, giving the house a wide berth as they ran generally toward the Toyota.

Behind came a loud crash from somewhere within.

The rot had fallen away.

3

Gunn backed the truck down the driveway and pulled out onto the relative safety of the road. But that was as far as she went. Neither of them cared to remove their eyes from the house. The night was dark enough that no details could be discerned, but it was fascinating, in a morbid and surreal sort of way, what was taking place within it.

Amazing, Morgan thought, how the mind, no matter what, immediately begins the rationalization process. Already she was trying to piece together how it *was* possible, and it all started with the guitar pick—except it didn't. It went back much, much further than that. Nevertheless, the guitar pick… it had gone from Dolores Gunn's pocket to Renee's hand, nothing but a timeless parlor trick, yet substantially more impossible. Cheap magic, Renee might say, to reveal a tiny sliver of mystery. *You don't know anything, much less understand.*

Gunn put the truck in drive and crept back up the driveway.

By the time Morgan acquired the ability to ask her what she was doing, she was already pulling up next to the shed at the edge of Uncle Rawleigh's back yard.

Gunn left the truck running, got out, and went into the shed. She returned with an axe and a two-foot crowbar. She tossed both items in the back seat, climbed back in, spun the truck around, and drove across the street to the old house.

The light was no longer on.

"If it's foolish, it's foolish." Gunn reached back and grabbed the crowbar. "I don't care."

4

There was a chain and padlock on the front door, but both the door and its frame fell inward after Gunn put forth a modest effort with the crowbar.

Their flashlights revealed nothing but dust, trash, a few remaining pieces of furniture, and a number of dead animals—birds, mainly, though one carcass looked to have been a four-legged land dweller back during its time on Earth.

Morgan hung back by the door as Gunn started in amongst the dusty death.

On the other side of what had likely once been a den, Gunn stopped and looked down.

"Stuff's drawn on the floor," she said. "Black lines and shapes." She moved toward a doorway on the opposite wall. "There could be more."

She proceeded on, and Morgan followed.

5

At the end of the corridor beyond the doorway was a small room not much bigger than a closet. Part of the ceiling and roof had collapsed. Two of the walls were covered floor to ceiling in writing and symbols and drawings, little to none of it discernible.

In a corner, lying amidst pieces of the ceiling and roof, was a book.

Gunn picked it up.

It was an old book, leather binding, pages of both paper and cloth, many of them frayed and brittle; the volume was not bound professionally but tied together with string and wire. It was filled with material that looked like the gibberish on the walls; the top corner of one page had been folded down, and red handwritten script in the outer margin read: ANIMATION OF AILMENTS.

Gunn replaced the book where she'd found it and said she was satisfied.

XXXIX
Toklat's Daughter

1

HE SLEPT FOR HOURS AFTER they finally stopped the bleeding. Or he thought it was hours. Hard to tell. The pain was immense, and he remembered almost everything, though there was no organization to the memories, and most of them were little more than flickering images. He remembered well the awful realization that he'd been hit, and whether it was the impact, or shock, or blood loss, or all of the above, he'd crumbled and been out. They took him away and stopped the bleeding. He remembered some of that, too. He remembered voices and the sound of an engine. Mainly, he remembered going to sleep. And now... Now, it was almost four 'o clock in the morning; he'd just spoken with an investigator, a friend of Pearce's, supposedly, who'd agreed to find him again when he was closer to his right mind. And he was checking out of an emergency room in Anchorage with an immense headache and no vehicle.

"Somebody called for you, sir," the receptionist said. "She said her name was Gunn and to call her back at this number."

She handed him a piece of paper with a number written on it.

He felt around for his phone, but he already knew he didn't have it.

"Can I use yours?" he said.

The receptionist turned the phone around and told him how to dial out.

He dialed the number on the paper.

"Mountaintop Lodge," said the man who answered.

"Dolores Gunn, if she's staying there. I need to speak with her."

A few seconds later, the man put him through to her room, and yes, Gunn answered. He did not expect her reaction; she gasped as she said his name, then broke down and started to cry. *Cry*, this woman he barely knew. When she finally calmed down, she said he was dead.

"No, not dead, I don't think. Is Morgan with you?"

"She's right here. Asleep. I've been with her since, well, this last evening. I left the park looking for you, and I found Morgan in her cabin. She told me what happened. She told me he shot you."

"He did. Morgan dove at him. I'd be dead if not for her. As is, I have a trench down the side of my skull, and I'm nearly blind with a headache."

"I can't believe I'm talking to you."

"I want to be up there. And I want to talk to you and Morgan. This is unbelievable."

Silence.

So much silence.

"What is it?" Wallace said.

"'Unbelievable' doesn't describe it, Wallace. You have no idea."

2

He fell asleep for a couple of hours on an uncomfortable sofa in a waiting room. At six, he awoke and bummed some mouthwash from a nurse's station, found a coffee pot and poured himself a cup of remarkably fresh and delicious coffee, and went outside. He walked four blocks to a bus station and caught a shuttle bus en route to Denali.

Gunn was waiting for him in the Mountaintop's sunlit lobby.

She hugged him, pulled back his hair, and inspected the network of bandages plastered to his head above and behind his left ear.

Satisfied that the ER doctor had indeed known what he was doing, she said: "I went down to that gift shop between here and the Salmon Catch and got us some fresh clothes. They had pants and shirts and socks, no underwear. But I'll wash what you have."

They sat down in a sofa before an unlit fireplace.

"Morgan?" he said.

"Still sleeping. We went to Fairbanks last night, to her uncle's house. If you're ready to hear what happened up there, I'll tell you. I'm prepared to do it. I'm prepared for whatever reaction you have. You'll think I'm crazy, but Morgan will reinforce the whole thing."

"I won't think you're crazy."

"No, you will, because it is."

"Tell me."

She proceeded through a story that was indeed very insane. The woman, Mary Rawlins, Renee, the guitar pick, the egg, and everything after that—including their findings in the old house across the street. Had it come from anybody else, in any other setting, amidst any other set of circumstances, he'd have laughed and walked away. But here and now, he believed.

But he had no comment for her story.

He simply looked into the dark and empty fireplace.

"I won't talk to Morgan yet," he said.

"Give her a day or two. You too."

He nodded again.

She reached into her jacket and withdrew his phone, handed it to him.

Then she said: "I'll be honest with you, Wallace: I want out of here. I care about you, and Morgan, but…"

"It'd be a good idea," Wallace said. "Get out of here, go home, get back to normalcy. When you're okay, call me. I want you to tell me your story again. Just not right now."

"I'll leave tomorrow, I think. Will you watch out for Morgan?"

He nodded and told her he'd do his best.

"And will you come over tonight?"

He told her he'd do that, too.

3

He drove up to Fairbanks and went to Rawleigh's house. There were two police cars in the driveway.

He did not pull in. He drove casually past and followed the dirt road to another highway that led into Fairbanks from the south. Once in town, he ate lunch and went to various stores stocking up on practicalities: snacks, clothes, toiletries. This done, he found an Irish Pub and drank down a few beers. The pub was nearly empty, and he spent the time keying Gunn's story into the phone's Notes app. He called the investigator who'd been at the hospital, answered a few questions, and lied when the investigator asked him about Mary Rawlins. *No, I don't know.*

When he thought enough time had passed, he drove back to Rawleigh's house.

The cops were gone.

He used a credit card to force open the back door, entered, and took pictures of the ruined living room: the rotted floor, the thousands of random blood splatters, the strange dark markings all over the walls, ceiling, and furniture. Across the street, he found exactly what she'd said he would find: the entire front door unit was leaning inward, and in what had once been a bedroom, there was a bizarre book still lying amidst a pile of rubble.

The cops would find this eventually and take it.

He took pictures of the cover, spine, and back, then flipped through it and took pictures of several pages—including one marked ANIMATION OF AILMENTS.

Finally, he snapped a few pictures of the markings on the walls and floors.

"She's right," he said. "This is crazy."

4

He returned to the Mountaintop Lodge in the early evening hours. But he did not go straight up to Dolores's room.

He dialed his editor's number and paced the front parking lot talking to her.

"It's been so long!" Patricia Weaver said. "How is the book? I admit, I have a blurb typed up and ready to go for the website. It's never too early to start building hype."

"My book is changing as we speak. I can't begin to explain to you the turn it's taken. I've been shot at and nearly killed. I've seen evidence of black magic. I've seen dead girls hauled out of glaciers. God willing, I can write the book. It will be based on fact, and nobody will believe it. I suppose that doesn't matter."

No reply from Weaver. Not right away.

Not until she said: "Are you okay, Wallace? Really okay?"

"I'm fine."

"Do you feel you're safe?"

"I think so."

"Wallace, you should get the information you need and get back to New York. This sounds like a daunting project, and I think you can pull it off. But not if you're dead."

"I think the danger has passed."

But then, he'd never known it was there to begin with.

5

"I'm worried about her," Gunn said.

She was sitting on the edge of the bed, lightly strumming her guitar with her right thumb, wearing only socks and a long tee shirt. Her hair was down and swept behind her left shoulder.

Wallace was sitting in a chair in the corner.

He'd brought up a couple of beers from the downstairs bar. His was on the table next to him, hers on the floor between her feet.

"She's a ghost," Gunn continued. "She hasn't called her parents, and I doubt she intends to. She's not interested in talking to anybody. I don't think she's suicidal or anything, but she *loved* him." She stopped strumming and set about fingerpicking a G chord. "Do you hate me for leaving?"

"No."

"I dread going to sleep tonight. I know what I'm going to see. Maybe it can't happen, but I need to escape these dreams. And I have an apartment to return to, bills, family and friends. I have shows lined up. I know you need to write your book, and I'm glad you're going to be here with her. Do you think she'll go back home?"

"Maybe."

"I hope she talks to you." She set the guitar aside and reached for her beer.

Wallace studied her. She was a frail thing, cute in her own off-kilter way. He knew damned well he'd grown attached to her, hated that she was leaving... but here she was, one more time, and he could see clearly through the tee shirt. There were yellow panties under there, and that was apparently all.

She drank her beer and watched him watch her.

"I've never been much for modesty, Mr. *New Yorker*," she said. "Are you interested?"

Wallace finished off his beer and went and sat down next to her.

Perhaps a bullet tearing through his scalp had opened him up, or maybe it was just a cocktail of alcohol and confusion. Whatever the cause, every part of him wanted her.

When he told her so, she looked him over and explained he really had to lose some of those clothes, or this was going to be very difficult.

6

The next day, he and Gunn spoke to the authorities.

And then he went with her while she said goodbye to Morgan.

They hugged in the Mountaintop's lobby. It would have been a sad moment if there was any emotion at all on the girl's face. Wallace told Morgan he had to return to Denali, if only for a short time.

"But I'll be around tomorrow," he said. "Maybe we'll talk?"

He returned to the park entrance and took a bus out to the Toklat Station, where he stared at walls and slept. He barely ate, drank substantial amounts of coffee, and refused to work on his book. Because the next step was talking to Morgan. He wasn't sure he was ready for that, and he *knew* she wasn't.

That night, the voice of Emily Rawlins jarred him from his sleep. She was singing. He heard it from the darkness near the ceiling. He heard it through the cracks around the window. He sat up in bed and knew she was close.

He sat in the darkness. Chilled. Hearing nothing.

But she was close.

"Emily," he said. "You can talk to me. Why did this happen?"

He got out of bed and waited to hear her again, and when he didn't, he went to the door and opened it, and the bear was there.

The grizzly stood in the dark, cold night on the other side of the threshold, directly in front of him.

The moment was silent, and it went on forever, until the bear raised a front paw and touched it to his chest. She kept it there for just a few seconds, then turned and started off in the direction of the river.

Wallace stepped out and watched her walk away. The bear was a faint smudge... and she was gone.

The sky was full of stars, and there was a faint, billowing curtain of yellow and pink over Pendleton.

It could mean anything, he thought.

Including nothing.

It could mean that, too.

7

He sat down at the table.

He did not delve into the book, but he did scribble out UNTITLED on the Moleskin's first page.

He replaced it with TOKLAT'S DAUGHTER.

XL
Denali

1

SHE WONDERED ABOUT HER UNCLE, and the wonder became worry. Never mind what he'd done. If he were a liar and a killer—and he was—that changed absolutely nothing regarding her memories of him.

The owner of the lodge had given her the room for as long as she needed it. He had plenty of rooms, he'd said, and the tourists weren't yet arriving in droves.

She'd accepted because she had nowhere else to go, and after drifting in and out of several shallow but lengthy periods of sleep, she lost track of time. She tried to keep herself well and nurtured and motivated; she showered and dressed and kept food in her stomach. She talked to a police officer, and she talked briefly with sweet Dolores Gunn. She told the writer how glad she was he was okay. And she meant it, because by some meaning of the word, she *loved* both Gunn and the writer.

She told herself she was young and healthy and educated and *okay*. What she *needed* to do, then, was get out of this God forsaken wild and empty place and go back home and make peace with her parents and get ready to retake the Arkansas bar. Sure, she could stay in touch with the writer, and if she ever found the willpower, she could have the talk she knew he wanted to have—maybe that would one day help her exorcise all this. Regardless, get *out* and get *on* with her life.

Such practical thoughts. Such practical, empty thoughts.

Everything—absolutely everything—was nothing at all.

2

After Gunn left for the airport and Wallace left her alone with the vague suggestion they might talk the next day, she decided a walk might assist in breaking up the clouds in her consciousness. She went downstairs and stepped out of the lodge, turned left, and started along the perimeter of the grounds. As she proceeded through the garden behind the building, she took a brief detour from her circular path and went to the wall at the back. From here, the jagged pillars of Healy's summit ridge rose into a faultless blue sky. The ridge gave way to gentler slopes of trees and grass, all of which plummeted dramatically down to the rushing Nenana.

She'd been through the garden once before. But this was her first time to stop and study the valley.

The view, she decided, was better for her than the exercise. The view reminded her that this place was beautiful, and there was still a lot here for her. Certain things she could not help. But she *could* help herself.

She continued on her original path.

When she made it back around to the front doors, she did not go back inside. She walked out to her uncle's Frontier, got in, and drove out toward the Denali park entrance.

She entered the Visitor Center and walked immediately over to a large map of the park hanging on the wall near the main desk.

A young ranger who was assembling a new corner book display approached her and asked if she needed any help. She asked him if Denali were visible today.

"Based on what I heard from Eileson, Denali was out in full force as of seven 'o clock this morning," the ranger said. "I'd say you should be able to see it from anywhere that offers a view. That can change in minutes, I'm sure you know."

She thanked him, checked her watch and saw that it wasn't yet noon.

She stepped back outside and set off across the parking lot to the start of a trail she'd noticed numerous times but had never hiked. She'd had her reasons: too close and obvious, go further out with your adventures… the trail is steep, and Denali is obscured today… that was usually the reason. But today, the Mountain was out.

The trail wound steeply up the massif's south slope and terminated at the top of the ridge. Healy's true summit was at the other end of the ridge, a mile or so to her north. The overlook was a rock outcropping with a single bench upon it. She went past the bench and sat down on the edge of the rock. Her feet dangling in open air above a slope of evergreens was exhilarating.

For the first few minutes, she looked and barely blinked. The great snowy monolith was there, to the southwest, far beyond the instant slopes of trees and row after row of lesser peaks. With the exception of a few light gray wisps hovering just below the top of the North Peak, there were no clouds whatsoever. It was *there*, as it had always been, as it always would be—for all her ability to comprehend.

She was not alone on the overlook, but she felt that way. The talk and laughter and shuffling footsteps, along with just about everything else, were irrelevant.

3

The afternoon wore on, and eventually she *was* alone. A few more clouds had built near Denali's summit, but they were inconsequential.

The air was considerably colder.

She barely thought to wonder what the others had thought of her. That strange girl, sitting alone on the edge of the rock. Just looking. Yes, it's a beautiful mountain, but look at her, just looking... These thoughts entered her mind, lingered for a few seconds, and dissipated.

Morgan did not know how long she sat. She hadn't a phone, and that was a blessing. Perhaps for the first time in her life, certainly her *adult* life, time—and cell phones—didn't matter.

A woman came up from behind her and sat down next to her. Morgan hadn't heard her approaching, because it was Renee. She was dressed in dark gray nylon hiking pants and a white Under Armor shirt. Her hair was in a ponytail. She was subtly beautiful.

"I'm glad you're okay," Renee said. "It's nice to see you going about things."

Morgan found the strength to speak.

She asked about her uncle. He hadn't been down there. Where was he?

"He's okay, Morgan. That's what's important."

"You won't tell me where he is?"

"There is something I'd like you to think about."

Renee put a hand on her back, and Morgan listened.

Her words were sweet, and like the light on the mountain, they grew fainter and fainter as meaningless time wore on.

4

The visitor center was dark when she came down off the ridge.

But the side door was propped open with a rock, and when she stepped inside to check the time and see about buying a bottle of water, she found an older park ranger behind the counter, leaned into a small lamp, reading a book. He looked up and told her to come on in, and yes, sure, she could buy a bottle of water.

The book, she saw, was the one she'd seen the ranger preparing to stock before her hike. It was about the Athabascans.

"They're an interesting people," the ranger said when he caught her eyeing the book as she paid for her water. "Natives of this part of the state, the interior. If you're interested, we just put up an exhibit right over here."

She was *most* interested in getting back. The Salmon Catch had reopened today, and she was tired and hungry, but to be polite, she followed the old ranger—*Merkin*, his nametag said—across the dark room to a display in the corner. The "exhibit" consisted of two large, framed black and white photographs and a glass case that contained a number of artifacts. The artifacts were likely very interesting in one way or another… But she never got a chance to concern herself with them.

Because when Merkin turned on the lights, her eyes went straight to the picture on the left side of the glass case, as well as the information card below it. An Athabascan shaman sitting in a chair outside a teetering old building (at the sight of the present day Salmon Catch) talking to a young American woman, circa 1916.

She studied it for so long that Merkin grew concerned about her.

Without removing her eyes from the picture, she told him she was okay, just tired. Too much time in the sun, probably.

5

It was nearly eleven before she made it to the Salmon Catch.

Ellis was behind the bar that night. He told her he'd of course get her a drink. What would she like? She requested a vodka tonic with a lime, and at first she sipped it. Then she drank it down. It felt good. It hit her hard. With the vodka on her brain, she almost decided Renee had never been there; she hadn't heard what she'd heard, hadn't seen what she'd seen. She almost convinced herself the young lady talking to the shaman in the circa 1916 photograph hadn't been a younger version of the woman named Mary and Renee. All these things... almost.

"Can we talk?" Ellis said when he returned to her.

Morgan said yes and followed him to his office.

He shut the door. His office was dark and dank and smelled of mouse shit and cigarettes.

Neither of them sat down.

"My son died," Ellis said. "He wasn't a nice boy. He had his own sins, and he paid for them when he shot himself. Your uncle had his sins, and he thought my boy was a good one to lay them on. Me too, I suppose, since he came in here and took my gun. Consider all this, and I *shouldn't* be okay. And I'm still not. But I'm getting there, because I'm here." He leaned against the front of his desk and looked her over. "Maybe you need to be here too. Or maybe you feel like you need to get as far away from here as you can. Either way, I get it. But all those folks up there in the bar, you did well with them. You can go back to work up there any time you want."

Her head was still spinning. Just slightly, not so badly she couldn't comprehend him.

"Thank you," she said.

"Think about it all you want. I just wanted to tell you that."

She wiped tears from her eyes and said it again—thank you.

The old man approached her, hugged her, and told her she had plenty of time.

"You'll be okay," he said. "Just let it come to you."

6

She had another vodka tonic, then another, and glanced up and down the bar several times as she drank. She looked for Cork and Uncle Rawleigh. She felt remarkably melancholy, but at least she wasn't crying.

Her head was floating, turning in the open air. God yes it was. If she could find somebody with a lighter, she now thought, indulging the vodka-fueled ramblings that were festering in her brain—if she could find a lighter (and somebody had to have one), she could take it and tell them she was going out to smoke, and she could set the place on fire. The restaurant, this bar, the cabins—*all* the cabins, the whole ones and the leveled ones and the half-rebuilt ones, all of them—and she figured the whole damned thing would go up with very little effort, because the remnants of the sickness Mary had shed had to be fucking flammable.

She could do it. She was somewhere between buzzed and totally drunk, yet she was surely sober enough to know better. But what harm would a little fire do, besides (potentially) ruining everything? Ellis was, last she heard, going to close down the cabin part of this operation; that was a good plan that would have to be enough. So drink up, she thought. Drink up, dear girl, because there are other things, certain things, important things, for you to consider—like fate—and the vodka will gladly be of assistance.

She took a few sips. She was not ready to go, but she did not (she thought) want a fourth drink. She wanted to feel pleasant, not gone—just sip.

Again, she felt like crying.

Screw it. She asked for another drink—just one more. She hadn't indulged like this since her first semester of law school, but what did *that* matter? She would be fine, or she would not be fine, and having a fourth drink tonight wasn't going to drastically (if at all) change whichever road she was on.

Ellis frowned.

But he got her the drink.

At the end of the night, though Morgan said she was fine (and she was, kind of), he insisted on driving her up to the lodge. No, it wasn't far, she was right about that, but it was steep—not a path she needed to be driving after a few too many.

She nearly fell asleep during the ride.

Ellis parked in front of the building and told her he cared about her. Please be careful. He would call her in the morning, maybe ten or eleven, and they could talk about things if she wanted to.

She spoke slowly, cautiously, not wanting to fuck it up. She thanked him for being nice to her. She was, she admitted, as she climbed out of his truck, pretty drunk. It was getting worse before it got better.

She noticed his frown.

It was sad and very obvious.

XLI
The New Child

1

WALLACE O'BRIEN SLEPT TILL NEARLY noon. It had taken him till nearly six a.m. to fall asleep, and he did not feel rested. Nevertheless, he was awake, the day was halfway gone, and there was no sense trying to force another round of sleep that would not come.

So he got out of bed, freshened up, dressed, and caught a bus bound for Eielson. Maybe he'd talk to Merkin. Maybe he'd start walking down some narrow and insignificant trail and never come back.

At Eielson, he helped himself to a cup of coffee and stepped out on the overlook. The morning was gray and the clouds over the mountains were low, dark, ominous.

Nevertheless, he imagined somebody trekking along one of those distant, icy ridges. Not a hiker or climber. Somebody else. Somebody likely not dressed for the occasion.

When he went back inside, one of his new friends, Makayla, was waiting for him just inside the door. After they exchanged pleasantries, she told him Mr. Everett was on the phone.

"He can't believe he actually caught you here. You don't mind to talk to him, do you?"

Wallace—in quite a bit of disbelief—told her no, of course not. He followed her behind the front desk, where she handed him the phone and pushed a button.

"Hello?" Wallace said.

"I'm glad I caught you there," the old man said. "I don't guess you know where Morgan is? I hope she's with you. I know she's not, I really do. But I hope so."

"No. She's not. I talked to her yesterday, when we told Dolores Gunn goodbye. That's the last time I saw her."

"Damn it. I'm worried. She was not in good spirits last night. I told her I'd call this morning and check on her. No answer, and she's not in her room."

"I don't know, Mr. Everett." He looked out at the tourists as if she might actually appear amongst them. "I'll be in touch soon."

2

He got back on the bus and rode it for four hours to the park entrance. There, he spent almost an hour searching the area, recalling how she used to come here to jog along the Park Road.

Not now.

He drove up to the Mountaintop Lodge, took the elevator up to the third floor, went down to her door, and knocked. And knocked.

A staff member emerged from the room next door, her arms loaded with towels.

"I was just in there, sir. She's out right now."

"Do you know where?"

"I don't. I'm sorry."

Downstairs, the receptionist could not help him, either.

Wallace thanked him for his time and stepped out.

He was walking out to his vehicle when he had an idea, pivoted, and went back inside

"Who was here last night?" he said.

The kid flipped back a page in the notebook in front of him.

"It was Nate," he said. "He was here till five this morning."

"Can you give me Nate's number?"

The kid studied him for what seemed like a long time, then scribbled a number on a sticky note and handed it to him. Wallace nodded in appreciation and went back out.

He keyed the number into his new phone and set about pacing the parking lot.

One ring. Two. Three. Four. And then, sorry, *Nate hasn't yet set up his voice mail.*

"Shit," he said.

What now? He could call Ellis, though he had nothing to tell the poor old man. Or maybe the old man now knew where she was? Or, fuck it all (and he stopped pacing), Wallace figured he could go back out to the Toklat Station and start writing. If this book wouldn't (couldn't) properly launch, he could dive into a lousy collection of poetry about his deep appreciation for the glaciers and wildlife of Denali National Park. Maybe he could even compose a Shakespearean sonnet: "Sonnet 18: Shall I compare thee to a blond grizzly?"

Morgan was a nice girl. He hoped she wasn't hurt. And God knows his book, as he imagined it, *depended* on her, but she was *not* his responsibility.

Was she?

His phone rang. It was Nate.

Wallace answered and began pacing again.

"Who is this?" Nate said.

"My name is Wallace O'Brien. I'm looking for a girl named Morgan McCown who's staying at the Mountaintop Lodge. I can't find her, and I wonder if you can help me."

"Blond, no charge for her room? I saw her last night. First time was, I don't know, between midnight and one. She'd had some drinks at the Catch, I assume, because she looked pretty gone. She didn't speak to me when I told her to get some rest. Then she came down a few hours later, four or five. She went out to the garden."

"What else?"

"That's it."

"She never came back in?"

"I'm not saying she didn't come back in. I'm saying I didn't *see* her come back in."

Wallace thanked him and hung up, then walked around the building to the garden.

An old couple stood at the back wall. They were speaking softly and taking pictures.

Otherwise, the garden was silent. No sign of Morgan.

He approached the wall.

"Gorgeous view of the valley, isn't it?" the old man said.

Wallace agreed it was.

I just don't see what I'm looking for, he did not add.

3

He called Ellis Everett and drove down to the Salmon Catch to pick him up, and the two men spent the afternoon and early evening searching everywhere they could—the cabins and the hillside behind them, the banks of the Nenana, even the Dragon Canyon area. At the end of it all, Wallace called Ted Stevens International and asked if she'd been there. Nothing.

"And here we are," Everett said as they pulled back into the Salmon Catch. "Not a bit of it's believable."

The Salmon Catch bar was back to normal. The tourists were starting to pile in thickly.

They found two empty stools and ordered drinks.

"She could be in Fairbanks," Wallace said, perhaps only to himself, "or she could be somewhere in that mine. She could be lost in the words, or out in Denali. She could be in the ground somewhere. I suppose she could be halfway to Canada right now, if she wanted to be. Or out in the ocean. Or maybe she got tossed into Ship Creek."

He realized he'd spoken all this aloud when he glanced to his right and saw Ellis staring at him.

"And that's not all," Wallace said.

"Like what?"

"I can't talk about it, because *I* don't get it."

Everett didn't press the issue.

They drank and did not talk.

A moment later, the bartender approached. Wallace expected him to ask if they wanted another round. Instead, he placed a folded piece of paper in front of Ellis and said: "A guy from the lodge just left this. Told me to tell you it was in her room."

The bartender left the paper and walked away.

The folded sheet was taped shut, and *Mr. Everett* was written across it in blue ink.

Ellis looked gravely at Wallace, then broke the tape with a finger and unfolded it.

The message was short and kind:

Thank you for being good to me. I have to go. Love, Morgan.

They both looked at it for a long time, until Ellis folded it again and shoved it away.

They drank in silence.

4

After he stepped out of the Salmon Catch, as he was considering whether or not he wanted to call Gunn, his phone sounded its ugly *da-dunk* noise that signaled he'd received a text message. He saw it was from Patricia Weaver... and the text was a long one. His stomach was soured from the beer, and he had no desire to read what she'd sent.

"Later," he said.

He tucked the phone away and drove back to Denali.

5

He called Gunn as he was waiting for the bus.

He sat on a wooden bench near the start of the trail to the Healy Overlook, partially hoping she wouldn't answer. After all, what ungodly hour was it where she was?

But she did answer, and she sounded very much awake.

"I need to talk to you," he said. "I can't do it. Not without talking to Morgan. It would all be a lie."

"Then don't do it," she said.

"I'm going back to New York. If nothing else, I'll look for a teaching job. Maybe something will come to me. Something new."

"Can I meet you there?" she said. "I could line up some shows, and we could meet." She paused. "See what happens."

"Please meet me there," he said.

After he was back at the Toklat Station, he packed up his notebooks.

If this was indeed the salvation of his literary career—this place, this book—then maybe his career wasn't meant to be saved.

He sat in the dark and went to Patricia's text message.

Tell me what you think, it began.

The rest of the message was the blurb she'd composed for the website:

Award-winning author Wallace O'Brien will soon be taking the publishing world by storm with a foray into suspense and true crime. Inspired by the real-life disappearances of two women in central Alaska, O'Brien has described his coming work as a "nonfiction novel" in the tradition of IN COLD BLOOD *and* THE EXECUTIONER'S SONG. *This is the work that could make Wallace O'Brien a true voice of his generation.*

Wallace set the phone down.

Perhaps, at one point, not all that long ago, or in a reality not all that different from this one, this would have been the blurb he was looking for. But not now.

The story he'd come here to tell was not complete, not even close, and he would not tell lies, not about Morgan, the young lady who'd spared him a bullet to the brain—not about any of them. He'd stolen from that miserable book *The Power Play*, and he would not steal again. He would not pluck from the lives of other people for the sake of salvaging his so-called literary career.

He would tell their stories completely and honestly, however bizarre, whatever the consequences, or he would not tell them at all.

And so there was no book.

December

1

HE RETURNED TO HIS APARTMENT, and things were as they'd always been, which was, truly, not that bad. He got a job as an adjunct professor and forced himself to write. Anything. There were multiple false starts. These were maddening but only moderately depressing. Returning to normalcy at least placed a blurry, dreamlike film between the present and his time in Alaska.

Gunn arrived at the end of summer. She lined up multiple shows in Manhattan and Brooklyn and spent the fall living in his apartment. He listened to her play, she taught him a few songs, they went to bars and made love and eventually joked about getting married. He read her passages from the novella he eventually started.

He felt okay about it. He'd likely finish it. And Gunn said it was good.

But the unspoken truth between them was obvious: Yes, it was good, and it would pad his bank account at a time when it really needed padding... But it wouldn't change anything.

"Do you ever wonder about the book?" she asked one night.

Yes. He was still hung up on it. He didn't want it to be the only way, but you don't experience something like that and expect anything else to suffice.

"How can I not?" he said.

2

The forty-thousand-word novella was between them on her desk.

Weaver had just finished the first round with her red pen.

"This is good work," she said. "It's well written. But what else would it be? You're a talented writer. It's just *not* what we talked about. It's not what I've been preparing for. You've turned in forty thousand words about a bisexual prostitute." She stacked the manuscript though it didn't need it. "But it's good. It's relevant."

"Thank you."

"Have you abandoned the Alaska work entirely?"

"No," he said. "It abandoned me."

3

He zipped his jacket and stepped out on the sidewalk. December's first snow was falling. It was not heavy, but it was blowing in a bitterly cold breeze. He turned left and braced himself against the chill.

He'd avoided this building, this sidewalk, he realized. How could he not? Patricia Weaver hadn't wanted novellas about prostitutes. How do you market that? And how big would they have to make the font, and how wide would they have to make the margins, just to inflate the book to a size they could sell?

Nevertheless, it was a sale. It would pay a few bills. And if it garnered even a few decent reviews, maybe it would rejuvenate his confidence.

It abandoned me.

He stuffed his hands deeper in his pockets and pulled his jacket tighter around him. He and Gunn were celebrating tonight. They were going to see the Nets, and then they were going to hop from bar to bar and drink like he'd just won the fucking National Book Award.

But for now, he realized he'd come to his old haunt, Shavano's, and it looked warm in there, and there was nothing wrong with having a beer in solitude to celebrate the sale of a book that probably didn't deserve to sell.

Because the prostitute novella was, in its own way, pathetic. It would be lumped in with other SERIOUS FICTION, but who was he kidding? It tried too hard. It wanted to sit proudly alongside the stuff put out there by Ian McEwan, Cormac McCarthy, and Don DeLillo. But Jesus Christ.

It was nothing. It would die an obscure death, and he'd be back to praying for salvation to a muse who'd left him high and dry.

He stepped inside.

Business, as usual, was light.

Shavano's had always done just enough to get by, and back when Peevey had been alive, that's all he'd wanted.

Wallace sat down at the bar.

The bartender placed a napkin in front of him and asked what he wanted.

He told her a Miller Lite would be fine, just one and he'd be going, and he went through the novella in his mind, wondering if he should have ever sent it to Weaver to begin with. What was it, exactly? Did he really think his oh-so-conflicted harlot was even comparable to literature's other great prostitutes? Wallace O'Brien, always with something to prove—yet he never proves it!

The young bartender set his beer down, and he looked up at her.

His reaction was as clichéd as the novella he'd just sold.

She smiled sincerely.

"I can help you," she said. "If you'd like me to."

March 9, 2016

Author's Note

TOKLAT'S DAUGHTER WEARS ITS INFLUENCES on its proverbial sleeve. This story was born out of the four-month gauntlet that followed my graduation from law school, in which I was studying for, taking, or waiting on the results of the Arkansas bar exam.

In the midst of this stretch, I took a week's vacation with my wife and her parents to Alaska. This book is as much an ode to that beautiful wilderness as it is a ghost story and murder mystery. I hope this aspect of the tale is both obvious and nonintrusive.

I took liberties, mostly slight ones, with the areas described in this story. Many of the locales are real, some are not. A few are both.

As I always state at this point in the book, I greatly appreciate all those who take a few minutes to review my work. Whatever your thoughts on this story, and I of course hope you enjoyed it, please post a review on Amazon.com or send me a few lines of feedback.

Most importantly, thanks so much for spending your time with something I wrote. It means a lot.

Mitch Sebourn
http://badwaterpress.blogspot.com
Twitter: @mnsebourn
mnsebourn@hotmail.com